KILLER MOUSSE

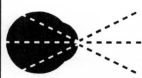

This Large Print Book carries the
Seal of Approval of N.A.V.H.

KILLER MOUSSE

MELINDA WELLS

WHEELER PUBLISHING
A part of Gale, Cengage Learning

GALE
CENGAGE Learning·

Detroit • New York • San Francisco • New Haven, Conn • Waterville, Maine • London

GALE
CENGAGE Learning™

Copyright © 2008 by Melinda Wells.
A Della Cooks Mystery.
Wheeler Publishing, a part of Gale, Cengage Learning.

Wheeler Publishing Large Print Cozy Mystery.
The text of this Large Print edition is unabridged.
Other aspects of the book may vary from the original edition.
Set in 16 pt. Plantin.
Printed on permanent paper.

LIBRARY OF CONGRESS CATALOGING-IN-PUBLICATION DATA

Wells, Melinda.
    Killer mousse / by Melinda Wells.
      p. cm. — (A Della cooks mystery) (Wheeler Publishing large
   print cozy mystery)
    ISBN-13: 978-1-59722-783-4 (pbk. : alk. paper)
    ISBN-10: 1-59722-783-8 (pbk. : alk. paper)
    1. Women cooks — Fiction 2. Cooking schools — Fiction. 3.
   Santa Monica (Calif.) — Fiction. 4. Cooking shows (Television
   programs) — Fiction. 5. Murder — Fiction. 6. Large type books.
   I. Title.
   PS3623.E4765K55 2008
   813'.6—dc22   2008014509

Published in 2008 by arrangement with The Berkley Publishing Group, a member of Penguin Group (USA) Inc.

Printed in the United States of America
1 2 3 4 5 6 7 12 11 10 09 08

To Norman Knight

ACKNOWLEDGMENTS

I want to express my heartfelt gratitude to:

Wonderful editor Kate Seaver, who inspired this book. It's a joy to work with you.

Literary agents Rebecca Gradinger and Morton Janklow. Thank you for everything you do.

Claire Carmichael, gifted writer and instructor. How lucky I am to learn from you.

D. Constantine Conte, mentor, treasured friend, and "godfather" to my pets.

Carole Moore Adams, Hilda Ashley, Regina Cocanougher and Carole Cook, Ramona Hennessy, and Barbara Rush: Thank you for contributing those delicious recipes.

The following people read the early manuscript and shared their invaluable reactions. Thank you Arthur Abelson, Carole Moore Adams, Dr. Rachel Oriel Berg, Christie Burton, Rosanne Kahlil Bush, Carol Anne Crow, Peter Crow, Ira Fistell, Judy Tathwell Hahn, Nancy Koppang, Susan Magnuson, Mari Marks, Jaclyn Carmichael Palmer, Judy Powell, Corrine Tatoul, and Kim La-Delpha Tocco.

Wayne Thompson of Colonial Heights, VA: You continue to inspire.

Robyn Astaire: Thank you for using your knowledge of standard poodles to choose "Tuffy," "Tuffy II," and his sister, "Robyn," for my late husband and me.

Always and forever: Thank you, Berry Gordy.

1

Through my earpiece, I heard the director's voice: "Take your place, Della. Thirty seconds to air. . . ."

Emerging from the Better Living Channel's backstage shadows, and faking confidence I didn't feel, I strode onto the TV kitchen set to polite applause. So far, so good; I didn't stumble, as I had during the last rehearsal. Now I just had to get through the next forty-six minutes — a TV hour minus commercials — without making a fool of myself.

I stood in my designated spot behind the food preparation counter and tried not to imagine that the two big television cameras facing me were actually a firing squad in disguise. As instructed by the director, I sent a cheerful smile at the thirty people in the studio audience and raised my right hand in a "hello there" wave.

Uh oh. . . .

My hand froze in mid-gesture when I saw Mimi Bond sitting in the middle of the first row. Impossible to miss, she was in her late fifties and had platinum hair piled high in a meringue-like swirl on top of her head. The seams of her purple satin dress strained against her ample curves, making her look somewhat like an eggplant.

After the fit Mimi had thrown at me less than an hour ago, I thought she had gone home, or headed for the nearest bar. No such luck.

Tonight would be the biggest challenge I'd ever faced. If I failed, I'd lose everything I'd worked for, and the presence of this angry woman threatened to make me so nervous that I could ruin what would likely be my only chance. I forced myself to continue the wave and the smile past Mimi as I replayed our bizarre scene in my head.

I had been alone in the tiny dressing room behind the set, trying to keep my hands steady enough to put on TV makeup, when she burst in without knocking. Reeking of alcohol, she'd shouted, "You ruined my life!"

Although I'd never met her, I knew her to be Mimi Bond. Until recently, she'd been the Better Living Channel's Cooking Diva. The rumor was that she'd been fired for

10

putting too many 100 proof liquids into the food she made on camera. I had been hired to replace her.

"You must be sleeping with him," she screeched.

That accusation surprised me more than her sudden appearance, because there hadn't been a man in my life since my husband died two years ago.

Genuinely puzzled, I asked, "Who?"

"Don't try to deny it. Mickey Jordan is *who*. Why else would he give you my TV show?"

I saw a hint of wildness in her large and slightly protruding brown eyes. Even though I was more than ten years younger, and in pretty good shape, this woman was *scary*. I hoped that if I stayed calm and spoke in a gentle tone, it would pacify her. "I've only seen Mickey Jordan four times," I said, "and his wife was always with him."

She wasn't pacified.

"Well, you must have slept with *somebody* to get my job — that's how I did it. When I find out which SOB is taking care of you, I'll make him pay."

She'd grabbed the leopard print makeup bag with the initials *MB* that lay on the end of the table and stomped out of the room, slamming the door behind her.

The seconds were ticking down toward broadcast time. I told myself firmly: *Forget Mimi Bond. If the public likes this show, I'll be able to keep paying the rent on my cooking school space in Santa Monica.* I needed this additional source of income because I'm a better cook than businesswoman, and I've strayed into the danger zone of debt. *Don't think about that now.*

A two-woman rooting section was here tonight to support me. One was sitting in the audience in the chairs set up between the two big cameras in the Better Living Channel's low-tech, no-amenities cable TV production facility. That was Iva Jordan, a relatively new friend. I'd met her about a year ago when she enrolled in my cooking school. Iva is the much younger fourth wife of Mickey Jordan, owner of the network — the man Mimi had accused me of sleeping with. A glance at Iva didn't give me much encouragement; she looked as anxious as I felt. Beneath her cap of pale gold hair cut in a pixie style, her face was tight with tension, and she was chewing her bottom lip. It was Iva who had talked her husband into hiring me for television. If this show failed, she would only be embarrassed in her social circle — I would lose my entire business.

My other friend was Liddy Marshall. With

her twin sons in college, she worked as an extra in movies for fun, so she was used to being on sets. Standing a few feet behind Camera Two, she was smiling at me like a proud parent and giving the "thumbs-up" sign. An attractive honey blonde with big green eyes and a smile so warmhearted it was contagious, Liddy had been Miss Nebraska twenty-four years ago. She'd come to Hollywood to be a movie star, but she'd switched goals when she fell in love with a sweet Beverly Hills dentist who told great jokes, and she traded the life of an actress for a happy marriage. Liddy had been my best friend for more than two decades.

In my ear: "Five seconds to air, Della. . . . Four . . . three . . ."

Prerecorded theme music was piped into the studio. It was almost surreal. *I have theme music.* Under the heat of the powerful TV lights, I shivered with anticipation.

Camera One's red light came on, signaling that my face was now appearing on thousands of TV screens. I hoped viewers weren't reaching for remotes to switch channels.

"Hi," I said. "I'm Della Carmichael. Welcome to *In the Kitchen with Della.* Tonight, I'm going to make a main dish, a veggie side, and a really fabulous dessert, and all three won't take any longer to fix than the hour we'll be spending together. First up, because it has to chill in the refrigerator after we put it together, is my own special chocolate mousse. A woman who took my cooking course nicknamed it 'Killer Mousse,' because she said the taste was 'to die for.' Don't worry if you can't write down the instructions while you're watching — just go to my website: DellaCooks.com. You'll find all the recipes there."

As I explained what ingredients I'd be using, Mimi Bond stared at me with the intensity of a vulture waiting for something to die. Much as I tried to ignore her, she succeeded in rattling me. The stainless steel mixing bowl I was holding slipped from my fingers and clattered to the studio's concrete floor.

"Ooops." I swooped down to retrieve it and heard a nervous titter from the studio audience. Ernie Ramirez, operating Camera One, swung the big glass eye around to follow me to the sink on the right side of the set.

Quickly washing the bowl, I flashed the audience an embarrassed grin. "I was about to tell you that this is my very first time on television, but I guess I don't have to do that now."

There were a few sympathetic chuckles from the spectators in the studio but not so much as a twitch of the lips from Mimi.

Her hostile attitude was exactly what I needed for my fighting Scottish spirit to kick in. Stage fright and concern about Mimi being there vanished. I smiled at the audience with genuine pleasure and uttered what I hoped was going to be my signature phrase: "Okay, people, let's get cooking."

Increasing the flame under a pot of water, I said, "I've been making meals since I was ten. Because I was the oldest of four kids, with folks who both had to go out to work, it was my job to fix dinner. Growing up, I read recipe books while the other girls were reading movie magazines.

"A few years ago I realized a dream when I opened a cooking school in Santa Monica. It's called The Happy Table. I chose the name because I think that's what family mealtimes should be."

I was comfortable moving around on the set because the studio designer had duplicated my old-fashioned kitchen at home: the butter yellow walls, the stainless steel double sink, a big white GE refrigerator, and two white enamel and chrome O'Keefe & Merritt gas stoves. They were manufactured during the Eisenhower administration

— before I was born — and still worked perfectly. In sharp contrast to mine, the TV kitchen for Mimi's *Cooking Diva* show had been as high tech and as full of expensive gadgets as a restaurant.

"We start the mousse by melting seven ounces of semisweet chocolate and one ounce of unsweetened chocolate in the top part of a double boiler." I demonstrated. "You don't have to own an actual double boiler. Just put a heat-safe bowl over a pot of boiling water, like I'm doing here. In my family, I was known as the Queen of Making-Do."

The yellow light next to the stove started flashing. That was my signal to get out of the way so the overhead, automated "stove cam" could show a close-up of the melting chocolate.

Camera Two, operated by a young African American woman named Jada Powell, followed me as I moved to the preparation counter.

For the next few minutes, I talked and demonstrated until all of the ingredients of the mousse were folded together.

"Now we pour the mixture into a pretty serving bowl." I flicked the rim with my fingernail and produced the *ping* that identified genuine crystal. "A fancy presentation doesn't have to be expensive; this bowl cost five dollars at a yard sale. I love yard sales. You can find real treasures, and I like pieces with history, pieces that look as though they might have stories to tell."

The director's voice came through my earpiece. "Ten seconds to commercial. Nine . . . eight . . . seven . . ."

I said to the audience, "I'm going to put the mousse in the fridge, and when I come back, I'm going to make our baked chicken main dish. Then I'm going to show you how to get children and those meat-and-potatoes men in your life to eat vegetables."

Theme music up. The camera's red light went off. In the glass-enclosed control booth above the audience, the director flipped switches and sent the scheduled commercials out over the air.

Carrying the just-made chocolate mousse, I hurried around behind the set to put it into the large refrigerator backstage, where two hours ago I'd placed the mousse I'd prepared at home. That one had to be kept refrigerated until it was time to show the audience the finished version and let volunteers taste it. Coming all the way back here was inconvenient, but the refrigerator on the set wasn't working today. I'd have to ask somebody to have it fixed before the next show.

I cleared a place among the plastic-wrapped sandwiches, cups of yogurt, and cans of soda that the studio staff kept there, and shoved in the unchilled mousse. This one would stay here at the studio. After the show, I'd tape a little note to the bowl, inviting the staff to enjoy it tomorrow.

The area behind the set gave me the creeps. Used mostly for storage, it was a jumble of old furniture, props, and machinery covered by sheets and canvas drop cloths. A path had been cleared that stretched from the set, past the fridge, past a small dressing room and the partitioned-off toilet, all the way to an outside door leading to the loading dock. I didn't linger; it was too dark and eerie. The only illumination came from a low-watt bulb in the ceiling.

Grabbing the package of chicken pieces I needed for the next demonstration, I closed the refrigerator door and rushed back into the bright lights of the set. Through my earpiece I heard another countdown. I got to my place two seconds before Camera One's red eye went on. We were broadcasting again.

"For our main dish, we're having Easy

Cranberry Chicken. I call it that because it's easy to fix and easy on the budget. I've taught children as young as eight how to make it in my Saturday morning Mommy and Me cooking class. All you do is stir together a sixteen-ounce can of whole-berry cranberry sauce, one envelope of onion soup mix, and half a cup of Russian dressing. Then you dip your chicken pieces into the blend and swish them around a little. The kids love to do this."

With the chicken pieces fully swished, I tore a length of foil from a roll on the preparation counter, lined a baking sheet with it, and placed the dredged chicken on the foil-covered surface. "If you have any liquid left, drizzle it over the chicken pieces. About the ingredients: You don't need any particular brands. I save money using manufacturer's coupons and taking advantage of in-store specials. That's how I buy all my hair care and house cleaning stuff, and laundry detergents, too."

At the sink, I squirted my hands with antibacterial soap and ran hot water over them. "Always wash your hands after working with poultry, meat, or fish before you touch any other food." I added lightly, "I think I must scrub more than the average surgeon." Drying my hands with a paper

19

towel from the roll on a spindle next to the sink, I went back to the prep counter. "The tray of chicken goes into our preheated three-hundred-and-fifty-degree oven to bake for about an hour and a half — that is if you use both white and dark meat pieces as I did here. If you just want skinless, boneless chicken breasts, then the baking time is about an hour."

Time for another commercial break. "I'll be right back, and then I'll show you how to transform a basket of vegetables into an unexpected treat."

As soon as I was off the air, Liddy Marshall quick-stepped up to the right side of the set and motioned frantically for me to join her at the sink where she whisked a brush from her shoulder bag and tamed loose strands of my dark brown hair.

"Listen," she whispered. "You're always telling me I shouldn't eavesdrop, but this time you'll be glad I did. During the first commercial break when you went backstage, I overheard your producer talking to the girl on Camera Two. He told her Mimi Bond — that bad bleach job in the front row — is going to be your *taster* at the end of the show tonight. He wants her to be sure to keep the camera on Mimi."

I felt my mouth drop open.

Liddy said triumphantly, "I didn't think you knew about it."

"No." And I wasn't happy to find out this stunt had been kept from me.

"By the way, you look great," Liddy said. "I was afraid your hair would photograph too dark and dull on TV, but it doesn't. The lights are catching all the shades of brown. I'm glad I talked you into wearing the blue shirt that matches your eyes."

"Do I *sound* okay? Am I making sense?"

"You seemed a little nervous at first, but only somebody who knows you well would catch that. After you dropped the bowl — and that was a hoot — you seemed more like yourself. Natural."

"Can you believe this? At the age of forty-seven I'm starting my third career."

"And no one's going to shoot at you, like they did when you had to teach at that awful high school in gang territory."

If I lose my cooking school, I'll have to go back to teaching anywhere the district sends me.

In my earpiece, I heard, "Ten seconds to air, Della. Nine . . . eight . . ."

"Gotta go." I gave Liddy's hand an affectionate squeeze.

As Liddy scurried back into the shadows, I took my place behind the counter.

When the camera light went on, I said, "Now we're going to take this eggplant" — I had to force myself to keep a straight face, because the vegetable I was holding really did resemble Mimi Bond in her purple dress. I put it down and indicated the rest of the ingredients lined up in front of the camera. — "and turn these into a beautiful one-crust pie."

I kept up the conversational patter as I sliced, chopped, sautéed, and seasoned. Setting aside the pan of cooked vegetables, I began to put together a simple piecrust.

"You can use a store-bought crust, but it's really so easy to make one from scratch. To moisten this mixture of flour, salt, and Crisco, I use three or four tablespoons of ice water. A lot of cookbooks will just say 'water,' but the colder the water, the lighter the crust. And if you don't happen to have a rolling pin, use a wine bottle or a beer bottle, but soak the label off first. If it's an empty bottle, fill it with cool water before using it."

With the dough rolled out and draped in a pie pan, I demonstrated how to layer the vegetables, adding Parmesan cheese. "Last, I take the red and the green pepper that I've cut into strips and arrange them on top, alternating the colors in a sunburst pattern.

You could use a yellow and an orange pepper, too, but they're usually too pricey for me. When I have time, I'm going to make a little vegetable garden in my backyard and grow my own."

In my earpiece, I heard, "Ten seconds to the final commercial break."

I told the audience, "I'll keep putting this together and pop it into a three-hundred-and-fifty-degree oven. When I come back, I'll show you how the three dishes I've made are going to look when they're ready to serve."

While the commercials played, I made another quick trip backstage to the refrigerator, took out the pre-prepared chocolate mousse, and brought it onto the set. As the director had rehearsed with me, I moved the other two pre-prepared dishes that I'd had sitting on the rear counter up to be displayed next to the mousse. The overhead camera would take close-ups of the food for what the director called "beauty shots."

When we were on the air again, I said, "Here are the Easy Cranberry Chicken and the Sunburst Vegetable Pie — all baked and ready to eat."

There was enthusiastic applause from the audience, but when I glanced at Mimi, I saw her hands remained in her lap, her fingers curled into claws.

"If you're like me," I said, "the star of any dinner is *dessert*. I just have one more thing to do before we can dig into the chocolate mousse."

I picked up a piece of semisweet chocolate and grated it over the mousse. "You can be extra fancy and decorate the top, but this is how I like it best — with just a dusting of freshly grated chocolate." That last touch completed, I put down the grater. Now I asked the question to which I already knew the answer: "Who'd like to have a taste?"

"I would!" Mimi Bond propelled herself out of her front-row seat and rushed to the set. A second before she'd spoken, I saw Camera Two swing in Mimi's direction. It was absolute proof that Liddy was right about this being prearranged.

The former Cooking Diva smiled broadly as she waved at the camera. "Hello, everybody. I'm Mimi Bond, and I'm taking a little vacation from my own show, but I wanted to be here tonight to help Della. I'm volunteering to be the very first one to taste her famous Killer Mousse."

Mimi bustled around the counter, subtly elbowing me out of the TV frame. Jada Powell pulled Camera Two back so that her shot included both of us.

24

Pretending that I was delighted to have her there, I scooped some mousse into a dish and handed it and a spoon to Mimi. I was thinking how desperate for attention she must be to have arranged to taste the mousse, just so she could be in front of the camera again. Instead of being annoyed, it made me feel sad for her.

"Oh, it looks so yummy," she cooed. She took a big mouthful and screwed up her face in disgust. "Eeewww. This is *awful.*"

"It can't be. When I made it this afternoon, I scraped the sides of the mixing bowl and licked the spatula clean. It was delicious."

I snatched up another spoon and plunged it into the mousse, but before I could taste it, Mimi gasped and dropped her dish. It landed sharply on my foot. Some mousse plopped out, but the bowl rolled off my shoe and onto the floor without breaking.

"Mimi? What's the matter?"

Her answer was a deep moan. She pressed her fists hard against her chest as her face twisted into an expression of agony.

I yelled, "Somebody call nine-one-one!"

Mimi's body stiffened and her eyes rolled back in her head. She started to sway. I reached out to keep her from falling, but she was too heavy for me. She slipped from my fingers as she fell forward and crashed facedown onto the studio floor.

I fell to my knees beside Mimi. Grabbing her by the shoulders, I lifted her head to help her breathe. But she wasn't breathing.

I felt for a pulse in her neck. No pulse.

George Hopkins, the show's producer, loomed above me on the other side of the counter, barking the studio's address into his cell phone, demanding an ambulance. I'd last seen him a half hour before the show. He'd looked cool and bored, but now he was sweating, and his smooth brown hair was slightly askew. I hadn't known it was a toupee.

"What happened? What's wrong with her?" His small eyes blinked double-time.

"I think she's had a heart attack," I said. Remembered grief stabbed at me: My husband had died of a heart attack.

George pressed the phone to his chest and muttered a curse. "We don't have a doctor here, or a defibrillator. Do you know CPR?"

I stood up. "I'm afraid it's too late."

"How can you be so calm about this?"

"I'm not. But if I let myself go to pieces, it could start a panic, and people in the audience might get hurt."

Suddenly a female on the premises let out a wild cry. A pale, thin, young woman from the front row jumped up and rushed toward me. Her face was contorted into an expression of fury, and her voice was a wail. Before I could tell her to stay back, she screamed at me, "You killed my mother!"

2

"She's dead, isn't she?" Emitting a guttural shriek, she flew at me with her fists flailing. "You killed my mother!" I threw up my arms to ward off her blows. George grabbed her shoulders and pushed her away from me. The effort jarred his toupee farther off center.

"Faye, stop it." He gave her a shake. "Come on now, get hold of yourself."

"I'm so very sorry about your mother," I said, "but I swear that I didn't do anything to harm her."

The young woman George had called Faye stopped thrashing. Her arms fell to her sides, and she bent forward from the waist and dissolved into great, gulping sobs.

Small and slight, and probably no older than nineteen, she was the total physical opposite of her full-bodied, flamboyantly coiffed and attired mother. The daughter wore no makeup, not even lipstick or mascara. Her complexion, her knit pants suit, and her limp, shoulder-length hair were all beige. Even though she must have been sitting next to Mimi, I hadn't noticed her. Until this eruption, there had been nothing about her that was vivid or memorable.

Liddy, the warmhearted Earth mother, hurried up to us, gestured for George to step away, and put her arms around the hysterical girl. With soft, comforting words, Liddy gently drew her over to the right side of the set and dabbed at her face with soft tissues.

Members of the audience, curious to get a closer view of this unexpected real-life drama, were getting up and stepping over camera cables to approach the set.

I faced them and stiffened my posture. Using my old high-school-teacher voice, I said, "Take your seats." The authoritative tone must have startled them, because they stopped moving forward. "Sit down, everybody, please. Paramedics are on the way. We need to keep the floor clear."

There was some grumbling but no sitting. "I'm *waiting*," I said, in a vocal quality meant to strike fear in the hearts of students. It must have reached them on some visceral level, because those adults began to move back. Some sat; others formed small groups in the corners and whispered. I didn't care whether they sat or stood; all that mattered was that I'd quashed the rebellion. *I've still got it,* I thought wryly. *I just don't want to have to use it in a Los Angeles classroom again.*

I turned to George Hopkins. His globular face was usually red, but now he was almost as white as my roll of paper towels.

Lowering my voice, I said, "I know what we're supposed to do. I was married to an LAPD detective for twenty years. Call the police, then call security and have them guard the doors until the police arrive. No one leaves unless the investigators say so. And we've got to keep everything exactly as it is."

George made the calls. Upon disconnecting, he said, "I'll stay by the door until the cops get here," and hurried toward the entrance.

The show's director, Quinn Tanner, finally appeared in front of me from the control booth above the studio. British, in her thirties, and very slender, she had long black hair parted in the middle and held away from her face by a large tortoiseshell clip at the back of her neck. Normally, Quinn's personality was so cool and low-key that she was practically a cliché of British under-

30

statement, but now, with sparks of rage in her eyes, she was more animated than I'd ever seen her.

"Mimi keeling over — it went out over the air. I didn't have time to cut to a commercial or even to black. Then Mickey called and shouted at me for letting the viewers see it. What the bloody hell went wrong down here?"

"She collapsed," I said, stating the obvious. "George called the paramedics."

Quinn reached down to touch Mimi, but I put my hand out and stopped her. "Don't." Leaning close so as not to be heard by anyone except Quinn, I said, "I'm afraid she's dead. I asked George to call the police, too."

"This is bloody awful." Quinn glared at me accusingly. "What did you put in that mousse?"

"It's nothing to do with the mousse. I think Mimi had a heart attack."

"We'll see, won't we?" Quinn stormed away and got into a huddled conversation with the two camera operators, Ernie Ramirez and Jada Powell. Ernie looked distraught, and Jada was crying.

I couldn't understand Quinn Tanner lashing out at me. She hadn't been exactly warm during our several days of prebroadcast rehearsals, but she'd at least been polite. Yet in an instant, nice Dr. Jekyll had turned into nasty Ms. Hyde. I wondered if she and Mimi had been close friends, and if her anger was really grief.

I remained standing next to Mimi to make sure no one came near her. By keeping people away as much as possible, I could try to give her a little dignity in death. She didn't have much; when she fell, her skirt had bunched beneath her, revealing her legs up to the middle of her thighs. For the sake of her modesty, I wanted to pull the dress down at least a few inches, but I knew that disturbing her body in any way was the wrong thing to do.

My take-charge bravado was purely fake. George had asked how I could be so calm. What a joke. The truth was that my insides were knotted with anxiety. Mimi Bond had just died during the debut of my show, in front of thousands of people — on live television. It was terrible enough for the woman to die, and for me to see it, but now her daughter was accusing me of killing her.

Even during the worst of my prebroadcast nerves, I had never imagined a catastrophe like this.

There was no time to think about that now. At the entrance, George Hopkins admitted a two-man team of paramedics. He pointed to where Mimi's body lay sprawled. Guiding a gurney piled with equipment, the paramedics rushed forward and sprang into action.

The older one had gray hair that stood up in rows of one-inch spikes, like a garden of nails. He ordered me, "Out of the way."

Obediently, I moved over to the right side of the set, next to the sink.

Liddy had persuaded Mimi's daughter to sit down at the end of the empty front row. The girl was quiet, staring off into the distance with a stunned expression. Liddy gave her a pat on the hand and came over to stand with me.

"You poor thing," Liddy whispered, nervously clenching and unclenching her hands.

"I'm all right, really." I hoped that saying it would make it so.

Liddy hooked her arm through mine as we watched the medics try in vain to revive Mimi.

A uniformed female police officer in her twenties arrived a few moments behind the paramedics and went straight to confer with them.

A tall, beefy Better Living Channel security man named Al Franklin came in and replaced George at the door. He glanced at the producer's head, bent to whisper something, and George quickly straightened his toupee. Jolly and avuncular, Al was the night security man. I met him for the first time this evening, just before he ushered the audience into the studio. The other times I'd come to the studio had been during the day.

Relieved of guard duty, George hurried across the studio to where Quinn was standing with the camera operators. He took Quinn's hand, but she pulled away immediately and turned her back to him. I wondered what *that* was about. No time to ponder. The older paramedic, his mouth set in a grim line, shook his head at the policewoman. They stopped working on Mimi.

The officer took the mobile phone from her belt and made a call. As she turned away from the medics and faced us, we heard the words "suspicious death." I knew she was reporting to her headquarters and asking them to send a detective.

Liddy tugged at the sleeve of my shirt and whispered, "She said 'suspicious death.' "

"That means this studio has just been declared a crime scene."

Liddy grabbed my hand and whispered frantically, "Oh, Del — that girl accused you. You're in serious trouble."

"That's ridiculous," I said. But icy prickles of fear were dancing around in my chest. "She's traumatized. She can't really think I'm responsible for her mother's death."

Or can she? And will anyone else believe her?

From her shoulder bag, I heard Liddy's cell ringing "Lara's Theme" from *Doctor Zhivago.* She plucked the phone out. "I had it off during the show," she told me. Flipping the top open, she said, "Hi, sweetie. . . . Oh, I thought you were Bill. . . . No, it was pretty awful, but we're fine. . . . She's right here. . . . She didn't answer her cell because she forgot to bring it." Liddy extended the hand with the phone. "It's for you — Big John. He saw what happened on TV, and he's been trying to reach you."

John O'Hara had been my late husband's partner and best friend for most of their law enforcement careers. His daughter, Eileen, lived with me while she was going to UCLA and worked with me at the cooking school. John was my best male friend and the one person I wanted to talk to at this moment. Just knowing he was on the other end of the line made me feel better.

I tried to keep any trace of fear out of my voice. "I'm glad you thought to dial Liddy's number," I said. "Where are you?"

"At your house. I watched the show with Eileen," he said. "What happened to that woman?"

"Mimi Bond. Unfortunately, she's dead. And don't ask what I put in the mousse. I've already had that question once tonight."

"A cop asked you that?" His warm baritone had turned cold. "If he wants to take you in for questioning, don't say anything. Call a lawyer, and have Liddy call me immediately."

"It was the show's director who asked, but I'm sure she was just upset."

"Who's on the scene?"

"So far, paramedics and a uniformed policewoman."

"She'll be from North Hollywood Station. That's the division where your studio's located."

"I imagine the detectives and the scientific investigation people will be here any minute," I said.

"You'll probably get two from SID but only one detective. North Hollywood doesn't have enough personnel for detectives to work in pairs. Do you want me to come out there, handle things for you?"

"Of course not." I could hear that he'd switched into full knight-protector mode, ready to gallop to the rescue of the innocent. My husband had sounded just like that. It was one of the many things I'd loved about Mack. "Thanks for the offer, but please don't worry about me. There *is* something you can do, though."

"Name it," John said.

"Walk Tuffy? I'm not sure when I'll be home tonight."

"We'll tour the neighborhood until old Tuff does everything he needs to do. But are you sure you're okay? This is rough."

"I'm handling it. Thanks for taking care of Tuffy."

We said good-bye just as a stocky man with bushy black hair and wearing a jacket that said "Coroner" entered, accompanied by a man and a woman who were both carrying small suitcases. The pair's matching windbreakers indicated they were from the scientific investigation division. The arrival of that trio set off a wave of excited chatter in the audience.

They came to a cooking show, but now they're watching real-life forensics.

The coroner spoke to the paramedics and then knelt beside Mimi. As the SID pair began taking photos of the body and the area surrounding where Mimi fell, the paramedics packed their equipment back

37

up on the gurney and left.

The departing paramedics passed a new arrival in the doorway, a man in his early fifties with a gold badge clipped to the pocket of his sports jacket. He had a commanding stride and a large head so perfectly bald that I was sure he shaved it. The air of authority that surrounded him was almost palpable.

"My Lord," Liddy whispered, "who does he remind you of?"

"*The King and I.* Yul Brynner," I said.

"If he looked any more like Yul, he'd have to pin that badge on his bare chest." She started humming "Shall We Dance," but I shushed her and she stopped.

I watched the detective survey the scene, and thought of Mack. My husband had been a hero to the innocent and a nightmare to the guilty. As hard as I tried to push fear away, it returned to roil my insides. I shouldn't be afraid, and yet I was. I hadn't killed Mimi Bond, but would this man who didn't know me believe I was innocent, or — like Mimi's daughter — think I was guilty?

The hero, or the nightmare?

3

The man with the gold badge stood at the entrance until the people in the studio became aware of him and the chattering quieted, then he went to confer briefly with the forensics group. The uniformed officer joined him.

George Hopkins scuttled over to stand beside me. We watched as the North Hollywood "Yul Brynner" asked the officer a few questions. She consulted her notes and then pointed to me. The detective advanced in my direction, but before he got very far, a middle-aged man with too little forehead and a double dose of chin strutted up to him, loudly announcing that he'd only been in the audience and demanding to be allowed to leave. Others joined in with a chorus of shouted complaints.

The detective ordered them, "Settle down." In a voice that was about as soft as a tire iron, he added, "I'll get to you all as soon as I can. The more cooperative you are, the quicker you can go home."

The protests subsided and the detective resumed his march in my direction.

He wasn't a big man, no taller than my own five feet seven inches, and he wasn't heavily muscled, but he had an aura of "don't mess with me" that was as intimidating as the mechanized battering ram a former Los Angeles police chief had used to smash down the doors of drug dealers.

"I'm Detective Hall." His voice was pitched low, with no discernible accent. Nor did his name, Hall, give any clue to his origins. He sounded like an everyman but looked a touch exotic. I wondered if Hall had always been the family name, or if had it been shortened for ease in spelling and pronunciation when his ancestors came to America.

Interrupting my speculations, Detective Hall aimed his dark — almost black — eyes at me. "And you are . . . ?"

George answered before I could. "I'm George Hopkins, the show's producer. This is Della Carmichael, the show's on-camera host." Indicating Liddy, who stood on the other side of me, he added, "I don't know who she is."

"This is my friend, Lydia Marshall. She's

my guest."

Detective Hall made no comment. "Who's the deceased?"

"Mimi Bond," I said.

George added, "She used to do the TV cooking show here."

"How well did you know her?" Detective Hall asked me.

"Not at all," I said.

George said, "I knew her pretty well. I produced her show, until it was canceled."

The SID woman held up the half-filled dish of mousse that Mimi had dropped and asked, "She was eating this when she died?"

"Yes," I said, "but that couldn't have killed her. I ate some of it myself before I brought it to the studio this evening."

Detective Hall scrutinized the substance with suspicion. "Exactly what is that?"

"Chocolate mousse." I thought it wise not to mention the dessert's nickname: Killer Mousse.

The SID man used one latex-gloved index finger to take just the tiniest dab of mousse and put it onto the tip of his tongue. He grimaced in revulsion and wiped the minuscule bit away with a piece of paper towel without swallowing any. "It tastes like that bitter chocolate laxative, Intesteral," he said. "And peanuts."

"That's not possible," I said. "I didn't put either a laxative or peanuts in that dish."

"Oh my God." George looked as though he'd been punched in the stomach. "Peanuts . . ."

"What about peanuts?" Hall demanded.

"Mimi had an allergy. Really powerful. If she even touched a peanut she broke out in a rash. She wouldn't allow anything with peanuts in the studio. She said if she ate even one it would kill her. . . ."

The SID woman used a gloved index finger to scoop a drop of mousse out of the dish, then examined it under the magnifying glass she had taken from her equipment case. "We'll have to test it at the lab to be sure, but it looks like we've got traces of ground peanuts here."

"Anaphylactic shock," I said. "Is that how she died?"

Hall's gaze pierced me with a look that was sharp as a boning knife. "So you knew Ms. Bond was allergic to peanuts."

"No, I didn't. I never saw her before tonight, except on some tapes of her show."

The detective then turned on George. "Who knew she was allergic to peanuts?"

George was sweating so hard he looked like an ice sculpture that was melting. He wiped his face, shrugged, and made a sweeping gesture with one arm. "Everybody who worked at the studio knew it. Camera people, technicians, staff, other hosts. She even talked about it on the air, warning people. She told them what they could substitute if a recipe called for peanuts."

Hall fixed his gaze on me. "You admitted you watched her shows, so you *did* know about her allergy."

"No, I didn't. At least, I don't think I heard her talking about it. I only watched a couple of the programs — to see how they were done technically. I didn't pay much attention to what she was saying. Besides, I don't have any reason to want her dead."

The scowl on his face made it clear he didn't believe me. Either that, or he was playing Good Cop–Bad Cop all by himself, except I hadn't yet seen Good Cop. Even though I know that interrogation can be a game of psychological intimidation, and that I hadn't done anything wrong, Detective Hall was scaring me a little. I told myself to be very careful about what I said, or I could be in trouble. Or in *worse* trouble.

The memory of something the SID man had said came back to me. I turned to him and asked, "You mentioned a laxative? Inter-something?"

"Intesteral. It's an over-the-counter bowel

relaxant. Pretty foul. You don't forget the taste."

"How in the world did those things get into my mousse? I made it at home and brought it here." I gestured toward Liddy. "My friend was with me." She nodded vigorously.

Detective Hall ignored her and stayed on me. "So, you're claiming you didn't put the ground peanuts in —"

"I'm not just *claiming* it, Detective. I will swear that I did not put either of those substances into my mousse." He'd made me angry. I was more comfortable being angry than being afraid.

"Why couldn't you tell that somebody had messed with it? Didn't it look different?"

He softened his tone, clearly trying to make his question sound casual, but I wasn't fooled into thinking that he had turned friendly. I was sure he was trying to throw me off balance and trap me into some damaging admission.

"Whoever put those things in my mousse only had to smooth the top with a spatula or the back of a large spoon, and it would have appeared undisturbed."

I couldn't tell if Detective Hall believed my explanation; his expression was impossible to read.

Instead of commenting, he studied the kitchen set. "Before the show, did you keep the mousse in this refrigerator?"

"No. It's broken," I said.

George looked startled. "What do you mean, 'broken'? It was fine this morning."

"Well, it wasn't working when we got here," Liddy said.

"I'll have somebody fix it," George said.

"No. You don't do anything until I say you can." Detective Hall's adamant tone discouraged argument. He took a pair of thin latex gloves from his jacket pocket and slipped them on. As we watched, he gripped the refrigerator near the top and rocked it gently away from the wall. When there was room to look behind it, he peered down and grunted.

I hurried over to see what he was staring at, and my breath caught in surprise. The refrigerator's electrical cord, which should have been connected to the outlet in the wall, was lying on the floor, with no plug on the end. I could see the ends of tiny copper wires inside the black rubber casing.

"The refrigerator was disconnected from the wall and the plug was sliced off," Detective Hall said. He gestured to the SID man. "Process this for prints — everything: back of the refrigerator, the cord, the wall, the

45

outlet. Look around and see if you can find the missing plug." Hall asked me, "If you couldn't use this refrigerator, what did you do?"

"The mousse and the raw chicken pieces I was going to prepare on air had to be kept cold, so I put them into the backstage fridge."

"Show me." He ordered Liddy and George: "Stay here."

I led Detective Hall and the SID pair around behind the set, through the poorly lighted jumble of props and equipment, to the appliance used by the crew.

I reached for the refrigerator's door handle.

"Don't touch that," Hall said.

"I already did — when I put things in and took them out."

The detective told the SID man to open it carefully. He did, using a pen beneath the handle to release the catch. When the door was open, Hall scanned the contents. "What's this bowl of chocolate stuff?" he asked.

"It's the mousse I made on camera."

"You mean you had *two* mousses?"

I resisted the temptation to tell him that the plural of mousse is "mousse." Instead I explained how a cooking show works. "Food that has to bake or, like a mousse, has to be refrigerated until it's firm enough to eat, is made in advance. That way the audience can see all the steps in how the dishes are prepared, and then they can also see the result, which they couldn't in just the time the show is on the air."

Nodding at the mousse in the refrigerator, he said sarcastically, "I doubt anyone's gonna want to eat that."

I bristled, but the SID man saved me from making a retort I might have regretted. He said, "Any prints here are probably smudged, but I might be able to get some partials."

"I'll give you my prints for comparison," I said.

Detective Hall's face was a portrait of skepticism. "You're being very cooperative."

"I know how hard your job is," I said. "My husband was a detective in the LAPD."

"*Was?* You're divorced?"

"He passed away two years ago. Mackenzie Carmichael."

"Didn't know him," he said. "I'm sorry for your loss."

I'm sorry for your loss. . . . The one-size-fits-all, standard phrase uttered to a person whose loved one had died. He didn't sound sorry, but since he seemed so suspicious of me, perhaps he was wondering if I'd killed Mack. I fought down the impulse to defend myself, to explain that my husband had a fatal heart attack while jogging.

Keeping a grip on my temper, I left Detective Hall and the SID team and returned to the set, just in time to see George grab a fistful of Ernie Ramirez's Los Angeles Lakers jersey. George's face was so red I thought he was about to have a stroke. I hurried to insert myself between the producer and the camera operator and pried George's fingers from Ernie's shirt.

"What's going on?"

"I just found out that Ernie, Jada, and Quinn knew that Mimi, the bitch, was going to play a rotten trick on you. While you were getting made up back in the dressing room, Mimi stirred that bad-tasting laxative into your chocolate thing."

"She wanted to make me look like a bad cook? To ruin my show?"

"Mickey Jordan told me Mimi wanted him to fire you and bring *Cooking Diva* back on the air, but he refused," George said, "even though they used to have a thing."

"A *thing?*"

George shrugged. "I shouldn't have said anything. Old news. Forget it."

I certainly wasn't going to forget it, but I

dropped the subject and turned to look at Ernie. The camera operator was staring at the floor.

"Ernie, look at me, please." Reluctantly, he raised his head. "If you all knew what Mimi was going to do, why didn't somebody tell me?" I asked.

"I'm sorry, Ms. Carmichael," he said. "I thought it was sort of funny — you know, good TV."

Good TV. Lord, what kind of a business have I gotten myself into?

I asked, "Did anybody else know what she was going to do?"

"Yeah, a few. . . ."

I surveyed the faces in the studio. Liddy had gone over to Mimi's daughter to sit with her, even though the girl seemed near catatonic, still staring into space.

Iva Jordan, who'd taken cooking classes at my school and persuaded her husband to put me on television, was in a whispered conversation with the grandmotherly woman who hosted the network's crafts show; I couldn't recall her name. I wondered if Iva knew that there had been some history between Mimi Bond and Mickey Jordan, or if it would matter to her if she did. Questions for another time.

I saw director Quinn Tanner talking to the

camera operators, and producer George Hopkins circulating among members of the technical crew. Several of the people knew Mimi was going to sabotage my dessert. I didn't know how far in advance Mimi's plot had been hatched, but it was long enough for someone to grind up peanuts and bring them to the studio.

There were two things I *did* know:

Nobody had warned me.

And one of them took that opportunity to kill her.

4

The coroner directed the removal of Mimi's body, but the SID kept doing their forensic things.

In spite of the trauma of the previous hour, an automatic switch clicked on in my brain and I remembered the ovens. I had a pan full of Easy Cranberry Chicken in one and Sunburst Vegetable Pie in the other. In a few more minutes, they would have burned. I took them out, placed them on the preparation counter to cool, and turned off the ovens.

Emerging from backstage, the SID woman sniffed the air and said, "Hmmm, smells good."

"If you're hungry, I'd be glad to fix plates for you and your partner."

"No, thanks," she said. "We have to take everything you made back to the lab, for testing."

Silently, I wondered if anyone was ever

again going to eat something I prepared. Or would I be known in tabloids as "The Killer Cook"? I shook my head in silent frustration and turned my attention back to Detective Hall.

In a methodical, thoroughly professional way, he was questioning the members of the audience as to how they happened to be here tonight.

Twenty-seven of the thirty said that they'd been approached last weekend, at various shopping malls in the San Fernando Valley, and offered free tickets to the premiere of a new live national TV show. The people who accepted the invitation had never heard of me, but the recruiter told them that the studio audience would be shown on camera, so they should tell their friends and families to watch from seven to eight o'clock Thursday night, which was tonight.

None of those twenty-seven said they'd known Mimi Bond personally, although some of them had seen her *Cooking Diva* show. Further, they told the detective that they had waited outside until being ushered in a few minutes before the show began. They said they had never been anywhere in the studio except where the audience was seated, or to the small guest restrooms behind the seating area.

Hall told them they could go home. "Officer Cutler took your names and addresses. If we have any further questions, we'll contact you."

Three spectators were left.

"This is Iva Jordan, Mrs. Mickey Jordan," I told Detective Hall. "Mickey Jordan owns the Better Living Channel."

Hall asked her, "Where's your husband?"

"He went to New York very early this morning for a stockholders' meeting. He'll be back tomorrow night."

Iva's face was normally pale, but right now she looked positively bloodless. There was a faint sheen of perspiration on her forehead and upper lip. I reached out to take her hand and discovered it was cold and damp.

"Iva, are you all right?" I asked.

"I don't feel well." Her voice had an unnatural hoarseness. "I need to go home."

It was obvious Hall didn't like that, but he agreed, albeit reluctantly. "If you're sick, I can talk to you tomorrow."

"There's really no point, Detective. I didn't know the dead woman, so there's nothing I can tell you that would be of help."

Hall's jaw tightened. I guessed that he didn't like being told what to do. I had a healthy streak of that myself.

"Sometimes people know more than they

think," he said flatly. "We'll be talking."

Iva looked so unsteady that I asked, "Do you have someone to drive you home?"

The woman sitting beside Iva spoke up. "She came with me."

"And who are you?" the detective wanted to know.

"Ah'm Lulu Owens. *All Things Crafty*? That's the show Ah do here." Her accent was distinctly southern, the hominy-and-honey tones native to Georgia and South Carolina. Lulu Owens, deep in her fifties and not trying to hide it, was lean and strong, with gray hair tied back in a ponytail that reached almost to her waist. She had muscles enough that I could picture her on a ranch, roping cattle, but her complexion was so soft and pink that I suspected she carried a parasol when she went out in the sun. Putting an arm protectively around Iva's narrow shoulders, and giving Detective Hall a flirtatious wink, she said, "Ah don' know anything 'bout what happened tonight, but you come see me anyway. Ah jes' love to talk to interesting men."

Hall ignored her flirting and gestured impatiently toward the door. "Go ahead. Take Mrs. Jordan home. We'll be in touch."

"Ah'll be lookin' forward to that," Lulu said, as she steered Iva toward the exit.

I'd listened to cop conversations for twenty years and learned that unless a murder was just a random act of violence, the best way to find a killer was to investigate the victim, concentrating on family and friends — some of whom had murder in their hearts. I was curious to know what Lulu might have to say about Mimi Bond as a person. Their shows taped in the same building. Definitely, I was going to get together with Lulu.

Detective Hall turned his attention to the last person left: Mimi's daughter. The girl was sitting slumped, her shoulders hunched forward, with her hands folded in her lap. She'd stopped staring into space and was now looking at the floor.

Before I could introduce her, Detective Hall demanded, "Who are you?"

Her lips moved, but I couldn't hear what she said. Neither could Hall. She flinched when he took a step closer to her. As though to keep some distance between them, she cleared her throat and spoke up. "Faye . . . Bond."

"Any relation to the deceased?"

"This is Mimi's daughter," I said.

When he responded, "I'm sorry for your loss," she began to cry again. Tears started sliding down her cheeks, and then came great, gasping sobs that shook her small frame. Her uncontrolled grief was like a punch to my own heart because I remembered the pain of losing not only my husband, but my dad, too. Their deaths had seemed like amputations, the hacking away of something from my own body. Silently, I gave thanks that my mother was still alive and healthy.

Faye Bond's weeping was so intense that Hall asked if she wanted him to call a doctor. She shook her head but kept on sobbing.

Liddy sat down next to Faye, opened a fresh package of Kleenex, and gave her a handful of tissues. The girl dabbed at the torrent gushing from her eyes, but that didn't lessen the hysterical crying.

Giving up trying to question Faye Bond tonight, the detective ordered Officer Cutler to drive her home.

It was almost four hours after Mimi's death when Detective Hall finally told Liddy and me that we could leave. Liddy could have gone home much earlier, after he'd finished questioning her, but she explained that we'd come together in her car. Hall offered to assign one of the police officers now on the scene to take me home, but she refused to leave me. Leave me alone with *him,* was what I knew she meant.

The SID woman took not only my finger-prints but my palm prints, too, then gave me a tissue to wipe my hands. It was a pleasant surprise to discover that investiga-tors now used the kind of ink that didn't stain the skin.

Detective Hall had continued to inter-rogate me long after he'd released George Hopkins, Quinn Tanner, the camera opera-tors, and the members of the crew. The same questions came at me — over and over — each time phrased a little differently. He was skillful, but if he was looking for dis-crepancies in my account, or hoping that I'd break down and confess to killing Mimi, he was disappointed.

"You can't honestly think that I murdered Mimi Bond. I didn't know her, and never met her before tonight."

"Maybe. Maybe not. If you did have any earlier contact with her, you can be sure we'll find out about it."

"All you're going to find out is that I'm telling the truth."

"Even if you didn't know the Bond woman, you might have wanted to eliminate a competitor. You can't deny that you fed her the mousse that killed her."

I couldn't believe what I was hearing. "You really think I'd murder someone just to have a TV show?"

Detective Hall's expression morphed from grim professionalism into a grimace of disgust. "I've seen victims who were killed for a lot less," he said. "Go. I'll be in touch. Don't leave town."

It angered me to be suspected of murdering a woman I'd only met tonight, but I stopped myself from asking sarcastically if he meant that I couldn't leave the town of North Hollywood and go home to Santa Monica. Instead, I remembered Mack. The job of a homicide investigator was hard. They saw the absolute worst in human beings: ugliness and evil that most of the rest of us were spared.

5

After Liddy steered her Range Rover away from the North Hollywood TV studio, heading toward Santa Monica to drop me off, she dialed her husband, who had watched the show and had called her half a dozen times to be sure she was all right.

Liddy let him know when she'd finally be home. "If you warm up my side of the bed, I'll make it worth your while, honey." She giggled at his response, told him he was "very naughty," and disconnected. "I swear," she said with a happy grin, "since the boys went off to college, it's like Bill and I are on our honeymoon again."

I wish I had someone to call; there wasn't anyone to warm up my side of the bed. But when we got to Santa Monica, there was a surprise waiting for me.

As soon as Liddy pulled up in front of my small, one-story little English cottage in the five hundred block of Ninth Street, I smelled the night-blooming jasmine that grew beside my front door. Then I saw a pair of silhouettes sitting on the front steps. Framed against the light coming through the living room window were the shapes of a two-hundred-pound man with broad shoulders and a seventy-pound dog with a rounded head.

Indicating the larger silhouette, Liddy said, "I see Big John is still here."

Both man and dog got up when I climbed down from Liddy's Rover. They were an impressive pair. John O'Hara was six feet four and Tuffy stood forty inches from shoulder to paws. The moment John let go of Tuffy's leash, my black standard poodle ran toward me, wagging his stubby tail. Actually, his whole body wagged. I knelt down and hugged him.

"Hey, Tuffy, you act like I've been gone for a month instead of seven hours," I said, scratching below his ears and stroking his cheeks. "Yes, I missed you, too." I stood up. Still wagging, Tuffy nuzzled his head against my thigh.

"You okay?" John asked as he stooped to pick up Tuffy's leash.

"The immediate answer is yes, I am. If you mean the bigger picture — do I still have my new career — I don't know."

"You were really good on TV. They'd be crazy to let you go," Liddy told me. "I'll call you tomorrow. Now I'm going home to my man."

We said our good nights softly, so as not to disturb sleeping neighbors, and Liddy drove away.

I asked John, "Where's Eileen?"

"In bed. She's got an exam in the morning. I told her I'd wait up for you."

"I appreciate that. Can you stay a few more minutes?"

"As long as you want. There's a nurse with Shannon tonight."

This was a painful subject to John, but because John and Shannon and Mack and I had been friends for so many years, I had to ask. "How's she doing?"

"The doctor just changed her medication. He thinks it will give her more good days than bad ones."

"That's encouraging."

"I hope so." John didn't look encouraged; I dropped the subject.

"Shall we go inside?" he asked. "If you like, I'll sit with you until you're ready to go to bed."

"I need to breathe in this clean night air. Let's take Tuffy for a walk. I want to tell you about tonight and get your investigators thinking."

"Such as it is, my brain is yours."

John handed me the end of Tuffy's leash, and we started to walk south down Ninth Street. Remembering my civic responsibility, I asked, "Do you have any more plastic bags?"

He chuckled and reached into the pocket of his jeans. "One. But I don't think old Tuff's got anything left to deposit."

It was an unusually soft night for the twenty-first of October: cool, but not cold enough to need anything heavier than the lightweight wool jacket I was wearing. As we strolled toward the lights on Montana Avenue, which was three blocks south of my house, I told John about the events of the night, including the fact that someone had cut the plug off the on-set refrigerator so I couldn't use it.

"I was thinking about this on the way home," I said. "My guess is that Mimi Bond did it so I'd have to use the crew's refrigerator. Back there, she wouldn't be seen sabotaging the mousse. It wasn't hard to maneuver the refrigerator away from the wall just enough to reach behind and disconnect it. Then cutting off the plug and inching the fridge back into place wouldn't have taken more than a minute, at most."

"But how could she know she wouldn't get caught on your set by somebody who wasn't in on her scheme?" John asked.

"It wasn't a big risk. Mine was the only show using the studio tonight, so there weren't many people around. When nothing's being taped, the work lights in the studio are minimal. The broadcast lights on my kitchen set weren't turned on and checked until about half an hour before the security man let the audience in. The killer knew Mimi was going to ruin the mousse. He or she must have been somewhere in the studio and saw Mimi sabotage it after I put it in the backstage refrigerator. As soon as Mimi left, the killer added the ground peanuts."

"How many ways are there to get into the studio?" John asked.

"Three. Through the front office where a security person sits at a monitor watching the front gate, through the back entrance to the loading dock, and through a side entrance where the studio audience lined up before being let in. The people in the audience were watched and then brought in by the night security man."

"How did Mimi Bond get in before the broadcast?"

"Detective Hall asked that. The night

security man let her in. Even though her show had been canceled, he said she still came to the studio, looking for things she said she'd forgotten. He felt sorry for her, so he always let her in."

"So the killer either works at the studio, or has easy access to it. I don't like the thought of you being around a murderer. I think you should quit."

"I appreciate your concern," I said, "but this job is important to me."

"You staying alive is important to *me*. And Eileen. You've been a second mother to her."

The warmth in John's voice made me a little uncomfortable. If Eileen had been present, I would have hugged him, but during times we were alone together, by unspoken agreement, John and I kept a certain distance between us. Perhaps it was an old-fashioned sense of propriety. As we walked, I told John as much as I knew about the people at the studio who knew Mimi Bond. I ended by telling him about Detective Hall's intensive questioning of me.

"Do you believe he *seriously* suspects me of murder?" I asked.

"Unless cops find the killer standing over a gunshot victim with a smoking gun, or holding a bloody knife over somebody who's been stabbed — and that doesn't happen nearly often enough — we try to figure out who had a motive and who had the opportunity. Let's talk about opportunity for a minute. Who knew you were going to make chocolate mousse tonight?"

"Lots of people could have. The menu and ingredients had been posted on the wall in the production office for at least a week."

"Why was that?"

"So George Hopkins's assistant could buy the ingredients I'd need in order to make the dishes on the air. Then the prop person had to make new labels for everything."

"New labels? Why?"

"They fake the brands, so we wouldn't appear to be giving any real company free advertising. When I agreed to do the show, I had to turn in one hundred and fifty-six recipes — three dishes each for a year of shows — so they can design labels and plan when to buy what ingredients."

John was silent for a few minutes, his features creased in the pensive frown Eileen and I called his "thinking expression."

After we'd strolled a block or so, he said, "Hall knows that statistically speaking — and eliminating gangs and drive by shootings — stranger murders are rare. Someone in a victim's family is most likely to be the killer. Next come rivals, either romantic or business. The business rival category is where you come in. The way Hall may be looking at it is that you wanted to keep your TV show, and that you're the one who had the most opportunity to put ground peanuts in the mousse."

Exasperated, I said, "But that's absolutely ridiculous. I didn't know about her allergy, or that she would be there tonight."

"The problem with your story is that you can't prove a negative. You could have learned about her allergy from watching her show. You could have found out somehow that she would be there. Maybe you even called to invite her."

I started to remind him that there would be no calls to Mimi Bond from any of my numbers, but he anticipated me. "You could have used a public phone or a prepaid cell," he said.

I tried to laugh, but it was a weak attempt. "This is unreal. Me, a murderer? I don't even jaywalk."

"I know you couldn't kill anybody, but Hall doesn't."

"What should I do?"

"Go about your business," he said. "Let the cops do their work. I'll check in with North Hollywood and see how they're progressing."

That was a little too vague for me. Some-one had used my show — messed with my *life* — to murder a woman. I decided to find out what I could about Mimi Bond on my own. Maybe I could learn something that would lead to identifying her killer.

I smiled to myself in the dark. After Detective Hall's relentless grilling of me, it would be poetic justice if I solved the mystery before he did.

6

After John left, I found a note from his daughter, Eileen, telling me that my mother and my two sisters in San Francisco had seen the show and phoned, anxious to find out what happened. They wanted me to call them at my sister Keely's house where the three of them had gathered — "no matter how late." Those words were underlined. I smiled; in my head I could hear Keely dictating that message in her authoritative tone.

I hoped Keely meant that: It was now one o'clock in the morning.

She snatched up the phone after what couldn't have been more than half a ring on her end. Her brisk "hello" was followed immediately by two distinctive *clicks,* signaling that my sister Jean and our mother had picked up the extensions. Everybody started talking at once.

Although Keely is the youngest of the

siblings, she's also the bossiest. In seconds she had them quiet, then commanded me: "Tell *all*."

I related what I knew. Most of it. I left out the part about Detective Hall's bizarre notion that I might have murdered Mimi, and the other part — about my intention to do some investigating of my own, in case he wasn't seriously looking in other directions. I didn't want them worrying because they might all decide to arrive on my doorstep. I loved my sisters and my mother, but there was too much going on at this moment for me to enjoy a mass visit.

When their questions were finally exhausted, they began giving opinions about how I should dress in future shows, and what dishes I should make on camera.

Jean said, "Show a little cleavage." Her voice was typically soft and playful.

Keely advised sweaters. "Because your boobs are still defying gravity. Take advantage while you can."

Mom was practical. "Don't wear silk tops. Silk shows spots when you splash something, and you always splash. If you wear silk, you'll spend a fortune on dry cleaners, and it's not deductible." Even when giving such no-nonsense advice, I always thought of my mother as having a hug in her warm voice.

On the subject of what dishes I should demonstrate, Jean spoke first. "Your bread-less meatloaf. Absolutely. And that crème brûlée — teach people how to make the hard crust on top. It's fun to watch you work with that blowtorch."

Keely's pronouncement was: "The Gangster Chicken."

"Daddy and Sean always loved your shepherd's pie," Mom said. "Oh, good heavens — I forgot about Sean. Do you think he knows what happened?" My brother, Sean, was serving on an aircraft carrier in Manila.

"I don't think they get the Better Living Channel on his ship," Keely said wryly. "I'll shoot him an e-mail, Della — and tell him your first TV show was *murder*."

"That's not funny," Mom chided.

The four of us were on the phone together for forty-five minutes. By the time we said our affectionate good nights, I was barely able to keep my eyes open.

At last I was able to take off my clothes, brush my teeth, and collapse into bed. Tuffy was already stretched out lengthwise on his side, snoring softly.

I dreamed that I was Nancy Drew, searching under lilac bushes and exploring dark cellars, armed with only a flashlight and a ton of gumption. But in the dream, Nancy wasn't "titian-haired" anymore; she was a brunette like me. We — or I — or the Nancy–Della combination were getting close to solving a serious crime, when all of a sudden, from out of the darkness, I heard a dog barking. Barking . . . ?

Tuffy?

I fought my way to consciousness and realized that it *was* Tuffy barking — because someone was ringing the doorbell. I squeezed my eyes to focus on the bedside clock's inch-high red digital numbers.

Three a.m.? I'd been asleep for only a little more than an hour.

The bell kept ringing. I quieted Tuffy with a reassuring pat and struggled into a robe. I'd just managed to thrust one arm through a sleeve when I opened the door to the hallway and practically collided with my young houseguest and cooking school assistant, Eileen O'Hara. Twenty, tall, naturally blonde, and naturally slim, Eileen was so pretty that if I didn't love her like a daughter I might hate her, or at least feel depressed around her. Even in the middle of the night, in her rumpled old UCLA Bruins T-shirt and faded sweatpants, she looked fabulous. On the other hand, I must have been a puffy-eyed mess.

Eileen grabbed my arm and whispered, "What's happening?"

"I have no idea, but whoever's at the door isn't giving up."

As I went down the hallway, Eileen and Tuffy were right behind me, practically on my heels. At the entrance to the kitchen, Eileen thrust a big, heavy Maglite into my hand; it was part torch and part cudgel. "It's one of Daddy's police flashlights. He gave it to me to carry at night."

"Thanks," I said. "Take Tuffy and go stand by the phone in the kitchen. If I scream, call nine-one-one."

Eileen curled her fingers around Tuffy's collar and turned on the kitchen lights. I flinched against the brightness and saw that she'd kept one hand on Tuffy and was reaching for the wall phone with the other.

When I got to the living room, I flipped the wall switches that controlled both the brass ceiling fixture above my head and the outside lights. Clutching the hefty flashlight against my thigh, I looked through the picture window to see a man jabbing at my bell as though he was summoning a sluggish elevator. It was a relief to recognize him, but he was not anyone I would have expected to find at this hour standing on my doormat. No — "standing" was the wrong word. Shifting impatiently from foot to foot, he looked like a jogger running in place while he waited for a red light to turn green.

My surprise visitor was Phil Logan, head of publicity for the Better Living Channel. I'd met him two weeks earlier when he supervised the photographer who was taking pictures of me to publicize the show. Phil oozed energy the way some people ooze sweat. In his thirties and thin as the blade of a knife, he had an explosion of sandy hair. I imagined every calorie he consumed rushing right to his scalp.

I opened the door. In an angry whisper, I demanded, "What are you doing here at this hour?"

Phil brandished a leather file folder. "Sorry, Della, but this is a business emergency. I need information from you that I have to start e-mailing out in a couple of hours."

On one hour's sleep I was in no mood for a visitor, business or social, but I couldn't keep him out on the doorstep. "Shhh. Come in before you wake the neighbors."

Phil stepped inside, and stopped. He said, "Nice house," but he was surveying my living room with a frown.

Why is he frowning?

His expression annoyed me. I should have ignored it, but before I could stop myself, I was defending my home. "I decorated the living room so it would feel like a country garden, with lots of flowers and plants. That sofa is so comfortable I practically have to pry people out of it. One evening a woman came over, wearing the same floral print, and when she sat down, all I could see was her head."

Phil didn't laugh at my attempt at humor, or even acknowledge it. With brow still puckered, he said, "If we hide the TV, rent some antique pieces and decent art, and bring in a pair of settees in pale yellow silk, I might land an at-home photo spread for you."

"But then it wouldn't be *my* home anymore." At three a.m. I wasn't even trying to keep the edge out of my voice. "Isn't there supposed to be truth in advertising?"

"That's 'advertising' — I'm talking about publicity. Different animal entirely."

"I need coffee," I said, gesturing for him to follow me down the hall. When we got to the kitchen doorway and he saw Tuffy, he practically skidded to a halt. Tuffy stood beside Eileen, on guard. Seeing Phil, Tuffy's

74

lip curled slightly on one side, and I heard a soft growl low in his throat.

"It's all right, Tuff. Phil is a friend." Calling Phil a friend was an exaggeration, but Tuffy stopped growling.

Phil was gawking at Eileen with the enthralled expression I had witnessed often when men saw Eileen O'Hara for the first time.

Had I ever looked as good as Eileen in the middle of the night, even twenty-odd years ago? Mack used to tell me I was beautiful, but he was in love with me, so I never regarded him as an objective judge. I used to joke that I'd cast a spell over him with my homemade pastas and chocolate cheesecakes.

I introduced Phil and Eileen to each other. "Phil handles publicity for the network — and," I added pointedly, "he works very odd hours."

"I'm a business major at UCLA," Eileen said. "Publicity's important."

For the first time since he'd seen my living room and found it wanting, Phil looked pleased. "You're right. Without properly managed publicity, nobody would know what TV show to watch or which movie to go see."

"Sit down," I told Phil, indicating a chair

75

at the kitchen table.

Phil looked at Tuffy with concern and remained by the door, as though he'd taken root in that spot. "In the bio you filled out, you said you had a poodle. I thought you meant a fussy little hairball. Does he bite?"

"He's very gentle," I said. "Here, give me your hand." Without waiting for Phil to extend it, I took his wrist and guided him toward Tuffy. "Hey, Tuff, this is a nice man. See?" I let Tuffy sniff Phil's fingers. Apparently, Phil passed what I called "The Tuffy Test." My standard poodle did his version of a shrug, strolled over beside the kitchen table and settled down. He rested his chin on his front paws, but his eyes stayed open and watchful.

Eileen took a seat at the kitchen table. Phil glanced at Tuffy. Noting the dog's lack of interest in him, he looked relieved and sat down beside Eileen.

I turned on the coffeemaker and took mugs from the shelf.

"No coffee for me," Phil said, "but I need sugar. Do you have something sweet around?" With a laugh, he added, "Anything except chocolate mousse."

"That's not funny," I said — and realized that I sounded like my mother. *Aggghhh.* When did *that* happen?

Eileen, the human bridge over troubled waters, said smoothly, "How about some of Della's chocolate almond-butter fudge?" She took a plastic container out of the refrigerator. When she removed the top, Phil's eyes widened with desire for something other than Eileen.

"My mom used to make fudge," he said. "Not like the stuff you get in stores that tastes like gum erasers. You got any milk to go with it?"

I took care of Phil's milk request while Eileen put pieces of the fudge on a small plate and gave it to him with a paper napkin.

After the first bite, Phil said, "This is fabulous."

"When I was in college, I was so broke I couldn't afford to buy Christmas presents, so I made fudge for everybody," I said.

"You could make me a present of this anytime."

I poured coffee for myself and for Eileen. One of the traits my young friend and I share is the ability to sleep soundly after drinking coffee, even if we do it late at night.

Phil pushed his empty plate aside and placed his file folder on the table. "That'll keep me going. Now, let's get down to business. Damn, I wish I'd been at the studio tonight, but I thought your show was going to be dull."

"Phil, a woman was *murdered,*" I said.

"Oh, well, yes. I mean, that was a tragedy, of course. But it happened. We can't change that. Now we have to look on the bright side."

"What 'bright side'?" I asked.

"The Better Living Channel got ten thousand new subscribers before midnight, after the story broke on the national news. The head of sales thinks that by the end of today they'll have another fifty thousand." Phil wasn't trying to disguise the excitement in his voice. "What's happened is *big.* Maybe you wondered why you didn't do any interviews before the show went on?"

"No, I hadn't. This is all new to me."

"Well, the reason is that I couldn't give you away to the TV or print media even if I'd tossed in season tickets to the Lakers — not that they'd take a bribe," he said quickly. "They wouldn't. I couldn't even get you on local radio. But since the murder, you've become *interesting.*"

"I don't want to profit from a woman's death." The idea of it put such a bad taste in my mouth I pushed my coffee mug away.

"Let's think this through," Phil said calmly. "Did you kill Mimi?"

"Of course not."

"Then your conscience is clear, so don't worry about it. Right now you're *hot,* Della. We've got to take advantage — but we have to do some damage control."

I looked at him with suspicion. "What do you mean?"

"I'll get to that in a minute, but first . . ." Phil extracted several eight-by-ten photos from his file folder and placed them face-down on the kitchen table. "Ready for the big reveal?"

"Yes."

With a flourish, Phil turned the pictures over.

Eileen squealed in delight. "Oh, Aunt Del — you look *gorgeous.*"

Staring at the pictures, I asked, "Who is that?"

"It's you," Phil said. "Same dark hair, same nice eyes."

"Where are the little lines around my 'nice eyes'?"

"The retouch artist got rid of those. And that crease in the middle of your forehead — I stood over him until it was gone."

"My face looks frozen, like I wouldn't be able to frown."

"Della, sweetie," Phil said, "*nobody* looks as good as their publicity pictures. That's the whole idea of a portrait shoot: improving on real life." In spite of his upbeat attitude, I heard a note of strain in his voice. It made me feel bad about my negative reaction. Maybe I was so upset at seeing a woman die in front of me that I was being unreasonable.

"They really are lovely photos," I told Phil. "It was just that I hadn't expected to be all glamorized and retouched."

"Don't take it personally," Phil said. "You're very attractive for a . . . for a . . ."

"For a woman my age?"

"I mean for somebody who isn't an actress."

"Nice save," Eileen said dryly.

"Speaking of that dreaded subject 'age' . . ." Phil pulled a sheet of paper out of the folder. I recognized it as the bio form I filled out. "Now that circumstances have put you in the spotlight, I've got to create a hot new bio for you, to make you sound exciting. That's what I've got to start sending around this morning, and what you've given me won't do. See here, under 'age'? You put down forty-seven. How old shall we tell the media you are?"

"Forty-seven."

"You don't look it. How about we say . . . late thirties?"

"I can see that you're really good at your

80

job, Phil, and I appreciate that you're trying to be helpful, but I'm not going to lie."

Phil shrugged, giving in. "Okay, we just won't mention age. Let people guess. Next: Are you having — or have you had — a romance with anybody famous?"

Eileen giggled, which wasn't a particularly flattering reaction.

"No," I said. "I did meet Jay Leno a few years ago. One morning in Beverly Hills, when my car broke down. He was riding a motorcycle and stopped to see if he could help me."

Excitement lighted Phil's eyes. "Great. What happened between you two?"

"Nothing. I told him that I'd already called Triple A, so he rode off."

Phil grimaced in disappointment. "That's not enough to get you on the *Tonight Show.*" Then he brightened. "What if we drop hints in the press about you and a *dead* celebrity — somebody fabulous but who isn't around to deny it? I'd let it slip that you were the last great love of that guy's life. Of course, you'll deny it, but nobody will believe your denial. It's perfect."

"Absolutely not."

He deflated like a balloon character after Macy's Thanksgiving Day Parade. "All right . . . So what do you want to do about

81

the publicity photos?"

I felt bad that I was making his job so hard. "Go ahead, use them," I said. "They're really beautiful pictures. Maybe my actress friend Liddy will teach me some makeup tricks, so I'll be able to look a little more like the retouched me."

"Good idea." Phil scooped them up and put them back in the folder. "Now for the next item on the agenda." He extracted three folded newspapers and smoothed them out on the table. "I got the early editions. Mimi's murder made the front page of the *L.A. Chronicle,* is on page three of the *New York Post,* and on the front of the *L.A. Times* 'California' section. Mimi herself isn't such a big deal, but how she died is — *live* on a TV network, even if it is basic cable."

Eileen and I scanned the stories. Straight reporting; no accusation that I was suspected of murder. One paragraph caught my eye. "This paper refers to me as 'TV novice Delia Carmichael,' " I said. "They got the novice part right, but *Delia?*"

Phil waved a hand dismissively. "Yeah, well, they can get your name wrong when you're an unknown. But you won't be unknown for long. I'm lining up interviews — I already promised the *Chronicle* first crack at you. Promotion-wise, this is *huge,*

Del. I didn't think I'd be able to get you into the *Chronicle* for months — if ever. The reporter's name is Nicholas D'Martino. He wants to come over here at one o'clock today. Can you do it then?"

"Yes, but there won't be time for you to go out and rent better furniture and art."

Phil either missed the irony in my voice or he ignored it. "We can do that later. Nick doesn't do life and style pieces. His specialty is *crime*."

7

When the doorbell rang at five minutes past noon, I was on my hands and knees, vigorously scrubbing the kitchen floor, scouring away traces of the cooking and baking I'd done yesterday for the TV show. At the same time, I was trying to erase the image of Mimi Bond's agonized face as she died in front of me.

I'd put Tuffy in the fenced yard behind the house while I was washing the floor, but he must have heard the bell because he started to bark. To quiet him, I went to the back door, shushed gently, and assured him that everything was all right. His response was to settle onto the grass beneath the big elm tree and chew on a new tennis ball. From the time he was a puppy, Tuffy seemed to understand what I said.

The doorbell kept ringing. Stripping off my rubber kitchen gloves, I hurried toward the front of the house. I'd have to get rid of whoever it was quickly in order to have time to take a shower and dress before the *Los Angeles Chronicle* reporter arrived.

Glancing through the living room window, I saw a man in his forties, medium height with thick black hair. A wavy lock fell onto the middle of his forehead, brushing the top of black brows. He was attractive, if you liked the tanned, a little too good-looking, Las Vegas singer type with the beginning of a stubble on his face. All he needed to complete the image was a cigarette in one hand and a glass in the other.

But this wasn't Las Vegas. I guessed he had come to my door for one of the three usual reasons that strangers rang my bell: a) to try to convert me to their religion, b) to try to persuade me to list my house with their real estate office, or c) to offer to trim my trees.

He saw me peering at him and flashed me a semi-smile. The slight curl of his lips didn't seem in the least bit religious, and judging by the fact that he was wearing a sweater and sports jacket, I couldn't picture him trimming trees. That left real estate; this would be the third agent in a week inquiring if I wanted to sell. I decided that when I made a little extra money, I would have the front yard fenced and put a lock

85

on the gate.

I opened the door a few inches. "Yes?"

"I have an appointment with Della Carmichael." He passed a white business card through the narrow gap. "Nicholas D'Martino."

"Oh, no. I thought you were coming at one o'clock."

"Is this a bad time?"

I *wanted* to say: "It's a terrible time — I'm perspiring, I reek of ammonia, and I'm wearing ratty jeans and an ancient Dodgers' sweatshirt with a rip under the arm. Go away and come back when you were supposed to be here." But, remembering how excited Phil Logan was about this interview, I pasted a smile on my face. "No, it's fine. I was just — never mind. Please, come in." I opened the door wide and stepped back. "Sorry I'm not dressed for company. I was cleaning the kitchen."

"Don't worry about how you look," he said. "I like to get to know people as they really are. Stains and all."

It hit me. "You came early on purpose, didn't you?"

"Yes." He wasn't embarrassed.

What an arrogant, insensitive jerk. "Why did you do that?"

"To provoke an honest emotion. You're

annoyed. Now I can get to know you without slogging through a few hours of BS celebrity manners."

"I'm not a celebrity," I said.

"You weren't twenty-four hours ago, but now you're my kind of celebrity: a murder suspect."

I wanted to smack him with my rubber scrubbing gloves, but I kept my temper in check. "I was on the scene when the death occurred," I said patiently, "but I didn't even know the woman. It was just my bad luck that somebody chose to use my dessert as a murder weapon."

"Technically speaking, your bowl of chocolate whatever was the 'delivery system' for the murder weapon, which was peanuts aimed at a victim known to be allergic."

"She wasn't 'known to be allergic' by me."

He shrugged. "I'm inclined to believe you. You were married to a cop, so you probably know enough not to point the finger of suspicion at yourself."

"How did you know about my husband?"

"Logan gave me your uncensored bio. He's probably rewritten it by now." The journalist regarded me with amusement. "You actually admitted you're forty-seven."

I bristled. "What do you mean, 'admitted'? Forty-seven is an age, not a crime."

"For a woman in Hollywood, it's a crime."

"This is Santa Monica. It's a sanctuary city for women who've passed Hollywood's idiotic 'sell by' date."

He held up both hands in a mock gesture of surrender. "Let's change the subject."

"Fine."

He frowned at me. "I suppose you'll want to put on different clothes."

"Why? You've seen me at my worst. It's too late to make a good impression."

"Oh, you've impressed me," he said. "But I want to go visit the scene of the crime, and I'd like to have you walk me through it. You don't object to going back there, do you?"

"No. Actually, I was planning to do that later. In looking around, I'm hoping I can remember something that might provide a clue to who killed Mimi."

"We're on the same page. Go change."

"'*Go change'?* Please don't talk to me in that peremptory manner."

"Sorry," he said. "I didn't realize you were one of those sensitive women."

"What is that supposed to mean?" I felt my face flush red with anger.

He must have seen it, too, because he said quickly, "Look, I'm used to talking in a kind of shorthand. Why don't we start this part of the conversation over?" He cleared his throat and smiled. "Since we're going to your studio, would you like to change clothes?"

"Yes, I would."

"Okay. Friends again?"

"We're not enemies," I said, smiling. "I won't be long." But I hesitated, feeling uneasy about allowing this professional snoop a chance to look through my things while I was out of the room. . . . And then I knew what to do about it.

"Excuse me, Mr. D'Martino. I'll be back in just a few seconds."

"Call me Nicholas."

When I returned moments later, Tuffy was by my side. As I had expected, the journalist had begun studying the framed family photos on my bookshelves. Before he could ask any questions, I said, "I hope you like dogs."

"Yes, I do. That's a fine standard poodle." The genuine admiration in his voice almost made me warm to him. *Almost.* "I'm glad you don't have him shaved in one of those fancy show-dog styles."

"This is called a lamb cut, and his name is Tuffy." I gestured to one of the club chairs. "Make yourself comfortable while I get ready."

NDM — I didn't like him well enough to think of him by his first name — sat. I had Tuff sit down in front of him. "Tuffy's friendly," I said. "But I'd better warn you that he does have one little quirk."

"What quirk?"

"While I'm changing, you should stay exactly where you are. If someone moves around a room when I'm not in it, Tuff can get a little . . . aggressive."

That was a lie, but the reporter seemed to believe it. He settled back in the chair.

"Can I bring you something to drink?" I asked sweetly. "Coffee? A soda? I could whip you up a chocolate mousse."

He laughed. "No, thanks." Looking at Tuffy, he said, "He seems like a friendly guy. Dogs like me."

"But he doesn't know you yet, and he's very protective of me and his home. You'll be fine — just as long as you don't move while I'm gone." I said that with a smile, but the new look of concern in his eyes when he studied Tuffy was gratifying. This smug man who liked to play games with people deserved to have one directed at him.

After the world's quickest shower, I changed into a pair of good black slacks, a pink cotton shirt, and a black twill jacket, and grabbed the bag with my cell phone in it.

In less than ten minutes I returned to the living room. Nicholas D'Martino and Tuffy were still staring at each other. I was pleased to see that it didn't look as though either had budged while I'd been gone.

8

Parked in front of my house was a dazzling, luxurious, silver sedan, probably foreign. I'd never seen one quite like it. Narrow stripes in red and blue ran lengthwise along the side. NDM unlocked it and opened the passenger door for me.

"This looks like something James Bond would drive," I said. I got in and NDM settled himself behind the wheel.

The red leather interior was so soft to the touch that it was a sensual experience just to sit in it. "The only thing I know about cars is to have the oil changed every three thousand miles. What is this?"

"A Maserati Quattroporte."

I was brought up to be polite and not comment on the price of things, so all I said was, "Ahhh," but mentally I was figuring that this vehicle must have cost more than our little house had, when Mack and I bought it twenty-two years ago.

NDM must have guessed what I was thinking, because he said, "I got the car last year when the Feds were selling off confiscated vehicles for pennies on the dollar." He placed a recorder between us. "Let's talk while I drive. You don't mind being recorded, do you?"

"Of course not. I wish I'd brought a recorder of my own."

"To make sure I don't alter what you say? That's pretty paranoid."

"Being unfairly suspected of murder will do that to a person," I said.

NDM took off as though he were competing in the Grand Prix. I watched the speedometer go from zero to fifty in a *whoosh.*

I had to admit that he was a skillful driver, but he soared past speed limits as though the posted numbers were only suggestions. Reflexively, I pressed my right foot down onto the floor of the car. That was a ridiculous thing to do. I forced myself to relax and pretend I was on a ride at Disneyland.

The fact that I didn't hear a siren or see flashing red and blue lights behind us annoyed the hell out of me. Why wasn't an officer lurking behind a hedge or in the mouth of an alley to catch this man who *deserved* a ticket? A few months ago I'd been stopped for going six miles per hour over the speed limit, and I'd had to spend a tedious day in traffic school in order to keep the citation off my license and prevent my car insurance rates from skyrocketing.

As he zoomed onto the 405 freeway going north to the San Fernando Valley, I kept myself from imagining the Maserati becoming airborne by giving NDM my biographical basics: that I was born in San Francisco, where my two sisters and my mother still live; that my brother is a doctor in the navy, currently stationed in Manila; that I graduated from UCLA; that I taught high school English before opening my cooking school; and that I met my late husband when he was a new police officer who came in response to my 911 call. My little one room and one bath apartment had been broken into, my TV set and camera had been stolen, and I was blubbering about how terrible it was to be robbed. He had stopped writing in his notebook and told me, "You weren't home at the time, so you weren't robbed; you were burglarized." I stopped crying and told him that I didn't want a lesson in police semantics. Two nights later we started dating.

"Was it a happy marriage?"

"Very." Such warm memories swept over me that for a moment I forgot where I was.

NDM's voice yanked me back to the present.

"So you two were the couple with the happy marriage." His tone was sarcastic. "I heard there was one, somewhere."

"The rumors were right," I said. "And there are more of us happy married couples out there. We just don't advertise."

He ignored that. "What do your sisters do for a living? Or are they married?"

"That question is vaguely insulting," I said. "Are you implying that women get married so they don't have to have 'real' jobs? Did you have a mother?"

"Contrary to some opinions about me, yes, I did have a mother — *do* have. I'm glad to say she's alive and healthy. She's a homemaker, and the hardest-working woman I ever met, so my question about your sisters wasn't meant as a put-down."

The way he talked about his mother made me feel a little less hostile toward him. "My sisters — Keely and Jean — are both accountants," I said. "They work with my mother, who's also an accountant. I didn't inherit the 'numbers' gene, but it's nice to have relatives who can do your taxes."

"What about your father?"

"Dad passed away ten years ago. He was a veterinarian." I thought lovingly of his gentle manner with injured creatures. "We had lots of temporary pets growing up because we all worked at his hospital, in between having paying jobs. Dad didn't make much money because he couldn't bring himself to charge people who were down on their luck but had animals that needed treatment."

"Father a vet, brother a doctor . . . Why'd you take up cooking?"

"Because it's something I'm good at, and it's something I love to do. Why'd you become a journalist?"

"I heard it was a good way to meet women."

"Is it?"

"Yes, but a lot of them turn out to be felons."

He expelled an exaggerated sigh, and I laughed, even though I wasn't quite sure whether he was joking or serious.

"Tell me about the plans for your show," he said. "How did they decide on the time and why did they go live?"

"What's that got to do with Mimi Bond's death?"

"Maybe nothing, but I won't have any idea until I know something about how she happened to end up dead in that particular place at that particular time."

NDM was an experienced crime reporter. Perhaps I could help myself by following his line of thought.

I said, "The way Mickey Jordan explained it to me, my show would be aimed at people who go to jobs during the day. That's why he scheduled it for seven p.m. here in the west, which is ten o'clock in the east. I'm supposed to do one weekly live hour, with taped repeats of that show rebroadcast four times during the week, at different hours of the day."

"They tape all the other shows on the Better Living Channel, so why are they sending yours out over the air live?"

"It's new, and I'm not famous. Mickey said that doing it live where things could go wrong added an element of excitement for the audience. It was a gimmick that was meant to attract viewers."

NDM's lips curled into a cynical smile. "I think it worked."

"I've never heard of *murder* as a publicity stunt," I said sharply.

"Let's hope it doesn't start a trend. Go on."

His cavalier attitude annoyed me, but I suppressed the feeling in order to get through this conversation without losing my temper. I said, "Mickey Jordan told me that if *In the Kitchen with Della* showed signs of building an audience that he'd want me to do two additional thirty-minute programs a week. Those would be taped, and they'd be repeated several times during the week, too."

"It'll be hard for the audience to avoid you," NDM said dryly.

I'd been so intent on answering his questions that I hadn't noticed when NDM's flying Maserati left the 405 North and merged onto the 101 South until I saw that he was taking the Tujunga Avenue exit into North Hollywood. With very little decrease in speed, he proceeded over surface streets.

"When did you find out Mimi Bond was going to be at your show?" NDM asked.

"Not until I saw her in the audience." I told him about meeting her for the first time in the dressing room. When he asked the question John had asked — who knew what dishes I was going to make that night — I told him what I had told John: Anyone who looked at the schedule posted in the production office saw the menu.

"Mimi either checked the show's rundown, or someone told her what I'd be making. She had to know in advance so she could plan how to ruin the food. And I found out last night that several people at the studio were aware that she intended to be the 'taster.' Nobody told me."

"Lots of suspects — this is my kind of mystery," NDM said with satisfaction.

Abruptly, he swerved the car onto a short gravel driveway at the corner of Chandler Street and Lankershim Boulevard and eased his James Bond car to a stop in front of the gated entrance to the Better Living Channel's studio. I looked at my watch and saw that we'd made it from my home in Santa Monica to the production facility in North Hollywood — a distance of nineteen miles, through Los Angeles traffic — in nineteen minutes.

The Better Living Channel building, with its domed roof and lack of windows, resembled an airplane hangar, but it had been a warehouse before being converted into a television studio. It was secured behind a double row of heavy chain-link fencing and a pair of tall wrought iron gates. The fence was so formidable that I half expected to see a high guard tower with a sniper poised to pick off trespassers. A huge billboard hung outside the fence advertising to passing motorists three of the cable network's shows: *Car Guy, All Things Crafty,* and *That's Not Junk.* The on-air hosts were depicted in amusing caricatures. I liked the drawings, but I didn't know how the hosts felt about having their most cartoonable features so exaggerated. If *In the Kitchen with Della* caught on, I might be caricatured on a billboard one day, too. I didn't think I'd mind it, but on my forty-fifth birthday I didn't think I'd care anymore how bad my driver's license photo was. *Wrong.* I learned that vanity dies hard. Now I wished that Phil Logan's retoucher could have gotten his hands on that picture.

NDM stretched his left arm out to press the call button on the gate.

A man's gruff voice crackled through the gate microphone. "Who is it?"

He leaned toward the speaker. "D'Martino from the *Chronicle,* driving Della Carmichael."

"Carmichael? Oh, yeah — the killer chocolate woman," the voice said. "Okay. Keep right and go around to the back. Park in any space that isn't marked 'Reserved.' The guard will let you in the rear door."

We heard the buzz that released the lock, and the big gates swung open.

I muttered ruefully, "So now I'm the 'killer chocolate woman.' "

NDM chuckled. "Worse nicknames have been pinned on me."

I'm not surprised, I thought.

He followed the guard's instructions but

only up to a point. Instead of parking in a visitor's space, he pulled up next to the big barn-size double doors at the side entrance to the studio.

As we got out of the car, one half of the large doors opened and a young man wearing a dark blue security guard uniform and carrying a clipboard emerged to greet us. It was Stan Evans, the guard who had let me into the studio each of the several days when I came to the studio to rehearse for my TV debut. In his late twenties, good-looking in a bland, college yearbook way, Stan had the sinewy build of a long-distance runner and red hair of a shade that fell somewhere between carrot and rust.

Stan greeted me with a wide smile. "Hey, Ms. Carmichael."

"Stan, this is Mr. D'Martino from the *Los Angeles Chronicle.*" The two men shook hands. "We'd like to look around the studio."

"Sure." Stan extended the clipboard toward me. "Will you two sign in and put the time down?"

I signed my name first, then handed the clipboard to NDM. He scribbled his name, noted our time of arrival, and handed the clipboard back to Stan.

"It's too bad about what happened last

101

night, Ms. Carmichael," Stan said. "You going to keep doing your show?"

"I think so. I hope so."

"That's good." He seemed pleased. "Come on in. *Car Guy*'s not taping for another half hour. And Mr. Gil — the guy who makes the furniture — he won't start taping 'til four today. He's been on jury duty."

Stan glanced sideways at NDM, then looked at me. His eyes narrowed and he lowered his voice conspiratorially. "If you don't mind my asking, Ms. Carmichael, is there something special you came back for today?"

NDM replied before I could. "We're going to look around. Is there a problem with that?" He gave the young guard a hard look that dared him to object.

"Oh, no," Stan said quickly. "I was just wondering. Most people don't come here unless they're working." He opened the door to the studio and stepped aside for us.

I went in first, followed by NDM. Stan brought up the rear and closed the door behind us with what sounded like an ominous thud.

But the characterization of "ominous" might just have been my imagination due to the circumstances; I was about to begin

102

investigating a murder.

My pulse quickened with excitement, but that was accompanied by the soft *thump-thump-thumping* of my heart. I recognized the early warning sign of fear: What if Mimi's killer learned that I was trying to solve her murder — and came after *me?*

Resolutely, I pushed my misgivings down into that deep place where I kept emotions I didn't want to face. Given the precarious situation I was in right now, I couldn't afford to be afraid.

9

We walked from the relative quiet of the parking lot through the studio doors and into a flurry of pretaping activity. Closest to the entrance was a set twice the width of mine and outfitted like a car repair shop. It even smelled of cans of oil and the rubber tires stacked against the back wall.

Two electricians on ladders were adjusting lights suspended from the ceiling. A prop man inventoried equipment, checking off items on a clipboard. In the middle of the set was a hydraulic lift with a Toyota on it. A few feet away there was a Lexus with its hood open.

In a casual tone, NDM asked Stan, "Were you here last night, when Ms. Bond died?"

Stan shook his head. "No. I missed all the excitement. I sign out at five, when Al Franklin comes on. He's the night man, gets off at two a.m. The place is guarded electronically until I clock in again at eight in the morning."

"It's just you and Al?" I asked. "With all this expensive broadcasting equipment, that doesn't seem like very much security."

"The property's surrounded by that big fence." Stan leaned closer to us and lowered his voice. "It's electric. Not supposed to be — I think there's some kind of law against that — but it is." Straightening up and once again speaking at a normal volume, he said, "There's usually somebody at the front desk, watching the gate monitor. Three people altogether, each one working an eight-hour shift. But whoever is on, all they do is sit. It's Al and me make the rounds, open the doors, direct deliveries. Stuff like that."

"What about the janitors?" NDM asked. "When do they work?"

"Ten to midnight, five nights a week, usually. Not last night, though. I can tell by the trash on the floors."

"That's right," I said. "When the cleaning crew arrived, Detective Hall questioned them, but he wouldn't let them touch anything. He told them they could come back tonight and work."

The mobile phone clipped to Stan's belt flashed, signaling an incoming call. I knew that the light instead of a sound was to prevent the phone from interrupting a tap-ing.

Stan answered, listened, replied, "Okay," and put the phone back on his belt. "Gotta go," he said. "Mr. Gil's getting a delivery. If you should need me for anything, just tell 'em up in the office and they'll find me."

"Thanks, Stan," I said.

Stan gave me a jaunty salute, and hurried off on his mission.

"Do you want to see where she collapsed?" I asked.

NDM nodded. "But give me an idea of the studio layout here first."

"There are four standing sets. My kitchen is on the far side of this car repair area. The other two sets are up at the front of the building." I gestured toward the wall behind the chairs where the studio audience sat. "That wall is soundproof. It separates the two front sets from these two back here, for when they're taping or broadcasting two shows at the same time. The door in the wall has a lock on both sides. Whoever is taping locks their side of it, to be sure the show isn't interrupted by somebody coming in at the wrong time."

"What shows are done on the other side of the wall?"

"*All Things Crafty,* hosted by Lulu Owens.

The 'Mr. Gil' that Stan mentioned is Gilmer York. I haven't seen his show, but I'm told he builds furniture out of things people throw away. He calls it 'repurposing.' There" — I gestured to the thirty empty seats between the cameras — "is where the audience for my show sat. They just set up chairs because none of the other shows have an in-studio audience. Back behind the last row of seats, on the left, are two small restrooms. Over on the far right side of the building is the production office. It's really more of a large cubicle — enclosed on three sides, but without a door. All of our production schedules are posted there." I drew NDM's attention to the glass-enclosed loft above us. "That's the control booth. There's an identical one on the other side of the wall, for the other two shows."

"You learned a lot for your first time on TV."

"I thought that the more I knew, the better job I could do."

NDM indicated the car repair set. "I have my car serviced at his shop in Hollywood. Car Guy's good with high performance vehicles."

"Everyone calls him Car Guy. What's his real name?"

"Car Guy," NDM said. "It was originally

Eugene Shaw, but he had it changed legally when he started on local TV a few years ago. I checked his background then, in case there was a warrant out for him, but he's clear. He claims the name change was just a show business gimmick."

"Do you believe him?"

"I couldn't turn up a reason not to."

I led NDM past the garage area to my TV kitchen. It was a relief to see that it wasn't encircled by yellow crime-scene tape.

Studying my set, NDM said approvingly, "Nice. It looks like a real person cooks here."

"A real person does."

He leaned over to examine the stovetop but was careful not to touch it. "Do all of the appliances function?"

"Except for that one." I indicated the on-set refrigerator. "It was fine all week during rehearsals, but when I arrived late yesterday afternoon with the food for the show, I opened the door and discovered the inside was warm." I went over to where the appliance had been pulled away from the wall. It still stood at that angle, and the plug hadn't been replaced yet.

NDM followed me. "I thought the refrigerator going on the blink was just my bad luck, but later we found the plug had been cut off," I said.

"So you were forced to put the food into the refrigerator backstage."

"Yes. It was inconvenient. The path is narrow and the ceiling light is dim. With my chocolate mousse in that back refrigerator, anybody could have gotten to it without being seen."

We looked down at the electrical cord with the missing plug. Traces of the charcoal gray fingerprint powder was still visible on the back of the refrigerator, on the cord, and on the outlet.

NDM asked, "Did forensics get a lot of prints?"

"None. Whoever cut off the plug wiped everything down."

"The trouble with all those scientific investigation shows on TV is that the bad guys learn too much."

"What the hell are you two doing here?"

Detective Hall's bark made me jump, but I was even more surprised when I turned around and saw who was standing beside Hall.

John O'Hara of the LAPD Intelligence Squad was glaring at NDM. I started to introduce the journalist, but John cut me off.

"I know D'Martino," John said.

Detective Hall added, "So do I, I'm sorry to say." The glacial tone in both voices told me that whatever their common history, neither John nor Hall was pleased to see the journalist.

"I came to look around," NDM said. "The crime scene's been released."

"Not to you it hasn't. Out."

"Hey, wait a minute. I have every right to be here," NDM insisted.

"No." Hall planted his feet in a defiant stance and leaned forward slightly, like a boxer waiting for the starting bell to ring. "I'm investigating. Leave, or I'll arrest you for obstruction."

NDM shrugged. "You win. For now. I don't have time to fight your phony charge. But if you louse up this case, you can be sure the public's going to read about every stupid mistake you make."

Detective Hall's body went completely still. His voice was soft and almost without inflection. "Look at me — I'm shaking in my shoes."

"I'll take you home, Della," John said.

"No, you won't," I said. John O'Hara's sudden assumption that I would meekly do what he told me to do was annoying. I would have to put a stop to that before it became a habit. Turning to NDM, I asked,

"Will you take me back to Santa Monica?"

"Sure. Door-to-door service."

"Then let's go."

I wanted to get home. While the men were having their little turf war, I'd decided where and with whom I wanted to begin my own investigation.

But if I were going to learn anything useful, I would have to do it alone.

10

As soon as we zoomed up the ramp to the 101 Freeway, NDM cut left to maneuver the Maserati into the fast lane. Speeding past the slower right lanes, NDM asked, "How well do you know John O'Hara?"

"He was my husband's best friend for eighteen years."

"And now he's *your* friend?" I couldn't see the expression on his face, but I heard a smirk in his voice.

"John *and his wife and daughter* are my friends." To put an end to any further little insinuations, I asked, "Are you going to keep looking into Mimi Bond's murder?"

"You think I won't, just because Hall chased us away?" His short laugh was little more than a snort. "I've been thrown out of better places than the Better Living Channel."

"What are you going to do now?"

"Investigate. Use my resources. When I

find out who killed the Bond woman, I'll tell you all about it — after I give the *Chronicle* its front-page exclusive." He aimed a smile at me that I'm sure he thought was charming. I didn't.

What an arrogant jerk. Smiling back at him, I said pleasantly, "Someone famous in the media once described newspapers as the very best source of *yesterday's* news."

He was silent for the rest of the trip.

When NDM dropped me at my house, I saw Eileen's secondhand red VW Rabbit with the UCLA sticker in the driveway behind Mack's old blue Mustang.

After Mack died, I couldn't afford to keep two cars, so I sold my year-old Chevy Malibu and kept the Mustang that Mack had so lovingly restored on his free days. I still remember his voice describing the classic fastback profile and long hood, and how he'd customized the car with a rear spoiler. The last presents I gave him were on the list of "Santa Baby hints" he'd made for Christmas: a chrome exhaust tip and a new set of mudguards with the pony logo. I couldn't bear the thought of his car being driven away by some stranger.

Eileen was in the kitchen, making herself scrambled eggs. Tuffy was watching intently, waiting for the taste she always gave him.

After greeting her, I said, "Your dad told me you had an exam this morning. How did it go?"

She beamed with pride. "Aced it. The subject was business plans, which is something I want to discuss with you, Aunt Del."

She couldn't know how precarious my cooking school business was because I'd kept that a secret from everyone, so I looked at her quizzically. "What do you mean?"

"Want some eggs?" She transferred the contents of the pan onto a plate, then cut a piece for Tuffy and gave it to him. I watched as he gulped it down with pleasure.

I shook my head. "No, thanks. Business plan?" I sat down at the table opposite her.

She swallowed a forkful of egg and said, "Now that you're on TV, you'll get to be well known, so I think you should go into the fudge business."

"What are you talking about?"

"You make a menu of — to begin with — three or four types of fudge and sell them through your website. We could even fix up a display and sales counter in the cooking school. All we'd have to figure out is a name for the fudge, how to make it in big batches without losing taste quality, sketch out some designs for distinctive packaging, and check different types of shipping costs."

I said dryly, "That's *all*, huh?"

"Well, not exactly all. I'd have to look into what licenses we'd need, what the government regulations are about shipping edible stuff, find out what we'd have to do to satisfy the California Department of Health, suggest pricing, and work up an advertising budget." She finished her eggs and moved to the sink to wash her plate and fork.

I hated to disappoint her, but there was no way I'd be able to afford to start a new business. "Honey, I really appreciate your enthusiasm, but —"

Eileen sat down again and grabbed my hands. Her eyes were shining with excitement, and she was nearly breathless. "Oh, *please* don't say 'no.' Let me work out all the details and present you with a business plan. Today probably wasn't a good time to talk about this, but Phil Logan's reaction to your fudge last night, and your saying that you used to make batches to give as presents, just lighted my fire. And Aunt Del, think of the entrepreneurs who got rich by starting a little business on a shoestring, working in their kitchens or garages. UCLA has case studies. We can learn from what those people did."

I held up one hand. "Stop." Her face

started to fall. "I mean, 'Wait.' " She perked up again. "I don't know if I can do what you're suggesting —"

"I'll help. I even have some money I've saved from what you've been paying me —"

"No, absolutely not. I couldn't let you risk your money on this . . . idea." Just in time, I stopped myself from saying "crazy" idea. "What I mean is, if you do come up with some plan that looks possible, you'll certainly be a part of it. This was your idea. You'll have invested your business acumen." *Something I don't have.*

Her excitement soared back up to a boil. "You mean I have your permission to explore the concept?"

"Explore away. But don't neglect your studies."

"This will be my term project: creating a business plan for 'Super Fudge.' "

"We're *not* going to call it 'Super Fudge.' "

Eileen smiled impishly. "Gotcha."

I couldn't help laughing. Eileen had actually managed to make me talk about her wild idea as though it were a real possibility.

Glancing at the kitchen clock over her head, I saw that it was a few minutes before three.

"There's something I have to do right now," I said. "Can you go to the market for

116

me, pick up what we'll need for the classes this weekend?"

"Sure. In all the excitement last night, I forgot the schedule. What are you teaching?"

"Saturday morning, at the Mommy and Me class, we'll be carving a bunch of pumpkins with a variety of faces for Halloween." From a kitchen drawer, I took the shopping list I'd made yesterday and checked to make sure it was complete. "Buy sixteen pumpkins, mostly large, a few medium-size. I'll save one back for the afternoon class, to demonstrate how to cook them after they've served their jack-o'-lantern duties."

" 'Waste not, want not,' " Eileen quoted. "My mother used to say that."

"Mine still does," I said. "I'll puree the cooked pumpkin and then show them a lot of things to make with pumpkin: bread, muffins, pie, and that pumpkin pudding cake you like."

"Yum."

"If you don't have to study, I could use your assistance with the Sunday classes."

"I'm available. What are we cooking?"

"Easy-to-make comfort foods: chicken cacciatore, green peppers stuffed with a ground turkey mixture, latkes, and chunky cinnamon applesauce. Low calorie desserts in the afternoon."

"What are latkes?" she asked.

"They're like little pancakes but made with shredded potatoes." I reached into my handbag for my wallet, removed my business Visa card, and handed it with the shopping list to Eileen. Because she frequently shopped for me, she was authorized to sign on it, too.

Eileen folded the list around the credit card. "Any news about the murder investigation?"

"Not that I know of," I said.

What I didn't tell Eileen was that I was about to go out and — to use a cooking term — stir the pot.

11

Before I left the house, I dialed Iva Jordan's number. I wanted to find out how she was feeling after the distress of last night, and I was going to ask when her husband would be back from New York. A man answered the phone.

"Yeah?"

I recognized the rasp and the brusque manner. "Mickey?"

"Who's this?"

I heard voices in the background, but couldn't tell who was speaking. Then there was a burst of music and I realized the sounds were coming from a television set. Iva had told me that the first thing Mickey did when he entered a room with a TV in it was turn it on; sometimes he even did it in other people's homes. Of course I didn't comment about his habit — it wasn't any of my business — but secretly I thought he must be somewhat difficult to live with.

"It's Della Carmichael, Mickey. When did you get home?"

"Half hour ago. Why?"

"How is Iva?"

"In bed with a migraine. No wonder, after what happened at your show. By the way, Del, you did a f—ing good job."

"Thank you. Mickey, may I come over and talk to you for a few minutes?"

I heard a grunt on his end of the line. "What? You want a f—ing raise already? You think you deserve combat pay?"

"Of course not. I just need to speak to you about something."

"Long as the subject's not money. You know where we live?"

"Yes, I —"

"Then come on." He hung up without saying good-bye.

His abruptness didn't bother me, nor did the rude language he used as casually as punctuation. I'd learned those qualities were typical Mickey Jordan, "retired Marine and self-made quarter of a billionaire," as he described himself. Mickey was six inches shorter than Iva and twenty-five years older, and he always seemed to be in a hurry, but when Iva and I were together, she spoke of him in loving tones. If she was sincere, it was one more indication that in this world, there was somebody for everyone.

Mickey and Iva Jordan lived in a large, two-story Spanish-style home in the seven hundred block of Alpine Drive, in what's called "the flats" of Beverly Hills. Those are the blocks south of Sunset Boulevard and north of Santa Monica Boulevard. Below Santa Monica is the Beverly Hills business district, with its elegant department stores, European boutiques, jewelers, and art galleries.

I parked on the street, just to the right of the driveway leading to the open door of the two-car garage. Iva's sunflower yellow BMW sports car was parked inside. Mickey Jordan's four-wheeled behemoth was out in the driveway, being waxed by a heavy, middle-aged man in brown overalls. It was some sort of steroidal SUV, almost as big as a yacht, and painted a matching sunflower yellow to Iva's car. Iva had told me that yellow was Mickey's favorite color; it looked as though "big" was his favorite size. If I hadn't known whose SUV that it was, the "MICKEYJ" license plate would have been a pretty good clue. Iva's car had a vanity plate, too: "MRS M J."

I got out of the Mustang and walked up the brick path to the Jordan house. Its exterior was cream stucco, with the windows trimmed in cocoa brown. The heavy wooden front door sported large, hammered iron hinges and looked as though it might have come from an old Spanish mission. Along the top and down the sides, the wood had been carved with small figures of monks in robes. To the right of the door, a great swath of scarlet bougainvillea climbed to the edge of the curved red clay tiles on the roof.

Seconds after I pressed the bell, the front door was yanked open. I had expected to see the Jordans' urbane English butler Maurice (pronounced "Morris"), but Mickey himself was standing there. His full head of salt-and-pepper hair recently had been cut so short it seemed to be standing on end. At sixty, Mickey had the energy of an athlete less than half his age. His body was compact, with the muscular shoulders and the wiry lower body of a bantamweight prize-fighter. It was an image perpetuated by his habit of punching the air with his fists to make his points.

Mickey nodded a greeting at me while he barked into a hands-free phone fastened to one ear. Never a soft-spoken man, his New Jersey accent — familiar to fans of *The Sopranos* — grew more pronounced when he was angry.

"What the f— you trying to pull? . . . F— the FCC. I wanna know how I can get around the regs and pick up those two Texas stations. . . . By six o'clock tonight, Jimmy, or look for another gig."

Mickey disconnected and gestured for me to follow him through the foyer arch into the living room that was as large as a tennis court. It was a beautiful room: original Spanish tiles on the floor, heavy dark beams above, and a stone fireplace big enough to roast a side of beef.

"Sit, sit, sit," Mickey said, gesturing to one of the two matching yellow couches flanking the fireplace. Because of the width of the hearth, they were far enough apart to have separate carved wood and glass-topped coffee tables in front of each. Mickey plopped down on the one nearest the door. So we wouldn't have to shout at each other across the distance between coffee tables, I sat on the same sofa, leaving the space of a seat cushion between us.

Mickey looked as though he was still three-quarters dressed from his trip to New York, in dark brown suit pants, a pale yellow dress shirt — the top button undone — and one of his bright yellow silk ties loosened around his thick neck.

"Maurice is upstairs unpacking for me,

but when he comes down and asks you what you want, say tea — he makes crappy coffee."

"I know," I said, smiling. "Iva warned me when we had lunch here a few weeks ago."

Mickey slipped off his glossy brown Italian shoes, slung his feet up on top of the coffee table, and let out a sigh of relief. I saw that he wore yellow socks.

"So, what's the story, Del? Why'd you want to come over?"

"You can imagine how horrible it was to see Mimi Bond die. Even though she was a stranger, I'd like to know something about her."

He snorted. "She was a miserable old broad."

Trying to get him to be more specific, I said, "She seemed to be a very unhappy woman."

"She was a bitch, and a mean drunk." He folded his arms across his chest and glowered into space.

"How long did you know her?" I asked.

He leaned forward and took a cigar out of the handsome old humidor on the coffee table. He asked, "Mind if I smoke?" but he was already clipping the cigar's tip and reaching for a lighter.

"No, not at all," I said.

As he lighted the cigar, he turned to glance at the staircase in the foyer behind us, as though checking to see if either Iva or Maurice were on their way down. Satisfied that we were still alone, he leaned back and relaxed as he drew on the cigar.

I asked again, "How long did you —"

"I remember the question. I met Mimi about ten years ago. She was a real foxy babe then. She'd just started doing an evening cooking show on one of my radio stations, KLEX. Only five thousand watts, but we had a long reach at night when there wasn't much signal interference. I saw her at the station. We got kinda friendly."

Kinda friendly. I wondered if that was a euphemism for . . . one of Mickey's favorite words. "Was she good?" I asked. Realizing how that might sound, I added quickly, "I mean, was she good at her job, on the radio?"

Mickey smiled, more to himself than at me. "Let's just say she looked better than she cooked," he said softly.

"I thought she was very successful."

"When she got her own TV show — I was still in radio then, hadn't started buying my cable stations — she had a 'stunt cooker.' She called the woman her assistant, but that gal did all the real work, with the finished stuff and on the air. By herself, Mimi couldn't make instant oatmeal."

That surprised me. "The couple of her shows that I saw, she was on camera alone."

"Oh, yeah, by then she'd learned a few tricks about cooking, so long as the dish had booze in it."

"But if that was your opinion, why did you put her on the air?"

"I didn't," he said. "Mimi was on the Better Living Channel for a couple of years before I bought it. The first year she sponsored it herself, with her late husband's money. We hadn't seen each other for a long time, so you could say I sort of inherited her."

"She must have been very surprised when you let her go."

Mickey tapped cigar ash into a crystal ashtray and nodded. "You got that right. She threw a f—ing class-A fit. She thought she'd be able to write her own ticket because we had a kind of history . . . but I'm a businessman. Her show was crap on toast."

Inwardly I shuddered at that image, but I pressed on. "She accused me of getting my show by sleeping with you."

"I don't do that anymore. I'm a happily married man now."

That wasn't a subject I wanted to get into

because of my fondness for Iva. And I couldn't see how it had any bearing on Mimi's murder. "As terrible as it was to have Mimi collapse, it was even worse when I realized that her daughter was there and saw her mother die. I'd like to visit her, to express my condolences."

Mickey grimaced and shook his head. "You're a better man than I am. Accusing you of offing Mimi — that's one weird kid."

"I'm sure she was just in shock."

"Go see her if you want to, but in my opinion, that little girl's a whack-a-doodle. Always was."

"What do you mean?"

Mickey tapped some more ash off his cigar. "The girl was eight or nine when I met Mimi. One night I came to their house to take Mimi out. The kid was polite when she met me, but when we got back we found her in the living room. She'd shaved her head."

"Oh, the poor girl . . ."

" 'Poor girl' my left *toches.* Mimi said she'd been a problem since the dad died. A year ago, when I bought the channel, the kid was away at college. Mimi said Faye was doin' great — but then Faye had that meltdown with you at the studio."

Knowing that Mimi drank, and having

learned how she'd planned to ruin my show, I thought that being Mimi's daughter must have been difficult. "I'd still like to go see her," I said.

"Suit yourself." Mickey reached over to the end table for the note pad and pen lying next to the phone and started scribbling. "Faye lived with Mimi, so I guess she's still in the house. Here's the address. It's a little tricky to find, so I'm writing down directions." He finished, tore the page from the pad, and handed it to me.

"Thank you." I got up to leave and Mickey rose with me. "Please tell Iva that I'm sorry I didn't get a chance to see her while I was here," I said.

"Yeah, I will. She likes you. I'll take you two gals out to dinner soon."

As we walked to the door, I thought of a question. "Whatever became of Mimi's assistant — the 'stunt cooker,' you called her?"

"She did okay. Didn't really like cooking all that much. Maybe working with Mimi ruined it for her. Anyway, she came up with a gimmick for herself and she's pretty successful. Has her own TV show, and she makes tchotchkes to sell on one of those shopping channels."

"I wonder if I've seen her. What's her name?"

"Seen her — you've met her. It's Lulu Owens, our crafts lady."

The woman who was with Iva at the studio last night. The woman who took Iva home. The woman who flirted with Detective Hall and said how much she likes to talk.

I decided that after I saw Faye Bond, I would get to know Lulu Owens.

Mickey and I said good-bye at the door.

As I started down the brick path to my car, some instinct made me glance back at the house. A shutter on one of the upstairs windows opened a few inches. I caught a glimpse of blonde hair and realized that Iva was watching me.

Why hadn't she come downstairs?

12

On my way to see Faye Bond, I stopped at a florist's shop and bought a plant blooming with little white orchids. I had the clerk put it into an elegant black ceramic pot. Thus armed with a condolence gift, I headed west on Sunset Boulevard.

Reaching Rockingham Drive in Brentwood, I turned south. Several turns later, I reached my objective: a small residential street with homes set a generous distance apart.

The address Mickey gave me was a lovely old house in the French country style, bracketed by mature shade trees. A mantle of English ivy covered both sides of the front door and climbed all the way up to the underside of the peaked roof over the second floor above the entrance. More of the ivy was draped like a garland along the top of the row of casement windows on the first floor.

The only unattractive thing about the house was the local TV news van positioned in front of it. A man in a dark sweater sat behind the wheel. I recognized the woman with streaked blonde hair who occupied the passenger seat; she was an on-air reporter. I drove past their van and parked at the curb just beyond the mouth of Mimi's driveway.

When I got out of the car, cradling the potted orchid plant against my chest, I saw the reporter simultaneously climbing from the TV van. She clutched a microphone with the station's identifying letters on it in one hand and fluffed her hair with the other. The driver hopped out, too. He hefted a camera rig onto his shoulder and hurried behind her.

The woman reached the path leading to the front door just before I did and blocked my way. She turned toward the camera and beamed a professional smile at me, but the expression didn't reach to her dark, predator's eyes.

"I'm Teddi Ross from KUBS. Were you a friend of the murder victim?" She shoved the microphone toward me.

"Just an acquaintance," I said. *Barely even that.*

"Why are you here?"

"To pay a sympathy call."

"What do you know about Mimi Bond's murder?"

"Sorry." I hoped she wouldn't notice that I'd given her a nonanswer answer.

The man poked his face out from behind the camera. "Hey, Ted — she's the poisoned-chocolate woman."

Oh, great, another awful nickname. It wasn't quite as bad as when the gate man at the Better Living Channel referred to me as "the killer chocolate woman."

When her cameraman identified me, excitement lighted the reporter's eyes. She thrust the microphone closer to me, almost decapitating an orchid blossom.

Annoyed, I pulled the plant out of range. "Please be careful with that microphone," I said.

"Mimi Bond was killed on your cooking show. Tell us what happened to her."

"I don't know," I said firmly.

"Were the two of you enemies?"

"Absolutely not. I'd never met her before last night. If you want information about the investigation, you'll have to get it from the police. There's nothing I can tell you."

I stepped around Teddi Ross and was about to start toward the house when she grabbed my arm.

"I do 'The Two of Us' feature segment on

132

the news at six and eleven," she said. "We're number one in the ratings. An interview on my show could do your new little show a lot of good. How about coming on with me tomorrow, Delta?"

Delta? She didn't even know my name. I eased my arm from her grasp. "I don't make those arrangements. You'll have to talk to our publicity man, Phil Logan."

"I know Phil. He'd kill to get you on my show."

I flinched. "Under the circumstances, that's a pretty insensitive way to put it."

"It was just a figure of speech," she said defensively.

"I've really got to go now," I said, shifting the weight of the plant in my arms.

Teddi Ross lowered her microphone and signaled the cameraman to turn it off. "I'll call Phil," she said, "but if you're going to do an interview with me, you'll have to give me some exclusive information, or it's no deal. You don't want to make an enemy out of me, Delta." After tossing off that threat, the reporter and her cameraman trudged back to their TV truck.

Now that I'd met Teddi Ross, I thought she wasn't as appealing as she seemed on TV. While doing her reports, she appeared to exude warmth toward the people she interviewed. Her sympathetic smile made her features look soft, lovely. Threatening me, her face had hardened, and she lost several points on the beauty scale.

The path from the street to the house was lined with tall rose bushes in shades of pink and red. They were still bursting with this year's blooms. I'm not exactly a talented gardener, but several years ago I saw two parched-looking bare root rose bushes on sale in front of a supermarket. I didn't want to leave them there to die, so I bought them, along with some organic rose food, and planted them in the backyard.

Much to my surprise, those plants lived and started to grow. What a thrill it was to see them bud. Because there hadn't been any labels on their dirty plastic wrappings, I had no idea what to expect, but they turned out to be a type of big and gorgeous yellow rose called "Brandy." I made a promise to myself that when I could afford luxury spending, I'd buy a few more bushes. But first I had to keep my job, and that need had brought me to Brentwood to try to question the girl who accused me of killing her mother.

Out on the street behind me, I heard the engine of the TV truck start. Either they'd given up on the idea that anything interesting was going to happen here, or the team had received a call that some famous name had gotten into trouble. A celebrity "Ooops!" was always a good TV story, especially if there were unflattering photos to be had. The truck was out of sight before I managed to find Mimi's front doorbell, which was partially concealed in ivy.

Leaning close to the door, I could hear a faint chime inside the house, but it took three politely spaced rings before footsteps approached. The cover over a peephole slid aside and an eyeball peered at me.

"Yes?" asked a woman behind the door. Even though she'd uttered only that one word, something about her voice was vaguely familiar.

"I'm Della Carmichael. I came to express my condolences."

"Lord Almighty, Ah'm glad it's only you."

The eyehole cover slipped back, the door opened, and I was facing a woman with a soft pink complexion, tanned, muscular arms, and long silver gray hair tied back in a ponytail: Lulu Owens, the Better Living Channel's crafts lady, and the one-time "stunt cooker" for Mimi Bond. She grabbed one of my wrists and pulled me inside. If it hadn't been for the orchid plant between us, I think she would have embraced me.

"Hello, Lulu," I said.

We were in the entry hall, but I felt as though I'd stepped into a big, exploding blood vessel: wine red carpeting below my feet, scarlet felt wallpaper to the left and right, and a crimson velvet tented ceiling billowed above, swept up in the center and anchored by a brass chandelier. The gaudy décor was a surprise because it was so different from the sedate elegance of the exterior.

Lulu peered around me at the street. "Is that bottle-blonde polecat possi-*tutely* gone?"

"They just drove away in a rush. What's a polecat?"

Lulu wrinkled her nose as though reacting to a bad smell. "Country cousin to a skunk." She closed the door, slipped the dead bolt, and gestured at the orchid plant in my arms. "Is that for little Faye?"

I nodded. "How is she?"

"One heck of a Rocky Mountain mess, poor baby." Lulu took the orchids from me and said, "Come on." She started walking toward the back of the house.

As we passed the living room, I saw it was another symphony in red, with timpani notes of gilt and brass.

"Faye's in the kitchen. I got her to eat

something." Lulu snorted. "The kitchen's the only room in this imitation bawdy house that Mimi was hardly ever in. Ah wish you coulda seen this place before her husband died and Mimi redecorated. Faye's daddy was a real sweet man, an' he had real good taste — in everything except women."

The hallway we were walking through was lined in gilt-framed mirrors, but the glass had been tinted pink. Stealing a glance at myself, I realized that I looked better in Mimi's pink glass than in my ordinary mirrors at home.

When I followed Lulu through the door at the end of the hall, it was like entering a different house, and going back in time. The lovely old country kitchen had a faded mural of a vegetable garden on one wall, a wood-burning fireplace, a stove that might have been made a hundred years ago, and a rough-hewn oak dining table in the middle of the room. A wrought iron baker's rack held well-used pots and pans. It reminded me of the kitchen in a farmhouse Mack and I had visited when he took me to France for our tenth wedding anniversary. It was the delayed honeymoon trip we hadn't been able to afford until then.

Faye Bond sat at the kitchen table, sipping from a steaming mug, surrounded by the pleasant aroma of hot cocoa. A half-eaten grilled cheese sandwich was on a plate in front of her.

"What a lovely kitchen," I said.

She looked up at me with a fleeting smile. "Daddy designed it. He cooked all my meals until he died." Her face grew solemn.

"Look at these beautiful flowers," Lulu said brightly. She set the plant on the table in front of Faye. "Miss Della here brought them for you."

Faye stared at the little orchid blossoms. "Thank you," she said softly. She turned to face me. "Auntie Lulu told me I was wrong . . . you know . . . about what I said last night. I'm so sorry. . . ." Her eyes glistened with tears. "I'm so sorry. . . . My mother . . ."

"What happened was horrifying," I said. "There's no need to apologize."

Lulu pulled out the chair opposite Faye and gestured for me to sit down.

"Can Ah get you some cocoa or coffee?" Lulu asked.

"Thank you. That cocoa smells great. I'd really like a cup." While Lulu took a mug from the cabinet next to the stove, I asked Faye, "Is there anything I can do?"

The pale young girl pressed her lips together and shook her head.

"Ah'm taking care of everything," Lulu said as she brought me a steaming mug of the hot chocolate and sat down beside me. "Now why don' we talk about somethin' cheerful?"

Hoping to hear anything that might lead to a clue to the murder, casually I asked the first question that occurred to me. "Are you in college, Faye?"

"I went to Smith last year, but I dropped out. . . ."

"Didn't you like it?"

"Mother said it was too far away."

"Perhaps she was worried about you," I said.

She shook her head again. "When I came home last summer, Mother said she needed me here." Faye looked at the woman next to me. "Auntie Lulu, I'm very tired."

"Well, honey, you just go upstairs and get into bed. I'll come an' check on you in a little while."

Faye Bond stood up, and that simple act seemed to take most of her strength. She started for the door but turned back and said to me, "Thank you for the flowers."

Lulu watched her leave and sighed. "That poor little thing."

"It's sad that she's so young and has lost both of her parents," I said. "She's lucky to have you in her life."

"My own children are grown an' far away, but Ah love that little girl like she was my blood. Ah've known her as long as Ah knew Mimi."

"Does Faye have a boyfriend in her life?" I asked.

"Ah wish she did so she'd have somebody to cuddle with, but she's a shy little thing. Hardly dated even in high school." Lulu grimaced with distaste. "Not like her mother. Ol' Mimi had men running in and out of this house almost as soon as her husband died."

Now I was getting somewhere. According to Mack and to John, their experience as investigators had been that the most likely person to kill a woman is either her husband or her boyfriend. "Who was Mimi seeing currently?"

"Nobody. There was a guy a few months ago, but they broke up last spring. Ah know because we went out drinkin' together, so she could drown her sorrows. Mimi said she was makin' Faye quit college to come home an' be with her. Ah tried to talk her out of that, but Mimi was a stubborn cuss, had to have everything her own damn way."

"Who was the man?"

Lulu shrugged. "She wouldn't tell me. An'

that was strange, 'cause she used to brag 'bout who she was sneakin' up to the hayloft with."

Lulu and I talked for another hour. I heard a lot of TV studio gossip. Some bits were interesting enough for me to look into, such as Mimi's nasty confrontations with director Quinn Tanner.

Lulu glanced back at the kitchen door and lowered her voice. "It's true that Mimi wouldn't tell me the name of her last fella, but Ah got a theory 'bout who it was."

Acting like a young girl eager to hear the latest high school gossip, I leaned a little closer to Lulu and whispered, "Come on, you can tell *me*."

With a gleefully wicked gleam in her eyes, she opened her mouth to speak, but we heard shuffling and scraping noises upstairs. It sounded as though someone was moving furniture around.

Lulu stood up. "Faye's awake. Ah better go see what she's doin'."

"Shall I come with you?"

"No. I'll settle her down an' stay with her this weekend. This next cup'la days gonna be the worst for the poor little birdie."

"I've enjoyed your company, Lulu. Maybe we can do this again soon?" What I meant was: I want to hear who you think was the secret man in Mimi's life.

Lulu smiled warmly. "Ah'd like that, gittin' together. Gal talk. Why don' y'all come over to mah place for dinner Monday night?"

"I'd like that."

She grabbed a pad and pencil from the kitchen counter and scribbled something. "Ah live in Sherman Oaks. Here's the address. 'Bout six thirty?"

"Perfect. What can I bring?"

More sounds of something heavy being dragged across the floor above.

"Dessert," Lulu said as she hurried off toward the staircase, calling Faye's name as she went.

I let myself out.

It was after seven o'clock and completely dark when I went back down the path toward my car. All at once, I felt very tired. It had been an exhausting twenty-four hours, and now I was eager to get home.

Most of the houses on this quiet residential block had lighted windows, and that made me imagine families gathering for dinner. For a moment, I indulged myself in what I called my Jane Austen fantasy: that after their meal the family members would meet in the living room and read books — maybe even read aloud to each other.

I shook my head to clear it of that unlikely picture. The reality was that so many families, even if they had eaten together, would probably disperse to watch television in several separate rooms. Reading versus TV watching was a campaign I'd waged as an English teacher. Unsuccessfully.

At the sidewalk, I stopped to think. Brentwood wasn't an area I'd visited often, and streets looked so different at night. Considering how many turns I'd made to reach Mimi's address, I hoped I could remember how to get back to Sunset Boulevard. I looked in my purse for Mickey's instructions, but I couldn't find that piece of paper.

I closed my eyes for a moment and mentally retraced my route. Straight ahead into the next block, then a right turn, then a left, and another left, and a final right to get back to Sunset.

Okay, got it.

Behind the wheel of the Mustang, I strapped myself in and switched on the ignition and the lights.

I'd gone only a few yards and was slowing to pause at the corner stop sign, when I heard a car engine start up behind me. It caught my attention because it was making an odd sound — something like a low growl. Reflexively, I glanced into my rearview mirror and saw a vehicle that had been parked several lengths behind mine pull out into the street. I noticed that the driver hadn't yet turned on the car's lights.

I crossed the intersection and was almost to the end of the next block when I saw that the car was still behind me, and still running without lights.

With a piercing stab of fear, I realized that I was being followed!

13

My next thought was that I was being foolish. Maybe I was on edge because I'd seen a woman die last night.

Why would someone be following me, especially in an expensive neighborhood like this? The most likely explanation was that the driver had just forgotten to turn on his lights.

Still, I was uneasy. To test my "forgetful driver" theory, I made an abrupt left turn into the next residential street.

I expected to feel ridiculous. Then that darkened car with the growling engine turned into the same street. The vehicle was a mid-size sedan in some dark color. I couldn't tell the make of the car, nor could I distinguish anything about the driver.

My pulse quickened. Inside my chest it felt as though a cold hand were making a fist around my heart.

I sped up. At the next corner, I yanked

the wheel to the right and swerved into another street. I had no idea where I was now. All I was thinking about was eluding the car behind me.

Through the rearview mirror I saw an empty street.

I was about to let out the breath I was holding when I heard that soft engine growl. The dark car made the same turn. There was no doubt about it: *I really am being followed.*

Time to call 911. Even though I didn't know exactly where I was, the police had a telephone tracking system. They'd be able to find me. *Please, God.*

Keeping my left hand on the steering wheel, I plunged the right into my handbag, feeling around until I grasped my cell phone and pulled it out. I regretted that in one of my many economies I hadn't upgraded to a hands-free system. With trembling fingers, I pushed the nine and the one —

Suddenly, the other car rammed me from behind! The jolt caused my chest to smash painfully against the steering wheel and the little phone to fly out of my hand. I heard it land with a *thunk* on the floor of the Mustang.

Because the car was right on my tailpipe, I could see the driver through the rearview mirror — he was wearing a ski mask! That destroyed any hope this was just a kid out to scare a lone woman. My fear spiraled up into the red zone.

Gripping the steering wheel as tightly as I could, I pressed down on the accelerator.

The car behind sped up, too.

Make noise! Attract attention! I leaned my right forearm hard against the horn — but no sound came out. Oh, dear God — the horn isn't working! I pounded on it with my right fist, but the horn stayed silent.

Fighting terror, desperate to keep a clear head, I increased my speed and careened around the next corner. This new street was lined on my side with willow trees.

Weeping willows. Long, dripping foliage that partially concealed the homes. If I could find a place to hide . . .

Next to a dark house up ahead I spotted a two-vehicle carport with only one car in it, a big SUV. I turned off the Mustang's lights, swung into that partial shelter, and cut the engine. Squeezing my body down below the dashboard, I prayed that the person following me hadn't seen what I'd done.

Almost immediately, I realized this might have been a stupid maneuver. *If he finds me, I'm trapped.*

If I'd had any idea how to get to Sunset

Boulevard from wherever I was, I would have raced to the safety of lights and traffic and cruising police cars. But I was lost in a quiet area of big houses where the people probably wouldn't open the door to a stranger banging on it.

The car with the soft growl drove by. Slowly.

He's looking for me!

Holding my breath, I felt around beneath the front seats for my phone, and anything I could use as a weapon.

My hand closed around the handle of a screwdriver. I'd hoped for something heavy, like a forgotten wrench or flashlight. No such luck. But a screwdriver was better than nothing. It would help me put up a fight, do some damage. . . .

The sound of my pursuer's car faded away. Quietly, I let out my breath, but I didn't dare sit up yet. He might be parked, waiting for me to show myself. Maybe he had gotten out of the car and was looking for me on foot.

While I flattened myself into the Mustang's carpet, my fingers continued to explore until I found the cell phone.

Carefully, by touch in the darkness, I counted the numbers on the keypad and began to dial. Nine . . . one . . .

148

I heard the car again. It was coming back from the opposite direction. Driving slowly. Searching . . .

Without warning, the beam of a flashlight revealed my hiding place! I squinted against the brightness.

"Hey! Who are you?" It was a man's voice. Angry. All I could see of him was the outline of a stocky figure behind the light.

Out on the street, I heard the car with the low growl speed up and drive away.

The man's voice demanded, "What the hell are you doing here?" There was a loud *click*, and the carport was flooded with light.

I struggled to sit up, clutching the phone in one hand and the screwdriver in the other. The man with the flashlight was short and compact, with a neat gray beard and thick gray hair above bright blue eyes. He was wearing white tennis shorts and a red sweatshirt with the words "Outlast the Bastards" written across the chest.

"A man was following me in his car." I put the screwdriver down on the passenger seat and held up my cell phone. "I turned in here to hide and call the police. Your house was dark. I didn't think anyone was home."

"I was working in my office, in the guest house out back." He marched to the en-

149

trance of the carport and scanned the street in both directions. "I don't see anybody out there now. Are you all right?"

I nodded. "The man rammed the car from behind, but I'm not hurt."

He bent down to examine the back of my car. "Your trunk lid's mashed in."

"Oh, no!" I felt a pang of guilt. This was Mack's beloved car, and now it was damaged because I'd been playing detective. I got out of the Mustang and came around to look.

"It's not so bad," the man in the red sweatshirt said. "Some body work, but you'll need a full paint job. A car this age, they won't be able to match the color exactly if you just paint the back end. Does it drive okay?"

"Yes."

He must have seen my distress because he said, "Don't be upset, Miss — ?"

"Della. Della Carmichael."

"I'm Fred Priestly." Recognition lighted his eyes. "Oh, you're the woman with the new cooking show. I thought you looked familiar, but I wasn't expecting to find a celebrity hiding in my carport."

"You watched the show?"

"Since I've been alone I had to learn to cook. I set the TIVO for Bobby Flay and

Paula Deen. Now I'll TIVO you, too." His face assumed a sober expression. "I don't mean to be insensitive. Was that woman who died a friend of yours?"

"No, I'd just met her."

"I watched her show a couple of times, but I didn't like it. Do they know what happened to her?"

"Not yet. If you don't mind, I really shouldn't be discussing this."

"Okay, yeah, I understand." He nodded toward the Mustang. "The damage isn't so bad. You have insurance, don't you?"

"Yes."

"It looks to me like your car just needs some cosmetic work. Make a police report before you call the insurance company. Don't let them think you were careless. They'll do whatever they can not to pay what you deserve."

"I'm sure my insurance company will be fair," I said.

"Have you ever filed a claim with them?"

"No, not yet."

His lips curved into a cynical smirk. "Good luck. Hey, you want to come in for a cup of coffee and some Paula Deen cake until you're sure the guy following you is gone?"

"I appreciate the offer, but I've got to get

home. Would you tell me this address and stay out here with me while I call someone?"

Fifteen minutes later, John O'Hara pulled up in his personal car, a four-year-old black Lincoln that Eileen nicknamed "the tank." He parked behind the Mustang. When he got out, I saw that he was wearing his "blank" expression, but I'd known him so long I could read it. I knew he wasn't at all pleased to find me in this situation, but I also knew that he wasn't going to say so in front of someone else. I wouldn't get a lecture until we were alone.

I introduced John to my new friend, Brentwood homeowner and retired insurance executive Fred Priestly, who had remained with me while I waited for John. The two men shook hands and John went to examine the back of the Mustang.

During the time it took for John to arrive, Fred had told me about his retirement project: He was writing a novel that was going to, as he put it, "rip away the paper curtain to expose the dirty little secrets of the insurance industry."

"I'm calling it *UN-covered: The Rip-off Racket.* It's going to be *The Sopranos* with actuarial tables."

While John was studying the damage and

trying to open the trunk, Fred continued his stories.

"I was watching TV one night — one of those true crime documentaries — and the show starts with my former company, Guardian Insurance. They were refusing to pay off on a million-dollar life insurance claim, and hired their own private investigator to establish that the man's death was a murder. Once the PI found enough evidence to prove that the insured didn't die of natural causes, Guardian took him off the case and turned what he'd discovered over to the police. If I'd still been there, I would have wanted the PI to keep at it until he found out who killed our insured, but the evidence he came up with was strong enough so that the company didn't have to pay the dead man's wife any money. All they cared about was not paying the claim."

"Did the man's wife commit the murder?"

"No. The police found out he was killed by his secret tootsie. The wife didn't even know about her. That didn't matter to the company because the murdered man wasn't insured against being murdered. I've got a lot more stories. The hero of my book is an idealistic young insurance salesman who has no idea of what's really going on behind the scenes at his company. Of course, I have to change names and locations. I'm calling the company Protector Insurance."

I thought Fred was probably going to have a bestseller, but he might never be allowed to buy insurance again.

When John stood up from his inspection, I asked, "Did the other car leave any traces of its paint when he hit me? Something that could identify it?"

"He transferred a couple of tiny paint chips. I'll have a friend in SID process them to see if we can get a line on the vehicle." John turned to my host. "Can we leave Della's car here tonight? I'll have someone come pick it up first thing in the morning."

"It can stay here as long as you like. Nobody uses the other half of the carport." With a playful smile, Fred told me, "I'm in the phonebook — in case you need a place to hide again."

I thanked Fred Priestly for his help and added, "I look forward to reading your novel some day."

He responded with a beaming smile. "I'll be watching your next show."

Out of the corner of my eye I caught a glimpse of John scowling.

14

As soon as I got into John's car and fastened the seat belt, he demanded, "What kind of trouble have you gotten yourself into?"

Ignoring his angry tone, I asked pleasantly, "Have you had dinner?"

"What's that got to do with — ?"

"You answer my question, and then I'll answer yours," I said. "Have you had dinner?"

"No."

"I'll feed you and then I'll tell you everything, but right now you're cranky, and I don't want us to fight."

I took his unintelligible grumble as agreement.

Tuffy met us at the door with his usual high level of excitement. Whether I'd been away for fifteen minutes or for seven hours, his enthusiasm was the same. After I petted Tuffy to his satisfaction, I led John and Tuffy into the kitchen.

"There's a note on the table," John said. "Eileen's handwriting."

I picked it up and read it. "She says she walked Tuffy at six, she's gone to her study group and will be home late, so I shouldn't worry."

"You'll worry anyway, won't you?"

"Of course."

For the first time since he'd arrived in Brentwood to pick me up, John O'Hara smiled. "I know." He reached out and took my hand. "Thank you."

In that tiny, unguarded moment, I felt a tremor when he touched me — a little tingle of attraction. *Attraction?* That was an emotion I hadn't expected and didn't want to feel. Pulling my hand away, I was afraid to look at him directly, but out of the corner of my eye I saw a sudden flush of embarrassment color his cheeks. *Oh, Lord — he'd felt it, too.*

Before I could think of anything to say, John cleared his throat and turned away from me. Like the unofficial member of the family he'd been ever since he and Mack started out as partners, John opened the refrigerator door. Surveying the contents a bit longer than was usual for him — and still not looking at me — finally he asked,

"What have you got that's ready? I don't want you to fuss with cooking."

"Cooking relaxes me. It's how I release stress." *And it's how I push away uncomfortable feelings.* I did a quick mental inventory of my supplies. "I've got some leftover brisket that I can warm up," I said. "How about the brisket, and I'll make potato latkes?"

"Great. What can I do to help?"

I took two large potatoes and an onion out of the pantry and gave the potatoes to John. "Peel these while I grate the onion."

I handed him the peeler and took the grater.

While John and I worked together side by side — I was careful not to let our shoulders touch — I told him about my visits to Mickey Jordan and to Faye Bond.

"Could somebody have followed you from Jordan's to the Bond house?"

"I've been replaying that in my mind, and I don't think so. I stopped at a florist's shop after leaving Mickey's, to take a plant to Faye. Then I went to Brentwood. With the turns I had to make from Sunset to get to Faye's and Mimi's house, I believe I would have noticed anyone following me." I told him about my glimpse of Iva Jordan, looking down at me from a second floor window as I left, but that she hadn't come downstairs while I was there.

"Mickey Jordan could have told Iva where you were going."

"Iva's and Mickey's cars are painted such a bright yellow that I would have recognized them behind me."

"What about other cars in their household? A maid's?"

"They have a housekeeper and a maid, but the only live-in is the butler, Maurice."

"What kind of a car does he have?"

"I don't know. He probably has one, but I've never seen it."

"I'll find out. What the guy's last name?"

"Maurice is his last name. It's pronounced 'Morris' but it's spelled M-a-u-r-i-c-e. English butlers are addressed by their last names. Don't you watch *Masterpiece Theatre*?"

He frowned at my attempt at levity. "This isn't funny, Del. Jordan or his wife could have borrowed his car to keep from being recognized."

"That's possible, I suppose, but I can't picture Iva being so aggressive. She always struck me as fragile."

John touched a spot on his side where I knew there was an old scar beneath his shirt; six-foot-four-inch John had been shot by a sweet-faced five-foot-one-inch grand-mother. "I learned the hard way that most of the time it's impossible to tell what a person is capable of doing just by looking at them," he said.

I thought about that as I took the grated potatoes, combined them with the grated onion, an egg, some matzo meal, flour, salt, and pepper. He watched me as I formed the gooey mix into patties. I checked the vegetable oil in the skillet I would use for the latkes; it was just beginning to form tiny bubbles on the bottom. Perfect. I lowered the latke patties into the hot oil, then transferred the leftover brisket into a ce-ramic dish, covered it with plastic wrap, and put it into the microwave.

John moved the kitchen stool up next to the stove and perched on one hip. "Let's examine the possibilities," he said. "Mickey Jordan knew where you were going. He could have told his wife. That could have upset one or both of them enough to go after you."

"Mickey didn't seem concerned about my seeing Faye. The house is hard to find, but he gave me good directions. He did try to discourage me by saying he thought Faye wasn't very stable, but all he had to base that on was her shaving her head when she was nine, and accusing me of murder last night. Incidentally, she doesn't believe that anymore. She apologized to me."

"For the sake of discussion, let's say neither Jordan nor his wife went to Faye's. That would mean it was someone who saw you enter or leave Mimi Bond's house. Or it could have been somebody who lives there. Who lives there?"

"Only Faye, as far as I know. Lulu Owens said that Mimi hadn't had a romantic interest for the past several months."

As I quoted Lulu I realized that just because she said it, that didn't necessarily make it true. Mimi's love life was something to look into, but I would be very careful about it. I definitely was *not* going to be one of those "too stupid to live" women in movies — the kind who goes upstairs alone into a dark attic where everyone except that airhead knows the monster is hiding.

The brisket was warmed and the latkes were done. I filled our plates and John carried them to the table. After he pulled out my chair, he sat down himself.

"I don't want you getting mixed up in the investigation, Del."

"Detective Hall thinks I murdered Mimi Bond, so I'm already mixed up in it."

"He's looking at other people, too," John said.

"Because he's 'looking at other people, *too*'? Is that supposed to make me feel better? I'm still a murder suspect."

"Hall is a good investigator, but he doesn't know you. I told him he'd solve the case faster if he eliminated you and concentrated his energies in other directions."

"And what did he say to that?"

Instead of replying, he ate another latke.

"Come on, John. What did he say?"

"He's concerned that I can't be completely objective, because your husband and I were partners. But the thing here is that I'm right. You *are* innocent."

"And innocent people are never arrested," I said wryly.

John knew the answer to that as well as I did: Sometimes they were. Sometimes they were even convicted.

"Has Detective Hall confirmed or destroyed anybody's alibi yet?" I asked.

"Nobody's alibi is tamper-proof. Not even Jordan's. Hall got proof that he really was in New York when Mimi Bond was killed, but he could have hired someone to do it."

Doubtful, I shook my head. "It would have had to be someone with access to the backstage refrigerator, which removes the

161

possibility that it was a professional hit person. Besides, if a contract killer did it, wouldn't that person make her death look like a robbery, or an accident, or a mugging? Or even a drive-by shooting?"

"Probably."

"I don't believe it was an outsider. That's bad for me, because, so far, I'm the only one Detective Hall can *prove* went to that fridge."

"Hall is nowhere near an arrest yet," John said. "Let's talk about something else." He complimented me on our impromptu meal. I think I told him I was glad he was enjoying it, but I don't remember exactly what I said. After that exchange, we were quiet.

I didn't know what John was thinking, but I was quiet because of the "elephant in the room" that I couldn't mention. It materialized when John took my hand tonight and I felt that unexpected little shock of excitement.

When had a stirring of physical attraction to Mack's and my old friend — our *married* old friend — crept into my neurons? Right then I promised myself I would avoid spending any more time with John O'Hara than was absolutely necessary.

John broke the silence. "SID is going to have your car tomorrow. I've got the next forty-eight hours off. Want me to drive you to your cooking school?"

"No, thanks," I said quickly. "I'm going with Liddy. She's taking the pumpkin carving class so she can make jack-o'-lanterns to decorate her husband's dental office for Halloween."

That "blank" expression was back on his face. "Okay, as long as you're covered," he said.

I followed him to the front door to double lock it behind him, and purposely remained back a couple of feet. When he said good night, it was with a small salute. He didn't lean down to kiss me on the cheek, as he had so many times over the years.

The moment John left, I called Liddy and persuaded her to cancel her facial appointment tomorrow and instead come with me to learn to carve faces in pumpkins.

15

Liddy arrived at my house Saturday morning an hour before we needed to leave for the school. Even with her blonde hair tied up in ponytail and with no makeup, at forty-six she still looked like the former Miss Nebraska she had been.

She gave me a "hello" hug, then stepped back. Surveying me top to bottom and frowning with anxiety, she asked, "Are you okay?"

"Of course I am. Why are you looking at me like that?"

"Big John called about five minutes after you did. He said a car chased you and that you ended up hiding in the garage of some weird character in Brentwood."

"Why did John call you? Didn't he believe me when I said you and I were going to class together?"

"Of course he *believed* you — even though, technically speaking, you fibbed to him because you didn't talk me into coming to class until *after* you told him I was coming. It's a good thing you got to me first so I knew what he was talking about — I mean, about the cooking class part. Everything else he told me was a surprise." She stopped talking and shook her head. "That sounds pretty convoluted."

"Life is convoluted," I said. *Never again will I whine to myself in the middle of the night about being stuck in a rut.*

"And for the record," I said, "Fred Priestly is not 'weird.' He's a very nice retired man who watches food TV and is writing a novel."

"That sounds interesting. Is he somebody you might like to spend time with? You haven't had a date since . . . *forever.*"

"I'm not looking for someone to date. Life is complicated enough."

"You've got a lot of years left to live," Liddy said. "I'd hate to think that you were going to spend them alone."

"I'm not alone. I have friends and my slightly nutty family, and work I love."

"But you share your bed with a standard poodle," Liddy said wryly. "I'm not going to nag you about finding a nice man, I'm just saying you should be open to the possibility." She sniffed the air and headed for the kitchen. "Lecture over. I want a cup of coffee and whatever smells so good."

The coffee was ready, and I'd baked a dozen banana nut muffins early that morning because I'd awakened at twenty minutes after five and couldn't get back to sleep. As I was getting out of bed, Tuffy lifted his head, looked at me, closed his eyes, and lay down again. His preferred time to rise is seven am.

I set two large coffee mugs on the kitchen table next to the sweeteners and a creamer full of half-and-half. As we sipped coffee and each ate a banana nut muffin, I filled Liddy in on the events of yesterday, beginning with Nicholas D'Martino — NDM — surprising me by coming to the house early, and ending with my being pursued through residential Brentwood until I took refuge in Fred Priestly's carport.

Liddy listened without interrupting, but she was frowning with concern. When I finished the story, she said, "Now I understand why Big John was so worried about you that he had your house watched last night."

"He did *what?*" I was so astonished I almost tipped over my coffee mug.

"Don't get all huffy on me and act like Miss I-Can-Take-Care-Of-Myself," Liddy chided. "When John told me what happened, I wanted to come right over and stay with you, but he said not to, that he'd make sure no one bothered you last night. John asked me not to tell you about it, but — oops, it just slipped out. Don't tell him you know."

"I won't, but he's inclined to be overprotective. I'm going to have to talk to him about that."

Liddy started to reach for another muffin, but then pulled her hand back. "No, I better not." Pushing the muffin plate away, she said, "It won't do any good, trying to talk John out of acting like Sir Galahad. He told me last night that when he and Mack started out as cops they promised each other that if anything happened to one of them, the other would look after the widow. Like if John had died when that little old lady who looked like Betty Crocker shot him, Mack would have had to take care of Shannon."

"The big difference is that Shannon is ill; she can't protect herself. I can."

Liddy poured herself another mug of coffee. "I like Shannon. When she's on her medication she's a sweet person, but that time she went off it, she scared the hell out of me. Remember how she flew into a rage

167

and came at us with the fireplace poker?"

I shuddered at the memory. "But now she has a psychiatrist who monitors her medication levels, she goes to group therapy, and John has reliable nurses to stay with her when she needs it and he can't be there. I visited her last week. She was excited for me about the show." To get away from the subject of John and Shannon, I said, "Thank you for giving up your facial to help me today. You look great, by the way."

She expelled an exaggerated sigh. "It takes a lot of work. I'm using the couple of days Bill's away at that dental conference in Santa Barbara for some female maintenance. Last night I slathered my feet and hands with Vaseline and slept with socks and gloves on. Today I'm letting my face breathe. In twenty-one years of marriage, the only time Bill saw me without mascara was in the delivery room when I was having the twins. He doesn't know that I'm going gray because I keep having my roots touched up. Thank God I'm a natural blonde because those 'silver hairs among the gold' don't show so quickly on us."

"Bill would love you just as much if he saw you without makeup."

"Easy for you to say. Mack didn't care if you weren't dolled up, but when he went to work, he saw dead bodies and other awful stuff. Bill works on the teeth of some of the most gorgeous women in Hollywood. Tonight, I'll mix up an avocado and olive oil mask and keep it on while I watch TV. Want to come join me? I've got lots of avocadoes."

"No, thanks. I have to pay some bills and start making notes for the next TV show."

Liddy finished her coffee and took her mug over to the sink to wash it. "Let's get back to what's important. I've been thinking that if the person who followed you last night just happened to see you at the Bond house, then it must have caused him some alarm, and I can only think of one reason for that."

"He's afraid I might find out something that will expose him, so he tried to scare me off." I *hoped* he was only trying to scare me, but he'd already killed once.

Liddy dried her hands and came back to the table. "Sweetie, you've got to be careful until the murderer is caught. Today I'm going to be the eyes and ears in the back of your head."

I gave her fingers a little squeeze of appreciation.

Ten minutes later, as we were loading the dozen large pumpkins and six smaller ones that would be carved in class into the back of Liddy's SUV, she caught me by surprise. "So tell me what's going on with you and John. Why didn't you want him to take you to class today?"

My first thought was to keep what happened in the kitchen to myself, but the need to confide in my best friend was overwhelming. Holding a pumpkin against my chest like a shield, I leaned against the side of her SUV and told her about my rush of feeling when John took my hand — and about the elephant in the room.

"I've had glimpses of an elephant for the past several months," Liddy said.

The skin on my arms prickled with apprehension. "What do you mean?"

"Big John is nuts about you. You just haven't noticed."

"That's ridiculous. We've been good friends for years. He's married —"

"To a woman who hasn't been able to be a wife or a mother for at least a dozen years. You've mostly raised Eileen, months at a time when poor Shannon couldn't be trusted to be alone with her."

"She's a paranoid schizophrenic who wasn't correctly diagnosed at first. Mack and I spent a lot of time with them, before Shannon was sick, or before we knew it. They adored each other. John still loves her.

I can tell by the gentle way he treats her and talks about her."

Liddy said, "I'm sure John is too honorable to ever tell you how he feels, but there are times he can't hide it. I spotted it — but now that I think about it, *John* may not even know how he feels. Not consciously, I mean. Men, bless them, can be pretty dense about their emotions. Kings of denial."

"Then you agree I'm right about seeing him as little as possible."

Liddy nodded. "Definitely. Keep that elephant out of the room, hon, or someday it might come stampeding into the house and knock down the walls."

My struggling little business, The Happy Table Cooking School, was located in the back of an appliance store called Country Kitchen, on Montana Avenue between Fourteenth and Fifteenth streets. The owners, Mr. and Mrs. Tran, were refugees from Vietnam, but they had chosen to make the front of this one-story building look like a Norman Rockwell painting of an early-twentieth-century American general store. They had attached white clapboard siding to the façade, put up green shutters, and installed a red Dutch door. A glance inside showed the appliances arranged as they might be in someone's home — if the house had five kitchens and no living room.

A small poster in the front right window advertised: The Happy Table Cooking School. My classroom could be reached by walking through the store, past the array of attractive merchandise. I didn't suggest that my cooking students purchase special equipment — actually, I showed them how to improvise so they wouldn't have to — but most of the time they prefered to buy items from the Trans' stock, making my landlords happy.

Behind a line of refrigerators was the door with the school's name on it. The Trans rented me the space and the six working stoves on which the students learned to cook and bake. I supplied the four long picnic-style worktables and the folding chairs.

My annual pre-Halloween Mommy and Me pumpkin carving class was full to capacity, as usual. Women who'd heard about it from their friends registered well in advance. Afterward, some of them would sign up for other classes, or for a full six-week course, during which I taught complete menus, beginning with appetizers and ending with desserts. If one didn't want to commit for that much time, I also offer individual lessons in Italian or French cooking, one-dish entrees, vegetarian meals, and desserts.

After greeting everyone — and managing to evade whispered questions from the grown-ups about what happened to Mimi Bond — I began the class by showing the mothers how to carefully remove the tops from the pumpkins I'd distributed.

When the tops were off, Liddy and I put bib aprons over the children's clothing. "This next part is fun, but mushy," I said. "We're going to scoop out the pumpkin seeds."

There was always a certain amount of face-smearing and seed-throwing, but these kids were generally well behaved, and before they arrived I'd taken the precaution of spreading newspapers on the floor to catch whatever fell. Liddy never minded getting dirty, so she helped me clean up the resulting mess.

When the pumpkins were hollowed out, and hands and faces were washed, and what was left of the pumpkin seeds were put aside to dry, I passed out sheets of white paper and black Sharpie marking pens.

"As you're about to see, I'm not much of an artist," I said, "but you don't have to be; just draw what you want to carve into your pumpkins."

I demonstrated by sketching a grinning face with two top teeth and one bottom tooth, and showed them how to cut out their drawings. "Now you put the picture up against the side of your pumpkin and punch little holes around the lines of the sketch with these chopsticks," I said as I gave out one long plastic chopstick apiece. "Then you'll be able to carve your faces into the pumpkin by following the outline you've made."

I guided the hands of some of the children as they pierced the flesh of the big orange vegetables. There was lots of giggling and happy little squeals of excitement.

Families were working together with enthusiasm. I circulated around the tables, helping out whenever it was needed, pleased to see that the moms appeared to be enjoying the activity as much as the kids.

At the rear table, Liddy was bent over her pumpkin, carving industriously. She didn't seem to need any help, so I stayed with the mothers and children. Everyone was having so much fun creating silly jack-o'-lantern faces that for a few hours I was able to forget about Mimi Bond and the mystery of who killed her and who had chased me in the dark.

■ ■ ■ ■

It was finally the end of the day and classes were over. The mothers and children put their jack-o'-lanterns into the large paper bags I'd provided and went home. Liddy and I straightened the tables for the next day's classes, and bagged the trash and took it to the outside Dumpster.

"I'm exhausted," I said, as I locked the back door. Mr. or Mrs. Tran would lock the front when they closed the Country Kitchen for the night.

"I know you love teaching," Liddy said, "but you have to spend an awful lot of time on your feet while staying cheerful and encouraging to everybody. No way I could do it."

"I love watching people discover they can do things they've never done before."

When we got to Liddy's SUV for the drive home, she handed me the bag with her pumpkin in it.

With a grin, she said, "I made a present for you."

I took the pumpkin out — and discovered that Liddy had carved her jack-o'-lantern into the profile of an elephant.

16

I didn't see John over the weekend. He returned the Mustang on Sunday afternoon, while Eileen was helping me teach a class on how to make simple comfort foods look and taste like gourmet creations.

John had slipped the car key through the mail slot in my front door, in an envelope with a note telling me that his friend at SID had taken a paint sample from the car that hit me and would let John know if he was able to determine the vehicle's make and model. He asked me to tell Eileen he'd be by at seven o'clock to pick her up for dinner. Twenty minutes before he was due to arrive, I took Tuffy for a long walk.

After Tuffy did his stuff, I scooped it into a double baggie, deposited that in a trash container, and we went down to Montana Avenue, where there were lights and people. I was watchful and checked the surroundings frequently while Tuffy was relieving himself. No one followed us.

Tuffy and I strolled east along Montana, past open shops, restaurants, and sidewalk cafés. It was such a mild night for October that many of the outdoor tables were occupied; the chai and latte drinkers seemed in no hurry to be anywhere else.

Without thinking about it consciously, I found myself in front of Country Kitchen. Glancing through the open top half of the Dutch door, I noticed tiny Mrs. Tran speaking animatedly with a dark-haired man a head taller than she. I saw her in three-quarter profile. Her smooth face, with tight skin over prominent cheekbones, was tilted up, and she was smiling. I thought again what a remarkable woman she was. With all that she had endured in escaping her homeland and spending time in refugee camps before finally reaching America, she found pleasure in every day. I was about to walk on so as not to interrupt her conversation, when the man turned and I saw his face. It was Nicholas D'Martino!

What in the world is he . . . ?

At almost the same moment I recognized him, he saw me. "Hello," he said.

Mrs. Tran saw me then, too. "Ah, Mrs. Della." This time, her smile was for me as she gestured for me to come in.

"No, I can't." I knew her rule against allowing animals in the store. "I'm just out walking my dog."

"Then I'll walk with you for a while," NDM said. Turning to Mrs. Tran, he offered his hand — which was larger than both of hers — and told her what a pleasure it was to have met her. She inclined her head, smiled again at both of us, and disappeared into another part of the store.

"Nice woman," NDM said, coming out to the sidewalk and closing the bottom half of the door behind him. His Las Vegas singer looks were made more vivid this evening by his expensive outfit: red cashmere turtleneck sweater, navy cashmere blazer with gold buttons, and pale gray slacks. On Friday, there'd been stubble on his face. Now his cheeks looked glassy smooth, and I caught a whiff of musky aftershave.

I didn't bother to keep the edge out of my voice when I asked, "Shopping for kitchen equipment?" I knew he must be here to ask questions about me.

"I was asking questions about you," he said, and bent down to give Tuffy a scratch below one of his ears. "Hello, fella." He straightened up. "Mrs. Tran didn't want to talk to me because she thought I was from the police. After I convinced her that I had nothing to do with the police, that I was trying to help you, she opened up."

"Trying to help *me?* You're trying to get a story."

I turned around and started to walk back along Montana with Tuffy. NDM got into gear and caught up to me.

"The sooner the killer is caught, the better it'll be for you. Unless you did it," he said. "Personally, I think you're innocent, but I was wrong once before in my life."

"Only once, in all your life? That's amazing. Does the *Guinness Book of World Records* know about you?"

He had the grace to smile. "Okay, so maybe I've been wrong more than once."

"Too bad. You blew your chance at immortality."

Tuffy paused to sniff the base of a parking meter. When he'd satisfied his curiosity, we moved on.

Up ahead was a sidewalk café with empty tables. It was one of the places with a sign that said dogs were welcome to sit outside with their owners.

"How about some coffee?" NDM asked.

"Sounds good." We took the table next to the building, out of the line of foot traffic. Tuffy settled under the table as a waiter approached us. He was a slender young man

179

with spiked bleached blond hair and an inch-wide strip of dark beard that ran from just under his lower lip to the tip of his chin. His nametag said "Chance."

"What can I get you folks tonight?" he asked.

"Cappuccino for me," I said.

"The same," NDM said.

Indicating Tuffy, I said, "May we have a bowl of water?"

"Yeah, sure. No extra charge." Chance grinned and hurried into the café.

I asked NDM, "So what did you learn about me from Mrs. Tran?"

"That you keep your cooking school space clean and your landlords like you."

"It hardly seems worth your while to come all the way down here for so little."

"I have a date later. She lives on Seventeenth Street, so we're meeting at a restaurant across from the Santa Monica Pier."

" 'Meeting'? Don't men call for women anymore and escort them to dinner? I admit I haven't dated for twenty-two years, but have things changed that much?"

The waiter returned with our order and set the cups of cappuccino on the table. I took the bowl of water from his tray and put it on the cement for Tuffy, who lapped at it.

When Chance was gone again, NDM asked, "Why has it been so long since you've dated?"

"I was married for twenty of those years. It's bad form to date when you have a husband."

"And since he died?"

"I don't have time."

"That's a crock," he said. "You just haven't met anyone who interests you. Surely you don't believe in that one and only true love business. You seem like too sensible a woman."

Sensible . . . When did I stop being "foxy" — Mack's nickname for me — and become sensible?

I guess something must have shown on my face, because he said, "Hey, I didn't mean to hurt your feelings."

"Not at all. I just realized that there's a lot I don't know about the dating scene today. Tell me about the woman you're meeting."

"She's a model."

Of course she's a model. Or an actress. Or that Hollywood triple hyphenate: the actress-model-something-else.

"I meant what is she like as a person?"

He paused. "I don't know her very well."

"Let me guess: she's blonde, very pretty, and . . . twenty years old?"

181

"Twenty-one. You're being sarcastic, but she's very mature for her age."

"Hah! I knew you were going to say that because men in their forties want to think that girls of twenty-one are mature."

"Older women can't keep up with me."

"Intellectually? Tell me what your model likes to read."

"We haven't discussed books yet, but she's very smart."

"She was a *teenager* two years ago!"

"Why are you so angry about this?"

"Because I have an unofficial daughter that age and I'd lock her in the cellar before I'd let her get involved with someone like you."

"You don't have a cellar. Hardly anybody in Southern California has a cellar."

That stopped me, and I started laughing at the absurdity of this conversation. I looked up and discovered NDM was laughing, too. Maybe he wasn't entirely a jerk, but I certainly wasn't going to introduce him to Eileen.

When we finished our cappuccinos, NDM looked at his watch. "It's a quarter after eight," he said, meaning that he wanted to leave.

Good. Eileen and John would still be having dinner somewhere. "I have to get home," I said.

NDM signaled for the check and paid it. "Did you and your curly-haired friend walk down here?"

"Yes."

"To prove that I'm not entirely a social Neanderthal, I'll drive you home," he said.

NDM dropped Tuffy and me at my front door and sped off to meet his date. I hadn't shared the information about my visit to Faye Bond and being followed from Mimi's house.

As I unlocked the front door, I told Tuffy, "He doesn't need my information. One of his *mature* young models can help him investigate."

All I'd had with NDM was that cappuccino, and I was hungry. I made a fried-egg sandwich for myself, gave Tuffy a treat, and was in bed with the lights out before Eileen got home. But I didn't fall asleep as quickly as I usually did.

I realized how much I missed the easy camaraderie I'd had with John for so many years. His friendship had kept me from being lonely. Now, until whatever had flared up between us died out, I was truly on my own for the first time since I met Mack.

17

Monday morning I called the Better Living Channel. I knew I was due there at one o'clock to rehearse with the director for the next show, but I wanted to find out who else would be at the studio. I learned that, luckily, the person I wanted to talk to was also working today, and would be there at ten o'clock. I decided to go in early so that meeting him would seem casual.

Just as I was dressing to leave for the studio, the bedside phone rang. It made me jump. I didn't know to whom I was more reluctant to speak: John O'Hara, because I was unsettled by my conversation with Liddy, or Detective Hall, who might insist that I come to his station house for more questioning.

Neither man was on the other end of the line. Instead, it was Ed Gardner of Western Alliance Insurance, the man who handled my homeowner's and auto policies.

"Good morning, Della. I hope I'm not calling too early."

"No, I've been up for hours. Is there something more you need to know, Ed?"

"More?" From his puzzled tone, it was clear he hadn't heard about the dent in the back of the Mustang. I'd made my accident report over the phone to the insurance company's twenty-four-hour line on Friday night. A woman with the inflectionless voice of a robot had taken down the facts, but it sounded as though the information hadn't yet reached Ed. "I wanted to talk to you for a couple of reasons. First, congratulations on having your own television show. That's pretty fabulous."

"Thank you." I felt awkward hearing that, because I couldn't forget that a woman had died on the show four nights ago.

"Well, I suppose you know why I'm calling, Della."

"No, I don't."

"We have to write some new policies for you. Now that you're famous, you've become what we call in the business 'a target risk.' As a celebrity, you're going to have to carry significantly more insurance."

His words struck me like a blow to the chest; I couldn't afford to buy any more insurance. "I'm not a celebrity, Ed — I'm

185

just on a cable TV cooking show. I'm not even well enough known to be called 'obscure.' "

"You're being modest." I heard the unctuous smile in his voice and remembered that I'd described him to Liddy as resembling a self-satisfied lizard with a stomach full of flies.

Blissfully unaware of my image of him, Ed went on. "As a public figure, which you are now, you need a *lot* more liability coverage on your house and cars."

"Car, Ed. One car. And it's eighteen years old."

"It doesn't matter what kind of car you have. If you hit someone, because you're on TV, you'll be sued for millions. Not to mention the millions you'll be sued for if somebody trips at your house." On the other end of the line, I heard him chuckle. "That's the downside of fame."

The thought of being forced to pay more for insurance when I was barely making expenses now caused my mouth to go dry with fear. I hadn't received my first paycheck from the channel yet, and it was possible that the show wouldn't attract enough viewers to stay on the air. If my bills shot up even higher, what in the world was I going to do?

186

"Della? Are you still there?"

"Yes . . . sorry, I was just . . . How much more do you think I'll have to pay?"

"You're going to need *at least* a couple mil in liability coverage on your home and another two mil on the vehicle. Three million each would be safer. That'll let you sleep at night. I'll have the new policies for you by tomorrow. If you're having a temporary cash flow problem, you can make partial payments, but we'll want the first check as soon as I work up the revised figures. In your altered circumstances, you can't afford to be unprotected."

I'd read that the Mafia forced people to buy "protection." If they'd sold insurance, they could have stayed out of jail, and they'd probably have made just as much money.

While I was trying not to panic, Ed had kept talking. I made myself focus on his words to catch up.

"— and it's all too true, Della. The one sure thing in this world is that sooner or later we're going to be blindsided by the *unexpected.* That's when you'll need the sheltering arms of Western Alliance Insurance. Think of us as being something like Superman's Sea of Tranquility."

At that moment, I felt about Western Alliance the way Superman felt about kryptonite.

Outside in the daylight, I stared at the dent in the back of the Mustang and was hit with a fresh wave of guilt. Murmuring apologies to Mack's car, I drove to the Better Living Channel in North Hollywood.

I was on Lankershim Boulevard, near the turnoff onto Chandler Street, when I got a surprise that caused me to swerve over onto the side of the road and stop the car. I sat there, staring up in disbelief at the huge billboard on the corner. Each time before when I'd seen that outdoor advertising, it had featured caricatures of the Better Living Channel's three best known show hosts: Car Guy, Lulu Owens, and Gilmer York. But this was a new billboard, and *my* caricature was on it, too!

The second surprise was that my depiction wasn't unflattering. The artist had chosen to slightly exaggerate the size of my eyes and lips, had narrowed my waist, and had lowered my neckline. Lowered it too much, in my opinion, but I had to admit that I looked good in those brushstrokes. It occurred to me that maybe I wasn't too bad in real life. Not *yet.* I hadn't thought much about it. I was only forty-seven and naturally healthy, but good genes couldn't carry a woman forever without what Liddy called "female maintenance." Right there, under that billboard, I decided to start exercising so I'd have a waistline that was a little closer to my caricature. And, while I'd keep eating everything I always ate, I'd consume maybe 25 percent less. Full of resolve not to let myself go, I put the car in gear again and made the turn onto Chandler. When I reached the studio's gate, I pressed the buzzer and identified myself.

The woman who answered from the security desk inside responded with a cheery, "Hello, Ms. Carmichael. We weren't expecting you 'til later, but come on in." It was a relief that the staff had stopped referring to me as "the killer chocolate woman."

The gate swung open. I steered the Mustang onto the TV station's property and around the building toward the parking area. At least a dozen cars were lined up near the open double doors to the studio. I saw the big bronze Cadillac belonging to producer George Hopkins and director Quinn Tanner's shiny little red Mini Cooper, but the other vehicles weren't familiar. They were all bunched together because a glossy new blacktop surface had been put down on the parking area beyond. I remembered the notice I'd seen tacked up

189

in the production office, alerting all employees that a new surface was going to be laid last Friday. Everyone was instructed to park on public streets until Monday morning. The yellow caution tape was still up, which explained the line of cars outside the big lot.

As I pulled up to a few feet behind the last car in line, a man emerged from the open studio doors. He was about five eight or nine, in his forties, suntanned, and dressed in blue mechanic's overalls. He walked with a slight limp. I recognized him from the channel's big billboard: Car Guy. The jutting chin in his caricature wasn't much of an exaggeration; his jaw was nearly as square as Dick Tracy's in the old cartoons.

I smiled at him. "Good morning. I'm —"

"I know who you are. I'm Car Guy." He started to extend his hand to me but retracted it and instead wiped it on a rag tucked into his pocket. "Sorry, I just taped a segment on changing your own oil. You're Della. Glad to see you came back."

"Why wouldn't I come back?"

He shot me a quizzical look, shrugged, and turned his attention to my Mustang. "Nice wheels," he said. "I had a sweet ride like that, but my ex-wife took it in the divorce, 'cause I loved it. Now she leaves it out in the street to rust. You want to sell?"

"No!" I hadn't meant to sound so sharp. Softening my tone, I amended, "This car means a great deal to me. I was wondering if you could take a look at the dent in the back and suggest a trustworthy place I should go for repairs."

Car Guy moved around to view the damage. I saw that his left leg was a little shorter than his right, and his left shoe had been built up to compensate. He ran his index finger gently over the dent and raised the trunk lid. "The lock's been sprung, and the trunk and rear spoiler got a good bash, but it's all fixable. Who's your insurance carrier?"

"Western Alliance."

He grimaced. "Spineless weasels. But I'm one of their approved shops. You want me to do the repairs?"

"Absolutely! That would be great." I'd come early to see him, hoping to talk him into working on my car so I'd have an innocent-seeming excuse to spend time with him. Car Guy's set was positioned directly next to mine, which had once been Mimi's set. He might know something useful to the investigation. It was even possible that he'd been her mystery man. I would question

191

Lulu Owens about him when I met her for dinner tonight.

"I'll talk to your adjuster," he said. "What happened?"

"I'm not sure." *A limited truth.*

"Are you going to be here awhile?" he asked.

"Several hours. I'm preparing for Thursday's show."

A tiny smile twitched the corner of his lips. "You can't rehearse for everything. But I guess you found that out the hard way, didn't you?"

Car Guy left the Mustang and moved to the brown sedan I'd parked behind. I told his back, "See you later," and went into the studio.

My kitchen area was dark, but the studio's TV monitor on Car Guy's set was playing the show being taped at the front of the building: Gilmer York's *That's Not Junk!*

I decided to watch it. York was in his early thirties and as supple as a rubber band. The black shirt and black jeans he wore emphasized his lean frame. Holding up the jeans were red, white, and blue suspenders. One strap featured a vertical column of American flags. The other sported a similar line of Union Jacks, the British flag. Beneath a tangle of sandy curls, his face was slightly round and dimpled. If little Shirley Temple had grown up to be a man, she would have looked like Gilmer York.

"Hello, treasure hunters," he said to the camera. "Are we ready to turn some other bloke's throwaways into just what you've been looking for? You're in the right place, mates. People ask how I got into this business of rooting around in other people's trash. Well, I owe it all to me mum. I grew up in North London. We weren't posh, but Mum used to take me to museums from the time I was a tyke. One day we saw a Picasso exhibit. Not of his paintings, but what he called 'found art.' That meant he painted on and made things out of the bits and bobs he'd found: slats from a rotting wood fence, the leg of a table, the bottom of a packing case. Things people threw away. Picasso gathered up bags full and turned them into beautiful works of art."

He gestured to some scarred and scuffed old pieces of furniture littering the set. "You can do it with a splash of paint or a rag full of polish, a few knocks with a hammer, or twists with a screwdriver. I had a date the other night with a charming Irish lass — ah, yes, ladies, I am available again. The woman I thought might be *the one* dumped me. The problem was, she wanted me to take her out to clubs, but I'd planned to put a new duct in her attic."

From his slightly naughty smile, I wondered if that phrase might be a British euphemism.

He pulled a wooden chest toward the camera and displayed its peeling paint and missing hinge. "Today we're taking on this old chest somebody put out on the street for the garbage man. We'll strip off the paint, give it two licks and a polish, top it with a plate of glass I picked up at Goodwill, and we'll end up with a handsome coffee table. And, while the varnish is drying, I'm going to show you some tricks to do with wire mesh."

Suddenly, to my left, I heard a noise that sent a lightning bolt of fear ripping through my body. I turned toward the studio's open double doors and gasped. A dark brown sedan was driving into the building. With sunlight behind the vehicle, all I could see was the driver's silhouette at the wheel, but I would never forget that particular growling sound. It was the car that had chased me through Brentwood Friday night — and now it was coming directly at me!

18

Caught between the heavy worktable and the wall, I wouldn't be able to escape to safety before the car reached me. I opened my mouth to scream, but no sound came out. Even if I could have produced a cry for help, there was no one at this end of the studio to hear. The soundproof wall separated the two halves of the building; staff members were busy taping Gilmer York's show on the other side of it. Instinctively, I grabbed the nearest tool — a grease gun — and raised my arm to heave it at the oncoming car's windshield.

I was about to let go when the growling car stopped in the middle of the set. Car Guy opened the driver's side door, leaned out, and yelled at me. "Put that down!"

He scrambled out of the car. In spite of his limp, he moved fast, leaned over the table, and snatched the grease gun out of my hand. "These things are expensive. What the hell were you trying to do?"

Keeping the worktable between us and staying out of the reach of his hands, I said, "I thought you were going to kill me."

He stared at me with an expression of disbelief. "Are you cooking babes *all* nuts? Why would I kill you? I don't know you well enough! In a couple more days, I might want to."

Either he was a great actor, or he really hadn't been intending harm.

"You were driving right at me," I said. But I heard uncertainty in my voice.

"Jeez! I didn't expect you to be standing there. Why aren't you in your kitchen, where you belong?" His glare could have peeled the paint off a fender. "You're on my set — in my way. I have to put this car onto the hydraulic lift and get ready for my next segment."

"I'm sorry." I felt myself blushing with embarrassment, certain now that I'd been wrong and needed to explain. "I was watching the monitor, then the car was coming into the building. It startled me." *To say the very least!*

He shook his head and snapped, "I teach people how to fix their cars. How am I supposed to do that? By drawing pictures in *spaghetti sauce?*"

Hoping to defuse his anger, I smiled and played innocent. "Making television shows is all new to me. And I suppose I'm still on edge after Mimi Bond's murder."

"Yeah, okay, I guess I can understand that." Car Guy shifted his weight from his right foot to his left, as though trying to find a comfortable position. "Did you know Mimi?" he asked. His tone was milder now.

"I never met her before Thursday night."

He scowled again. "She was a grade A, number one, high octane bitc— I mean, a pain in the ass. I thought she'd finally be out of my hair when she was fired, but she's causing even more trouble now that she's dead. That bald cop is sticking his big nose everywhere, asking questions up the wazoo."

That meant John was right; Detective Hall *was* looking at other people, but if he didn't find the killer soon, I was sure he'd be coming right back to me. I wondered why Car Guy disliked Mimi so much, but decided not to risk asking him about it. I made a mental note to find out what Lulu knew when I joined her for dinner tonight.

"Detective Hall is making all of us uncomfortable. He's acting as though I'm his number one suspect, and I didn't even know Mimi Bond."

All he did was grunt. Clearly, he wasn't

going to say anything useful. I changed the subject. "Your show must help a lot of people who don't know how to take care of their cars."

"That's the truth." Flattery seemed to work; he smiled at me. "Ignorance of how a car operates is why unscrupulous repair shops can rip people off. Especially women. When some mechanics see a female coming, they get dollar signs in their eyes and try to sell them big-ticket repairs they don't need."

I gestured toward the car he'd driven into the studio. "That car was making a strange sound. What's wrong with it?"

He shrugged dismissively. "Just a dry bearing. It's no big deal, but if a crooked mechanic thinks he's dealing with an inexperienced owner — especially a woman — he could tell her that she needs an engine overhaul."

With an exaggerated comic shudder, I said, "Please don't say those words: 'engine overhaul.' "

Car Guy grinned. "Yeah, if you've got a car, those are about the two dirtiest words in the English language. I'm surprised the FCC lets me say them on the air."

If it hadn't been for what happened to me Friday night, I would have enjoyed our conversation. Car Guy's personality had progressed by degrees from grim to jocular. But until the killer was caught, I didn't know which of my new acquaintances to trust. I couldn't risk letting my guard down with him.

Car Guy began to tell me a horror story about a bogus engine repair.

While pretending to be interested in what he was saying, I had worked my way over to the front of the car and leaned down. As soon as I got a good look at it, I felt my pulse start beating faster. In the front of the car was a telltale dent. Not only that, but I could see flecks of blue embedded in the sedan's dark brown paint. It looked like the same shade of blue as my Mustang, but it would take an expert to say for sure.

I stood up, thrust my right hand into my bag, and gripped my cell phone. Keeping the sedan between Car Guy and myself, I moved closer to the outside door. If I had to, I knew I could outrun him in open space.

Trying not to sound nervous, I asked, "Is this your car?"

He nodded. "It's one of my props."

"Props?"

"Most of the machines I fix on the show belong to my shop customers, or people at the channel, but I have this Simba and an old Toyota to take apart when I need to illustrate a repair that's not currently in the shop. Like today, with the dry bearing."

"Are you going to fix the dent?"

"The dent in your Mustang?"

I indicated the front of the Simba sedan. "I mean the damage to this car."

"What damage?" Car Guy stepped around to look at the front end of the Simba. When he saw what I was talking about, he muttered one of the more colorful curses.

I said carefully, "Maybe somebody backed into you when you were using the car this weekend. Perhaps when you were parked outside a restaurant or a movie theater?"

"I don't drive this piece of Korean crap except for work. It's been parked on the street with the other cars since early Friday morning — or it should have been. I didn't look at it when I brought it into the studio today." He scowled again at the damage. "Jeez! Some miserable kids must have taken it for a joy ride. A few blocks north and it's gang territory. I'm surprised the bastards brought it back."

He was so convincing in his anger that I risked telling him part of the truth. "I believe you, but it looks like your car was involved in a crime Friday night. I'm going to have to call the police and tell them where it is."

So much for good intentions, I thought, as I pulled out my cell and dialed John O'Hara's number.

When John got to the studio half an hour later, he had Detective Hall with him. Hall was not in a good mood. I was almost relieved; the more difficult Hall was going to be, the less opportunity I'd have to worry about being with John.

After looking at Car Guy's Simba sedan and then at my Mustang, he called the North Hollywood Division and asked for SID to process the Simba inside and out, and see if the dent on the front of the Simba matched the damage to the back of the Mustang. I was certain the answer to that would be a yes.

After Detective Hall told Car Guy that he'd have to use another vehicle on his show today, John asked the mechanic to show him where the Simba had been parked on the street on Friday morning.

As they headed outside, Hall turned on me and demanded, "Why in the name of all that's holy am I only hearing about this *now?*"

I planted my feet on the floor of the studio and replied firmly, "Exactly what was I supposed to do, Detective? If I'd called you Friday night and told you a car chased me around Brentwood, you'd have blown me off — and you would have been right to do it." I added that last part to sound less confrontational.

His voice was heavy with sarcasm. "You were followed from the home of the murder victim. Didn't that strike you as significant?"

"I'd never seen that car before, and I couldn't make out who was driving it. It might have been some bully trying to scare a woman driving by herself, or even some thug trying to rob me. Honestly, isn't that what you would have thought if I'd called you then?"

He didn't answer my question, choosing instead to ask one of his own. "What were you doing at Mimi Bond's house?"

"I went to see her daughter, to pay a condolence call."

Detective Hall didn't reply, and he was hiding whatever he was thinking behind a poker face. I used to tease Mack sometimes by asking if the police academy had a class in being inscrutable.

At that moment, John and Car Guy returned.

"Where the cars were parked, it's pretty much an empty block," John said. "Anybody who knew how to hot-wire could have stolen one."

"Where were the car keys kept?" I asked.

Detective Hall scowled at me, but before he could say anything, Car Guy answered, "The keys to my cars stay with me. I don't leave them at the studio."

"Who drives that car?" John asked.

"Just me."

"I'll need to get your fingerprints for comparison," Hall said, breaking in.

"You already got 'em. I'm in the system," he said quietly.

"For what? Don't lie because I'll pull your sheet."

Car Guy looked embarrassed. "Grand theft auto — but it was seventeen years ago and I did twenty-two months. I'm clean since then."

"What were you doing Friday night?" John asked.

"Watching a ball game in a sports bar near my apartment. A lot of people saw me. I'm a regular."

Hall wrote down the name of the bar, and the names of the two friends Car Guy said could vouch for him being there from six pm until midnight Friday.

"Thank you," Hall said. "If I need to ask you anything else, I'll be in touch."

"No doubt." Car Guy's tone was wry.

John slipped on a pair of latex gloves. "I'm going to drive the Simba back outside so SID can go over it."

"You got a warrant?"

"I can get one," Hall said. "But it looks better if you cooperate."

Car Guy thought for a moment, then shrugged and moved toward the Simba. "Do what you want with it. I haven't got anything to hide anymore."

John climbed behind the wheel, turned on the ignition, and backed the car through the studio doors. Returning, he handed the key to Hall and stripped off the gloves.

Car Guy said, "Now will you all clear off of my set? I've got two shows to tape this afternoon and I have to find another car to take apart."

I led John and Detective Hall over to my set and turned on the work lights above the preparation counter just as Quinn Tanner came down from the control booth. Wearing tight gray slacks and a black leotard top, she might have been a ballet dancer between rehearsals instead of the television director that she was. As usual, her long black hair was parted in the middle, but today it was held away from her narrow face by mother-of-pearl combs. She was as pale as a vampire's entrée, and it looked as though in the several days since I'd seen her last, she'd lost weight from her already slender frame.

"I hadn't expected you for another two hours," she said. It sounded like an accusation, but then Quinn was one of the iciest people I'd ever met. Her British accent differed from Gilmer York's in that she sounded like the wealthy residents of "upstairs" and York more like the servant class of "downstairs."

"I thought I'd practice for a while before you took me through the camera moves," I said.

Her response was an emotionless, "Ah." She turned her attention to Hall. "Hello, Detective. Have you apprehended the murderer?"

"Not yet."

Indicating John, I said, "This is Lieutenant O'Hara from the LAPD."

Quinn bestowed on John a quick appreciative glance and then a regal tilt of her head. "Hello." Addressing Hall, she said, "I've told you everything I know, Detective. Is there something else you need from me?"

"Ms. Tanner, where were you Friday night?"

"Why in the world do you want to know

that? The murder occurred the night *before.*"

"Just answer the question, please."

"I attended the theater," she said. "The revival of Sondheim's *Into the Woods,* at the Dorothy Chandler. That's in downtown Los Angeles."

"I know where it is," Hall replied. "We're not entirely uncivilized here in the colonies. By the way, I hope you saved your ticket stub."

Quinn lost a little of her imperiousness as she admitted, "I'm afraid I threw it away."

"I'll want a timeline of your movements on Friday, from six p.m. until midnight, and I want the names and numbers of anyone who can substantiate your whereabouts."

She opened her mouth to speak, but Hall didn't give her a chance. "I want that timeline and the list in my office at North Hollywood Station by tomorrow morning." He handed her one of his cards. "Here's the address."

The tension was broken by the arrival of Stan Evans, the studio's daytime guard, who hurried in from the door to the security desk. He flashed a pleasant smile at me but addressed Detective Hall.

"Two of your people are here to look at a car," Stan said.

"Yeah, thanks." Hall turned to John and asked, "You coming with me?"

John glanced at me. "What are you going to do?"

"Rehearse for Thursday's show, and then go home." I neglected to mention that after feeding and walking Tuffy I'd be going to Lulu Owens's house for dinner.

19

Quinn Tanner decided that since I was there early, we should run through what I was going to do on the next show, before Car Guy's taping. She came out of the production cubicle holding a clipboard and a pen, and with a stopwatch hanging from a cord around her neck.

"We'll camera block on Wednesday," she said. "Right now, let me see what you'll be preparing so I can do an initial timing."

"Thursday's theme is 'Hearty and Light.' The main dish is chicken cacciatore; the side is spinach fettuccine with fresh spinach, garlic, and oil. For dessert it's just going to be raspberries and blueberries marinated in fresh-squeezed orange juice."

"Talk. Go through the motions. Use the equipment, but pantomime the food."

Positioning myself behind the prep counter, I greeted the imaginary audience and told the empty seats approximately what I was going to say to the real audience, about what I was going to make and something about how the dishes were created.

I related the story I heard from my grandmother, about when, as a teenager newly arrived in America from Scotland, she worked as a maid for a businessman who taught her how to make what he called "authentic Jewish-Sicilian chicken cacciatore." He had Grandma Nell memorize the ingredients and his special cooking technique, which was to bake the cacciatore, rest it for a couple of hours, and then bake it again before serving. He insisted she memorize because he didn't like to have anything written down. After the second baking, the chicken pieces came out so tender they could be cut with a fork. Grandma Nell made it for him and his guests several times. Then one night the front of her employer's house was sprayed with bullets by some rival "businessmen." That's when my terrified grandmother learned she'd been working for the famous gangster, Mickey Cohen. She quit her job but never forgot how to make his delicious cacciatore. She finally wrote the recipe down and gave it to me as a wedding present.

"I call it Gangster Chicken," I said.

It was encouraging that Quinn, who so far had never displayed much of a sense of humor, smiled when she heard that story.

From the drawer beneath the counter, I took my Berghof utility knife and began to pretend to slice the vegetables and split the chicken breasts, then I went through the motions of sautéing, incorporating, and putting the big casserole dish into the oven while Quinn timed my actions. She even timed me pretending to wash my hands after I cut up the chicken while I advised the audience to be careful not to "cross contaminate."

Indicating the on-set refrigerator, I asked Quinn, "Has someone fixed this?"

"Yes. It's working now. Just keep going."

I continued moving around the set and pantomiming preparation until we'd gone through the entire show.

"You're almost two minutes long," she said. "Have the majority of the vegetables cut up and ready to be used before we go on the air."

"Will do." I put my knife back in the drawer, and replaced the casserole dish, the pot for boiling the pasta water, and the pot I would use for the oil, garlic, and fresh spinach in the cabinet beneath the counter.

Now I could go home, take care of Tuffy, and then soak in a hot, foamy bath before I left for Lulu Owens' house.

As I drove out through the studio gate, I remembered that I'd promised to bring dessert to Lulu's. Looking up at the channel's new billboard, I got a fresh thrill, but the sight of my caricature's small waist convinced me to take fresh raspberries and blueberries for dessert, with a couple of juicy oranges I'd squeeze over the berries to marinate them.

Lulu Owens lived in a cottage that looked like a witch's house from a Disney fairy-tale movie. Nothing Grimm; all charm. The roof was peaked, but tipped slightly to the right; the windows were set at whimsical angles. The walls were facsimiles of gingerbread, created from wood and tile. An asymmetrical stone path led from the driveway to the front door, and it was bracketed on both sides by a chorus line of tulips. It was evening, and they were closed for the night, but it was easy to imagine how beautiful they must be during the day, with their little petal faces upturned to the sun.

Lulu met me at the door in a long, loose gray cotton dress that Mother Goose might have worn. It was perfect for the setting into which I stepped, and more imaginative than my dark blue running suit that had never been worn for running.

Inside Lulu's cottage, the wooden furniture looked handmade by an artist. The bright upholstery fabrics and throw rugs might have come from the antique loom I saw in the corner. Styles and colors were mixed with cheerful abandon.

"What a lovely home," I said sincerely. "Did you make all these unusual pieces?"

She beamed with pride. "Most. That lamp Ah picked up at a craft fair in Georgia, seems like a hundred years ago. The sideboard was mah mother's, but Ah painted the scene on the doors at the bottom."

Lulu showed me through what she called her "three-room enchanted cottage." In addition to the living room, there was a large kitchen and Lulu's bedroom, all decorated with storybook artistry. Opening the bathroom door was like looking into an arbor; the walls were covered with murals of wisteria vines, heavy with their lavender flowers.

"Ah got the claw-foot tub, the pedestal sink, and the wood-lid toilet just before they demolished an old hotel in Pasadena. Teardowns are a crafter's paradise."

After the tour, we sat down at her large

oak kitchen table.

"Ah didn't know what you like to eat, so Ah made lasagna. If a body doesn't like lasagna, Ah'd suspect they're from Mars."

"Lasagna's one of my many favorite foods."

"You're mah kinda gal. Let's eat. Ah'm up by five, so Ah go to bed real early."

Lulu's lasagna was delicious. "Frankly, this is better than mine," I admitted.

She grinned with delight. "Ah'll send you mah special recipe."

Much as I enjoyed Lulu's dinner, I wasn't here for the food. I needed to learn as much as possible about the woman who had been murdered right in front of me. We were having the raspberries and blueberries when I brought up the subject. "You said you'd known Mimi a long time."

Lulu made a face. "Oh, yeah. Since before she turned prematurely blonde."

"What was she like to work with?"

"Let me ask you a question first. What's the worst job you ever had?"

That was easy. "When I was teaching high school English in a gang area and a student shot at me. That's when I opened a cooking school in Santa Monica."

Lulu thought for a moment. "Okay, maybe you had it worse — but not by much. 'Less one o' them delinquents also run off with your husband."

I felt my eyes widen. "Mimi ran off with . . . ?"

"Actually, Ah caught 'em doin' the nasty, an' Ah run *him* off. Ah honestly think at that moment, if Ah'd've had a gun, Ah'd a killed 'em both. They broke my heart. . . ."

"That's terrible," I said. "I'm so sorry you had to go through that."

She shrugged. "Most chairs last longer than a lot of marriages. Ah stopped workin' with Mimi, an' took the bastard for everything Ah could get. At least the kids were already grown an' out on their own. The divorce was still hard on them, but not as bad as it would have been when they were little. Thank heaven for small favors."

"Mickey Jordan told me that you were the one who really did the cooking for Mimi, so you were valuable to her. Why did she go after your husband?"

Lulu smiled ruefully. "It's like that ol' mountain climber's joke: because he was *there.* Mimi was an alcoholic, but she was also addicted to men."

"When we were at Faye's, you said you had an idea about who her last man was."

She frowned and looked away from me. It seemed as though she was having an internal struggle. "Ah've been thinkin', but Ah'm not sure enough to say. If Ah'm wrong, it could hurt somebody who doesn't deserve a smack in the face."

I came at the question another way. "Did Mimi have a particular type?"

"Yeah — he had to be *alive*. After her husband died — the lucky bastard — an' she didn't need money anymore, she favored men who were young, but sometimes she wanted *rough*. Don' mention her to Car Guy, or he might throw a truck tire at your head."

"Her name came up this morning, and he seemed bitter," I said.

Lulu snorted. "No wonder! Ol' Mimi chased him like a hound dog after a bitch in season, 'cept the genders were reversed. Ah heard about the Christmas party she invited him to last year, while Faye was away at school. Car Guy got to the house an' discovered he was the only guest. Way he told it later, she practically pulled his pants right off an' said that if he didn't do what she wanted, she'd call the cops an' charge him with rape. She knew he had a record, somethin' criminal in his past."

"This is fascinating," I said. "What did he do?"

"According to what Mimi told ever'body

215

at the studio, they got down, so to speak, but he couldn't get it up — pardon my language. Ah heard he told Mickey Jordan it was Mimi or him. He'd quit if he had to be on the same channel as her. So Mickey fired Mimi. He used her drinking on the air as his excuse, but he was lookin' for a reason to get rid of her anyway. The viewers were complainin' that her recipes turned out like hog slop." Lulu chuckled. "You know why there's a lock on the studio's sound wall?"

"Yes. To keep someone from going into the studio and interrupting a taping."

"Nope. That cute limey, Gil York, installed it himself, so she couldn't come botherin' him. There used to be just the red light over the door. When it was on, ever'body knew not to open it. Mimi got so mad 'bout that lock — 'cause we all knew it was meant for her — she went around sayin' he was gay. Whether he is or isn't, nobody cares these days, so she didn't get any satisfaction out of it. Next she told people he was a druggie, but when he heard that, he threatened to sue her for slander. He got himself one of them celebrity attorneys. It shut her up, but only the good Lord knows what she would have tried next, if she hadn't died." Lulu hunched her shoulders and shuddered at the dire possibilities. "Mimi was a *baaaad* loser."

The picture that emerged in talking to Lulu was of a truly dreadful woman, but it was hard to believe it was the whole story. "Wasn't there anything good about her?" I asked.

Lulu considered the question for a good minute before she finally replied, "Well, after her last dog passed away of old age, she didn't get another, but she set up an anonymous fund for people who couldn't afford to get medical treatment for their pets. She had a good heart — for animals."

"There must have been some people who liked Mimi," I said.

"Yeah. Faye, of course; she loved her momma. An' Mickey Jordan liked Mimi. That surprised me, 'cause she usta brag that back when the world was young he'd dipped his wick in her hot wax — that's the way she put it. Mimi thought she was gonna be the queen of the channel when he bought it, but he didn't want his wife to find out about their past. Ah heard him tell her to shut the 'F' up. Other than that time, he was always nice to her. Mickey's foul-mouthed, but he's a gentleman."

"He did fire Mimi, though."

"Had to. Couldn't afford to lose Car Guy.

Car's ad spots bring in tons of money, lots more'n Mimi's did. Maybe with all this excitement, sponsors will start lining up for your show." Impishly, she added, " 'Course, you can't promise 'em murder every week."

God forbid!

Lulu was about to eat another mouthful of raspberries when she paused, her spoon in midair. "There's somebody else who liked Mimi, or at least is grateful to her: that redheaded security guard, Stan."

"Stan Evans. He's on the day shift."

"That's him. He worked for Mimi a few months last year as her driver. Then she got him the job at the studio. Security guard hasta be a helluva lot easier way to make a livin' than cartin' Mimi around."

"Who drove Mimi after Stan changed jobs?"

"She said she got disgusted with chauffeurs — they were always askin' for time off. Faye came home 'bout then, an' Mimi had her doin' the drivin'."

"Sounds like the poor girl didn't have much life of her own," I said.

"Faye tol' me she didn't mind 'cause Mimi paid her well. Faye was savin' up for her own apartment. That's one good thing I can say 'bout Mimi: She was never stingy with the salaries. By the time I quit doin' her cookin' an' took my cheatin' hubby to the cleaners, I could buy this house. It was just an ordinary cracker box then. Ah made most of the changes myself. Ah got a lot of pleasure slingin' a hammer while picturin' the faces of Mimi and mah husband."

She smiled, but I saw sadness in her eyes. Blinking it back, she continued, "Ah kept the foundation and the dimensions, an' just replaced the walls an' windows an' roof. Ah hired a couple big ol' boys to help sometimes, but Ah was mah own contractor, an' mostly mah own workman. By the time Ah finished, Ah felt better 'bout life. An' as time passed, Mimi an' me sort of made up. Ah figured she hadn't made the vows to me, *he* had. Ah always felt sorry for Faye, losing her poppa when she was so young. For her sake, Ah more or less forgave Mimi."

Dessert and coffee finished, we cleared the table together.

I said, "You did such a wonderful job with this house. I'll bet your neighbors are grateful to you for raising the property values on the street."

"Yeah, at first, but then not so much now that tourists drive past real slow, or stop to take pictures."

It was a few minutes after nine p.m. when Lulu walked me out to the driveway beside

219

her little witch's cottage. As I came near the Mustang, I saw a small shape curled up on the hood. If it hadn't been for the leaning lamppost at the end of Lulu's drive, I wouldn't have seen it.

"Oh, look, Lulu — there's a cat on my car."

"It's that poor li'l abandoned girlie comes around every day."

"Abandoned?"

Lulu simultaneously nodded and tsk-tsked. "She used to live up the block, but a few weeks ago the people who owned her moved out — an' just left her. They musta took her collar off 'cause she wasn't wearin' it when Ah saw her sittin' in their yard next day, waitin' for them to come back."

A surge of fury made my blood feel hot. "I hope somebody abandons those awful people someday and leaves them alone to starve to death!"

"She stayed in that yard for a few days. Ah brought her food an' water. A week or so later, she was at my door. Ah keep feedin' her, but Ah can't let her in the house 'cause Ah'm allergic. She needs a home."

The cat looked up at me and I saw big eyes in a pale gray face. I reached out to pet her. The cat shifted position and rubbed one of her cheeks and the top of her head against my index finger. She started to purr, and I felt something inside me melt.

"She's so sweet. . . ."

Lulu shook her head. "It's sad. Nobody 'round here seems to want to take her in. Ah know if Ah take her to a shelter they'll kill her, but that little thing's gonna be coyote food one night soon. We've had such a dry summer an' fall, the coyotes are startin' to come down outta the hills. One night they're gonna catch her an' rip her to shreds."

"Oh, no!"

"She likes you," Lulu said. "Why don' you take her in?"

"I already have a dog. . . ."

"Dogs an' cats can get along real well. All a matter of how you introduce them, and make sure you don' give one more attention than the other."

"I don't know. . . ." But I was still petting the cat, and she was still purring. I picked her up, and she pressed her head up under my chin. Unexpectedly, I had a cat. I glanced at Lulu and she was grinning.

"But I don't have any cat food, or litter, or —"

"Jus' wait here," Lulu said. "Don' move a muscle." She sprinted back into her house.

I stroked the cat and whispered, "Would

221

you like to come home with me and meet Tuffy? He likes cats. He has two cat friends at the veterinarian's." The cat kept purring, and I knew there was no way I could leave her here to some horrible fate.

Lulu rushed back outside and down the driveway, carrying a canvas *All Things Crafty* tote bag.

"Put her in this," Lulu said, spreading open the bag's wide top. "Ah don' have cat food — Ah've been givin' her tuna fish. There's a big Ralphs market on Ventura Boulevard. You'll have to go right past it on your way back to Beverly Glen Canyon."

With Lulu holding the tote bag, I gently lowered the cat into it. She didn't resist.

I asked, "What's her name?"

"Don' know. It might have been on her collar, but that was gone."

As I said good night to Lulu, I put the tote bag on the front passenger seat and folded the top back enough so that the cat could look out and wouldn't feel trapped or frightened. She was surprisingly calm. Perhaps some instinct told her she was safe now.

The supermarket was one that was open twenty-four hours a day, and so big and well lighted that it was impossible to miss. I parked, locked the car, and hurried inside to buy supplies for the newest member of my little household.

The store wasn't crowded at this hour. It didn't take long to fill a cart with bags of unscented litter, a large plastic dish pan to use as a litter box, two dozen cans of the best cat food they sold, a bag of dry food, and a few cat toys. I'd have to buy a proper cat-carrying case for trips to the veterinarian at a pet store; the market didn't carry those. In a couple of days, when she settled in, I would take her for an examination and for whatever inoculations cats were supposed to have. In my shaky financial situation, I realized that keeping this cat meant giving up the new pair of leather boots I'd planned to buy. *That's life,* I thought. *We can't have everything.*

Besides, who really needs boots in Southern California?

My last purchase was a large bag of Tuffy's favorite imitation bacon strips. I thought it might be a good idea to give him treats at the same time that I introduced him to our cat.

223

20

As soon as I opened my front door, Eileen hurried in from the back of the house. I knew she'd just come in from an evening jog because she was wearing an old UCLA sweatshirt over faded running shorts. Her fine blonde hair was tied up in a ponytail, and her beautiful face was flushed with healthy color.

"Aunt Del, there's something —" She saw movement in the *All Things Crafty* tote bag on my arm. "What's that?"

I put my handbag down, reached into the tote, and lifted the cat out.

Eileen gasped with delight. "Oh, how adorable! Where did you get him?"

"*Her.* She was abandoned near the house where I had dinner tonight. At least I was told she's a female." I turned the cat onto her back in my arms to get a look at the relevant part underneath. "Yes, it's a girl."

"I love cats." Eileen reached out to stroke

her gently. The cat responded by purring. I marveled at the animal's sociability, at her willingness to trust humans. Here she was, with two strangers, away from her neighborhood, just having riden in a tote bag, and now she was in an unfamiliar house, and yet she'd started to purr again. Even though her owners did a horrible thing in leaving her, they must have been kind until then.

Eileen asked, "What's her name?"

"My friend from the TV station didn't know, and she's not wearing a collar."

The light in the living room was giving me the first good look I'd had at the cat. She was a calico, with longish fur that was a soft, silver gray, with patches of yellow gold and white. All four of her dainty feet were white, as though she had walked through a plate of powdered sugar. Her eyes were large and yellow green.

"What a pretty face," Eileen said as she stroked the cat's fur.

I agreed. "She's really lovely." A name occurred to me. "Let's call her Emma," I said. "After my favorite Jane Austen novel."

"Hello, Emma," Eileen said, rubbing the top of the cat's head with her finger.

Holding Emma against my chest, I could feel her little bones. She was slim beneath her long coat, but not alarmingly skinny.

Apparently, Lulu had fed her well.

"Her coat's nice and thick," Eileen said. "She looks pretty healthy."

"I'll take her to Tuffy's veterinarian tomorrow or the next day, for an examination and to get her shots. I don't know if she's had any, so I have to assume she hasn't. If she's old enough, and hasn't been spayed, then I'll have him do that after she's been here for a couple of weeks. For her to be safe, she's going to be an indoor cat, so we'll have to be careful when we open the front or the back doors."

Eileen's hand flew to her mouth. "Oh my gosh — Tuffy. He's outside in the backyard. How do you think he's going to react to having a cat in the house?"

"He has two Siamese cat friends at Dr. Marks's veterinary hospital, and he's never been scratched. I think the odds are good they'll be okay together. Before we let him in, could you go out to the car and bring in the supplies I bought for Emma?" I handed Eileen the key to the Mustang. "I'll put her litter box in my bathroom, and set up her food and water dishes on that table in the corner of my bedroom, where Tuffy can't get to them. I'll clear the photos and magazines off. She can use my room and bath as her sanctuary, until she feels confident

226

enough to explore the house. And Tuffy can continue to have the kitchen for his drinking and dining."

"Sounds like a plan," Eileen said.

As soon as Eileen came back in with the supermarket bags, I handed Emma to her and we went to my bathroom. I placed the big plastic dishpan under the sink, out of the way of foot traffic, and poured in a mound of litter.

"Put her down, so she can see where her box is," I said.

No sooner had the cat's paws touched the floor than she padded over to the litter box and used her new facilities.

"Good girl," Eileen said. "That's such a good girl."

As soon as we'd completed Emma's new arrangements, I asked Eileen to bring Tuffy into the bedroom.

When my handsome standard poodle came bounding in to greet me, I was holding Emma in my arms. "Hey, big boy," I said, "look what I brought home to live with us."

Spotting Emma, his long ears arched a little, he drew back, and then moved forward cautiously. Emma squirmed in my arms, but didn't hiss or scratch to get away. Instead, she pressed herself closer against my chest.

I sat down on the edge of the bed, to bring the two of them closer together, but I was ready to pull back fast if there was trouble.

While Eileen petted Tuffy and told him what a wonderful boy he was, I freed one hand and offered Tuffy a treat, to associate our new roommate with his favorite goodies.

Tuffy sniffed at Emma, sniffed at the treat, and then took the imitation bacon strip in his mouth. He ate it while Eileen and I continued to pet the two of them and talk to them gently.

Emma turned around in my arms to get a better look at Tuffy. She seemed curious, not afraid. Gradually, I moved her closer to Tuffy. They lightly touched noses.

"Good boy, Tuffy," I said. "This is *our* cat." I gave him another treat. After about twenty minutes of stroking and talking to the two of them, I took Emma over to the table that I'd cleared off, and where Eileen had put down newspapers and dishes of cat food and water. While Tuffy watched, and had another treat, Emma began to eat. I stepped back.

"I think we did it," Eileen said.

I left Emma eating and sat down on the edge of the bed to pet Tuffy.

"They seem to like each other," Eileen

said. "Or at least not to mind each other."

As I watched Emma and scratched Tuffy behind the ears, I asked Eileen, "When I came home — what was it you started to tell me?"

"Oh, yes. I almost forgot. Momma called. She said she'd like you to come and visit her again, as soon as you can."

John's wife wants to see me.

For the first time since Shannon's psychiatrist had put her on the correct medication, I felt a tiny shiver of apprehension. Or was it a twinge of guilt?

"I'll call her first thing tomorrow morning," I said.

I made myself wake up several times during the night to turn on the bedside lamp and check on the pets. Tuffy was sleeping in his usual place next to me, and Emma was curled up on top of the cabinet that enclosed the television set.

At six thirty a.m. I awoke to start the day. It was a happy surprise to find that after the last time I looked at them, Emma had moved over to sleep in the space between the top of my head and the headboard.

Tuffy opened his eyes and saw where Emma was. He just sighed, and went back to sleep. I gave a sigh myself. Of relief. With

Tuffy's naturally sweet disposition, and Emma's apparent lack of fear of him, I was positive that the two of them would coexist peacefully and keep each other company when I had to be out of the house.

Remembering the message Eileen gave me, I intended to call Shannon as soon as I fed Tuffy and Emma and gave them fresh water, and let Tuffy out into the backyard for a few minutes.

Then I promised myself I'd call Shannon as soon as Eileen and I finished breakfast.

After breakfast, brushing my teeth, I vowed to call Shannon the moment I finished showering and got dressed. Well, I'd call her *no later* than after I gave Tuffy his usual morning walk around the neighborhood. If I called her too early, I might wake her up.

Brushed, showered, and dressed, I was putting on my shoes when the doorbell rang.

Eileen called out, "I'll get it!"

She was back and at my bedroom door in well under a minute.

"Daddy's here," she said. "That Detective Hall is with him. Aunt Del, from the way they're acting, I think something bad has happened."

Eileen followed me into the living room, looking worried. "What's the matter, Daddy?"

John said, "We need to speak to Della alone, honey." His tone was soft, but the expression on his face was grim.

"I'll tell you all about whatever it is, later," I told Eileen. "Right now, would you do me a favor and please walk Tuffy? Go out through the backyard gate."

"Okay." She retreated into the kitchen, but she wasn't happy about it.

As soon as the three of us were alone, Detective Hall demanded, "Where were you last night?"

"I don't like your storm trooper manner, and I'm not going to be treated like a criminal. Why do you want to know?"

Towering over both Hall and me, John assumed what Mack used to call his non-threatening "gentle giant" persona and said,

"Your Mustang was seen in a driveway on Fulton Street last evening. Were you visiting someone?"

"You don't have to be so roundabout with me, John. Yes, I had dinner with a colleague from the TV studio, Lulu Owens." A ball of ice began forming in the pit of my stomach. I was getting a terrible premonition. "What's happened?"

"I'll ask the —"

John cut Hall off. "Ms. Owens died last night."

"Oh, no! How did — ?"

"She was murdered," Hall said.

I gasped. "I can't believe it."

"What can you tell us?" John asked.

My knees felt weak. I sank down on the nearest chair. John sat down on the edge of the couch opposite me. After a moment, Hall took a seat, too, but he leaned toward me, as though ready to leap up and grab me if I tried to run away.

Wanting to be helpful, I took a calming breath and mentally re-created the evening. "Lulu invited me to have dinner with her last night, at her house. I got there at six thirty, and left about nine o'clock." I stared at Hall. "You said she was murdered? When did it happen? And how?"

Hall was tight-lipped, but John said, "We

should tell her. Della might have seen something that would help us."

We? Us?

John must have read the question in my eyes because he said, "I've been temporarily detached from the Intel Squad to work with Detective Hall. Two hosts from the same TV network killed in less than a week makes this a high-profile case."

"We don't have the medical examiner's report yet," Hall told me, "but his preliminary guesstimate of time of death, based on liver temp, is between nine and eleven p.m. When did you get home?"

"About ten thirty." I looked at John. "Eileen was here."

"At nine o'clock at night, it wouldn't take more than twenty or twenty-five minutes to drive from the victim's house to here. That leaves at least half an hour unaccounted for. What were you doing during that time? And don't try to tell me you were stuck behind a traffic accident because I can check that out."

Biting back a hot reply, I ignored his crack and explained about finding the cat on the hood of my car, and Lulu persuading me to adopt it. "I wasn't prepared for a cat, so I stopped at the Ralphs market on Ventura Boulevard, a few blocks east of Beverly Glen

Canyon, and bought what I needed for her. The checkout woman might remember me. I told her about unexpectedly acquiring a cat, and she said that she has two." I concentrated hard on trying to remember details about her. "She's in her late thirties, has dark, curly hair. I think her name tag said 'Mercedes.' I'm sure I have my receipt for the purchases."

"I'll want it," Hall said.

"Did you notice anyone around when you left her house?" John asked. "Walking, or driving by? Anything, even though it might have seemed insignificant at the time."

I shook my head. "I was excited about the cat and making a mental list of what I had to buy before I brought her home, but still I think I would have noticed someone walking, or anything that seemed suspicious. The street was quiet."

"The way it looks," Hall said, "you're the last person to have been with the victim."

"I don't care how it *looks*, Detective. I didn't kill her, so, obviously, someone else was there after I left Lulu's."

Hall stood up. "Let's talk about this at the station."

John and I stood up, too.

"Are you arresting me, Detective Hall?"

"Let's say I'm inviting you to talk about

this in a formal setting."

I gave silent thanks that I knew all of my rights. "That's an invitation I'm not going to accept, unless you tell me more about what happened to Lulu. How did she die?"

"She was stabbed to death," Hall said. "In the back. No chance to fight her attacker off."

The image of Lulu being murdered was horrible, but I willed myself to control my reactions, and to think. "What about fingerprints?"

"SID is processing the house," John said, "but Ms. Owens wasn't murdered inside her home. She was killed outdoors."

"Outdoors? Just before I drove away with the cat, Lulu went back in. I saw her close the door behind her."

Hall was staring at me with an expression of "so *you* say" skepticism.

John said, "She was found by her newspaper delivery woman, Alicia Reyes, a few minutes after five this morning. It was just getting light. The Reyes woman was about to toss the paper onto the driveway, when she saw the body lying facedown across the front step."

"Reyes thought Owens had fallen down," Hall said. "She got out of the car and went to help her, but then she saw all the blood and started screaming. The next-door neighbor heard Reyes and called the police. When the responding officer found out who the victim was, and that she appeared in a show on the Better Living Channel, it became my case."

John took his small investigator's notebook out of his jacket pocket and flipped to a particular page. "The neighbor who called it in is Phyllis Shay. Her husband saw your car in the driveway last night at eight thirty when he was walking their dog. Herman Shay said he noticed the car because it was an old Mustang, like one he used to have and is sorry he sold. He remembered part of the license plate."

"That was enough to determine the car was yours," Hall said. "There's one more thing. We have the murder weapon. The knife was still in the victim's back."

"Please stop calling her 'the victim.' She has a name: Lulu Owens."

"We know," John said gently. "No disrespect was meant."

Hall was staring at me, as though I was something under a microscope. "The medical examiner recognized the kind of knife it is," he said. "It's Norwegian — a chef's knife."

Oh, Lord, please don't let this be going

236

where I'm afraid it's going. "Lulu used to cook professionally," I said. "Did it come from her kitchen?"

"Ms. Owens was very neat, well organized. On her kitchen counter there's a block that holds knives. Nothing's missing," Hall said. "Do you have a Norwegian chef's knife?"

"I have four of them. Different blade lengths, for different purposes."

"Where are they?"

"Three of them are here. I'll show you."

Hall and John followed me to the kitchen, where I displayed them. "Do you know anything about knives, Detective?"

"Why don't you fill me in?"

"These are Laslo Berghof designs. He was a Norwegian machinist who developed them for perfect cutting and grip. The handles are ergonomically shaped for maximum control, and so the wrists don't get tired. These three are Laslo Berghof Multi Chef's knives: a six-inch blade, an eight-and-a-quarter-inch, and a ten-inch. They're manufactured by the Berghof company in Oslo, Norway, but anyone can buy them at a high-end kitchen equipment store, or on the Internet."

Hall picked up the slightly curved, Damascus-styled knife with the six-inch blade and examined it.

"Careful," I said. "That's very sharp." One night when I'd barbequed for Mack and John, John had admired my facility with a knife. I was grateful he didn't repeat the compliment now in front of Detective Hall.

"You said you had four knives. Where's the other one?" Hall asked.

I felt my heart start to pump faster. "It's at the studio, in the drawer below the preparation counter. I used it to slice the chicken breasts and the vegetables for last week's TV show, and I used it again yesterday afternoon, when I was rehearsing with the director."

I tried to sound confident, but I was quaking inside. If it turned out that my knife had been used to kill Lulu, I could be in the soup without a ladle.

22

We drove out to the studio in two cars. I'd managed to persuade Detective Hall to let me take my Mustang by making the case that unless he arrested me, I'd need a vehicle in order to get home. John's car was at the North Hollywood Station, and he and Hall rode together, in Hall's car. I was used to seeing police detectives drive undistinguished, blend-into-the-landscape sedans, but to my surprise Hall had a ten-year-old green Range Rover. Between his shaved head, his slightly exotic resemblance to Yul Brynner, and his distinctive wheels, Detective Hall was not exactly standard-issue law enforcement. I was hoping that beneath his carefully shaved dome, he would keep an open mind about me.

John, a gentleman to the core of his DNA, walked me to the driver's side of my car. As I slid behind the steering wheel, I glanced back at Hall and saw that he was watching us as he climbed into his Range Rover.

I asked John, "What do you think of Detective Hall?"

"Smart, but he's under pressure to clear this case. No matter what he says, keep your temper. If he decides to take you into custody, I won't be able to stop him."

We got to the channel a few minutes before eleven a.m. As soon as our two-car convoy rolled onto the studio lot, Mickey Jordan came running out to meet us. Right behind him was producer George Hopkins, clutching a clipboard to his chest and breathing heavily. Both of their faces were red. Mickey, who was trim and sinewy, just looked agitated, but I was concerned for George. He was overweight, a heavy smoker, and had the pattern of red veins on his nose and cheeks that suggested he drank too much. It was a lethal combination that made him ripe for a heart attack.

Before I could ask George if he felt all right, Mickey, ignoring the two lawmen behind me, said, "Della! I called you. The girl at your house said you were on your way out here. Thank God. We got a crisis. Lulu's dead."

"I know. Detective Hall and Lieutenant O'Hara want to see —"

Mickey interrupted by using his hands to form a "T," the classic "time-out" sign. While finally acknowledging the presence of the two investigators with a nod, he continued to speak directly to me. "I just taped an announcement that tomorrow's going to be our "In Memoriam" all-day marathon of Lulu's shows. Sunday we'll have a "Farewell Tribute" an' show her unaired tapes. But until I find an act to replace her, you an' Gil an' Car have got to do extra shows to fill the holes in the program plan. I need you to tape two half-hour shows today and two tomorrow. Then you'll go on live Thursday evening with your scheduled hour. We'll spot the half-hours around as needed, along with Gil's and Car's, and the couple extra shows I'm having them shoot on the East Coast."

Wheezing, George said, "Quinn will direct all your new shows, and Gil's director, Jerry Bobbie, will also do Car's." He squinted at his clipboard, then tore off a page and handed it to me. "From the hundred and some recipes you turned in, I picked out what you'll do on the new half-hours. Today it's just quickie stuff you don't have to make at home first. I sent my assistant out to buy the ingredients you'll need."

"Hey!" Detective Hall's tone was as sharp

as a guard dog's bark. "What am I — *lawn furniture?* Cut your engines."

Mickey barked right back at him. "This is my f—ing television network. Don't think you can come in here and order —"

"This is my badge," Hall said, flashing it. "The badge wins. Now we can do this the easy way, or we can do it the hard way. Since you like to be the boss, you get to choose which it's going to be."

Mickey clamped his lips together in silent fury. George just looked deflated. Neither said a word.

"I'm taking silence to mean you've chosen the easy way." Hall gestured to John. "Take Jordan and Hopkins somewhere and get an account of their movements last night while Ms. Carmichael and I visit her kitchen."

Like the laconic hero Gary Cooper played in *High Noon,* John shepherded Mickey and George toward the little production office.

Hall followed me to my kitchen set.

Switching on the work lights, I said, "My tools are in the cutlery drawer, beneath this end of the preparation counter. The knife is in a leather case."

With the detective practically Velcroed to my side, I opened the drawer. "There."

Seeing the case where I'd left it, a warm feeling of relief began to wash over me.

Then the warmth turned to frost when I opened the case and saw that it was empty.

Hall said, "Your knife is missing. Imagine that." He reached into his jacket pocket and pulled out an envelope containing a pair of five-by-seven color photographs. They showed both sides of a Laslo Berghof utility knife with a five-inch blade and the up-curved profile. That design meant faster prep time and less damage to the food being cut. When I'd last seen my knife it was clean, but this blade was stained dark rust. It took a moment for my mind to register what that discoloration was — and then I nearly retched. With effort, I managed not to throw up, but the impulse left the bitter taste of bile lingering in my mouth.

Hall was watching me intently. "Have you seen this knife before?"

I forced myself to study the picture. "It's mine." My stomach acids were roiling.

"You're sure about that?"

"There's a small plus sign scratched into the handle, up near the blade. The same little mark is on my other Laslo Berghofs." I wasn't going to tell Hall that it was Mack who had scratched in the plus signs when he gave me the set. He'd said it was like his carving our initials on a tree trunk, that it stood for "Mack loves Della."

I saw John coming back from the production office carrying two sheets of white Xerox paper. He stopped on the other side of the preparation counter from Hall and me.

Detective Hall held up one of the knife photographs and told John, "It's hers."

His triumphant "that's-it, end-of-story" attitude yanked me up from the emotional quicksand into which I'd been sinking since I'd realized that Lulu Owens's blood was on the blade of my knife.

"Yes, it's mine," I said with heat, "but look at this drawer. No lock. We're in a TV studio; people come in and out all the time. Oh, sure, Detective — I decided to commit a murder with a weapon that can be traced back to me. What's more likely — I'm that stupid *or* that someone's trying to frame me? Somebody with a powerful motive took that knife after I left here yesterday and used it to murder Lulu Owens. You're a detective — find out who that person is."

"Anyone who had access to the studio could have taken that knife," John told Hall. "There's no case against Della unless you can prove she had a motive to kill the woman."

"And you won't be able to, Detective, because I barely knew her. I think it's clear that the murders of Mimi Bond and Lulu

Owens are connected. *Find the connection.*"

John shot me a look I interpreted to mean, "Quit while you're ahead." He turned to Hall, whose face was reddening with anger.

"We've got a lot of work to do, investigating Lulu's friends, acquaintances, and her finances for some clue as to who might want her dead." John's voice was calm and reasonable. "Asking Della more questions can wait. She's not going anywhere."

Hall speared me with a look that Captain Ahab might have aimed at the whale. "Do you have a passport?"

"Yes."

"Let me have it."

From my years of marriage to a police detective, I was pretty sure that only a judge could force me to surrender my passport, but I played along with Hall and tried to inject some humor into this grim morning. "I'll give it to you," I said, "but only if you promise not to look at the picture — it's awful."

He didn't smile.

Good thing I took up cooking and didn't try to be a comic.

I glanced at John. "Eileen doesn't have classes today. She can get it out of my bureau and bring it here."

"Have her take it to the North Hollywood

Station and leave it in an envelope with my name on it." Hall slapped a card with the address into my hand. He removed a plastic evidence bag and a pen from another jacket pocket. He used the pen to pick up my knife case without touching it. "I'm taking this with me." Hall dropped the case into his evidence bag and sealed the top. "We have your prints for comparison." Turning to John, he said, "Let's go talk to Jordan and Hopkins."

"I kept them separated and had each of them write down their movements last night," John said, as he led Detective Hall back toward the production office.

I fished the cell phone out of my bag and dialed Eileen. In addition to finding my passport, there were some things I'd ask her to bring here to me. The plain black slacks I was wearing would do for the tapings today, but I would need separate tops for the two different shows.

Just as Eileen answered, I thought of another item I'd ask her to bring to the studio — something I was sure would make these hastily taped new shows more entertaining for the viewers.

23

A half hour before taping was supposed to begin, I had changed into one of the blouses Eileen brought, put on TV makeup, and was checking the cooking equipment on the set. But I was still waiting for George Hopkins's assistant to bring the groceries I needed for the show. George was nowhere in sight. I was about to call him on his cell, when Quinn Tanner came running down from the director's booth. With Shakespearean drama appropriate to her British accent, she pointed an index finger to a spot behind me and demanded, "What is *that?*"

I countered her haughty tone with an imperious inflection of my own. "*That* is a standard poodle named Tuffy. He's a five-year-old male, and he's well behaved."

The time had come to put a stop to her arrogance toward me. "This is *my* show, Quinn. When we tape without an audience, I'm going to have him with me." Her mouth dropped open in shock. I'm sure it was a reaction to my unexpected declaration of independence and not because there was a canine in the studio. I softened my voice. "Lulu's death is awful enough, but the situation is even worse because it's come so soon after Mimi's murder. We're all on edge. Tuffy's presence will lighten things up. I'd like you to make sure you get shots of him watching me cook because it will amuse the audience. He cocks his head, as though he's about to ask a question." For the sake of diplomacy, I added, "Don't you agree, Quinn? I value your opinion."

For a few seconds a kaleidoscope of emotions played across her face. The smile that finally settled on her mouth looked forced, but it was an improvement over the expression of cold disdain she'd aimed at me since the moment we met. I wondered why she'd decided to dislike me before getting to know me, but that was a question for another time.

When she spoke, Quinn's voice was carefully neutral. "I must admit that I hadn't thought of including a pet, but upon reflection, I believe it will add *charm* to the show."

She might have been implying that I wasn't supplying any charm, but I didn't care. What was important was that we weren't at war. I needed to have at least a superficially friendly relationship with her to be able to talk to her. Whether she was aware of it or not, she might know something that would fill in a piece of the murder puzzle.

Behind Quinn, next to Camera One, I saw Ernie Ramirez grinning and giving me the "thumbs-up."

"Quinn, I need your problem-solving skills," I said. "George told me he'd sent his assistant out to buy the food I'm going to cook on camera, but that was at least an hour and a half ago and it isn't here yet."

"Bollocks!" she said. "That wretched girl is a total nightmare. I'll go and sort this out." Pivoting away from me, Quinn was off to investigate. In spite of her personality deficit, she'd always struck me as capable at what she did, but I pitied the next object of her wrath.

I knelt down to scratch Tuffy beneath his ears and told him, "We won this battle, Tuff. Now just stay here so she doesn't have a legitimate reason to cut short your TV career."

As though responding to what I said, Tuffy sat up straighter on his dog bed. When I'd asked Eileen to bring him to the studio, I'd also asked her to get the big beige pad I'd bought him when he was a puppy from the back of my closet. He'd never used it at home, because from the beginning, he made it clear that he preferred to sleep on the "people bed." Now I was glad I'd kept it, because I didn't want him to lie on the studio's cold concrete floor while he watched the activities going on around us.

Gaffers on high ladders were adjusting the lights. A maintenance man was polishing smudges off the front of the refrigerator, and a plumber was running water in the sink to be sure everything was functioning.

Ernie Ramirez, having checked out his camera, came over to pet Tuffy.

"We're taping half-hours," he said. "That's twenty-two minutes of cooking and talking time for you, so we're only using the remote-controlled overhead stove cam, and Camera One today. I'll make sure to get some good reaction shots of your dog." He stood up again. "I got stuff to do, but don't worry about not having a chance to rehearse. If you make a mistake, we can stop tape and do it over."

"Thanks, Ernie." He left the set and I went back to making sure I had the pots, pans, and utensils I needed. Fortunately, what I'd be making today didn't require anything more than a paring knife.

I heard rapid footsteps on the concrete, looked up, and saw Stan Evans, the handsome young redheaded security guard, hurrying toward me. He was carrying two bags of groceries.

"This is the stuff Ms. Tanner told me you were waiting for," he said. Just like everyone else at the channel today, Stan was solemn.

"Thanks, Stan. Would you put them down on the counter?"

He was about to do that, but he froze, staring at Tuffy.

"That your dog?" he asked.

"Yes. His name is Tuffy."

He set the bags down on the counter. "Ms. Tanner doesn't like dogs."

"She'll learn to like Tuffy," I said firmly. "Let me introduce you to him."

"Okay. Sure." He didn't sound wildly enthusiastic, but he didn't say no.

I led Stan around the counter. Taking Stan's hand, I stretched it out toward Tuffy. "This is Stan," I said. "He's our friend."

Tuffy looked at Stan, sniffed his fingers, and then he went back to watching the man on the ladder above us.

"Nice-looking dog," Stan said. He went back around the counter and started to unpack one of the grocery bags. I began to unpack the other.

251

"Oh, no!"

"What's the matter?" Stan asked.

"Nothing that will stop the earth revolving around the sun," I said, "but the container of ice cream I was going to use on the first show has melted into soup. Where have these groceries been?"

Stan glanced down at the floor. "I don't want to get anybody in trouble. . . ."

"I won't make a complaint, just tell me what happened."

He looked up at me again. "It was Mr. Hopkins's assistant. She went shopping, but when she got back, she was still so upset about what happened to Ms. Owens, she got all hysterical and went home. Ms. Tanner sent me searching for the groceries, and I found the bags sitting outside the studio doors where she must have left them."

"This is a pretty bad day," I said. "I thought Lulu was a lot of fun."

"She sure liked to talk," Stan said with affection. "Car Guy called her our own *National Enquirer.*"

"Didn't he like Lulu?" I asked.

"Oh, sure. We all liked her. I was just saying."

I took the container of melted ice cream and put it into the freezer compartment of the on-set refrigerator. It wouldn't harden up in time for the first show, but it should be firm enough by the second taping that I could crumble some chocolate wafers into it — there was a box in the pantry — give it a few turns with the mixer and serve it up as crunchy soft ice cream. That would work with the second show's quick menu of grilled fish and microwave-zapped rice with fresh vegetables.

My grocery bag was empty. I asked Stan, "Did George's assistant get the strawberries?"

"Right here." He pulled a box of them out of his bag.

"Oh, those are luscious." They were so big and gorgeous that I knew what special thing I could do with them on the first show. One immediate problem solved.

Now all I have to do is get through a day of unrehearsed tapings — and solve two murders.

With no audience to look at, I faced the camera and just chatted at the lens as I would to Eileen or to Liddy, or to the students in my cooking classes.

After introducing Tuffy, I said, "When you get home from a long day of hard work, or when you've had a day of hard work *at home*

253

— and you moms know that what you do is as exhausting as digging ditches or smearing hot tar on a new roof — you need a meal you can make in a hurry with the least possible effort. Today I'm fixing one of the quickie dinners I pull together when it feels like I'm down at the bottom of my energy tank. The main dish is what I call Zapped Chicken and Vegetables because it's baked in the microwave. The side is angel hair pasta, which takes only three or four minutes to cook in boiling water and another minute to toss with a little oil, garlic, grated Parmesan cheese, and a sprinkling of fresh chopped parsley on top. And for dessert" — I held up one of the strawberries — "some of these beauties dipped in a coat of chocolate."

I managed to get through the taping without having to stop for a do-over. To my surprise, it turned out to be easier to just talk on camera than it had been when I pre-planned what I was going to say. The years of teaching had turned out to be the best possible experience for this new professional adventure. The timing of the three commercial breaks seemed to fall naturally between finishing one dish and starting another. Probably just luck this time, but now I knew when the breaks would come and could adjust my chatting accordingly on the next show.

After taping the first show, and while changes to the set were being made to ready it for the second, I grabbed some paper towels and a baggie, and took Tuffy for a walk around the studio property.

The yellow caution tape had been removed from the entrance to the big parking area and about a dozen vehicles occupied spaces on the handsome new blacktop. At the far side of the lot, behind two big SUVs that had been parked side by side, was a strip of grass that ran between the blacktop and the security fence encircling the property.

Tuffy pulled on his leash, leading me to the grassy region. I didn't think he could see grass at this distance, so he must have caught the scent. That was where he wanted to go, and I had to walk fast to match his pace.

Just as we were passing the two SUVs, I saw that someone was standing between the vehicles. Actually, it was two people, a man and a woman, and they were embracing, where no one at the studio could see them. A slight young woman with light brown hair had her arms around a man, her head bent, her forehead pressed into his chest. He had his arms around her, his fingers entwined, holding her close to him. The woman's back was to me, but I recognized the man: Stan Evans.

Stan saw me at that same moment. I must have startled him into making an abrupt movement, because the woman turned around to look in my direction, and I saw her face.

It was Faye Bond.

24

I recovered from the surprise first. "Oops," I said. "I'm sorry. I didn't meant to interrupt."

Stan and Faye sprang apart.

"You're not interrupting," Faye said.

"She was just upset," Stan said.

"I didn't want anybody to see me crying."

"You see, she heard about Ms. Owens."

"Oh, good Lord, Faye," I said. "I'm so sorry about what happened to Lulu. I forgot how close the two of you were." Silently, I kicked myself for not having realized what a blow Lulu's death would be to this delicate girl.

Faye nodded and tried to say something, but she couldn't get the words out. When she started to cry again, Tuffy went over to lean against her thigh. Faye immediately fell to her knees, hugged him, and buried her face in his neck. My Tuff stood there like a gentleman and patiently let her sob into his curly coat.

Seeing Faye in such distress, I felt terrible that I hadn't remembered her warm relationship with Lulu and realized what a devastating loss the woman's death would be for her.

Stan edged close to me and whispered, "Would you mind looking after her now?" He nodded toward the studio. "I should get back before somebody starts looking for me."

"No, you go on, Stan. I'll stay with Faye."

"Thanks, Ms. Carmichael. I don't know what to do when girls cry."

Most men don't.

Stan hurried off through the parking lot, and I leaned down to help Faye stand. She was only a couple of inches shorter than me — perhaps five feet five — but her head was bent, with her chin tucked almost into her chest. I stroked her hair and murmured words of comfort. She finally stopped crying and took a handful of tissues out of the fanny pack that doubled as her purse.

After she blew her nose and looked up, I said, "Come for a walk with us."

She stuffed the used tissues into her pack. "I won't be in the way?"

"Definitely not."

As we walked Tuffy around the inside

perimeter of the fence, Faye reached for my free hand and held on to it. She was like a sad little child holding on to a caregiver. Faye didn't talk, and I didn't try to push her.

She didn't let go of my hand until I had to stoop and scoop after my canine friend.

"He's a beautiful dog," Faye said, as she watched me. "Have you had him long?"

"Since he was a puppy. He's five years old now. His name is Tuffy."

When I stood again, holding a baggie with Tuffy's natural deposit in it, she clutched my upper arm. We continued our stroll.

Since Faye had begun to talk, I wanted to encourage her. "Stan seems very nice," I said.

She shrugged. "I suppose. I don't know him, not really. We met a few months ago when I took Mother's Bentley into Car Guy's shop to have him check the air-conditioning. It wasn't getting cold enough for her. Stan was there, with his motorcycle, and he recognized Mother's car. That wasn't hard — it's bright red, and the license plate says 'Mimi B.' He came over to talk to me while I was waiting, and told me he knew whose car it was because he worked at the channel. He just happened to come outside as I drove in today. When he asked me who I wanted to see, I started crying, so he took me over to where people couldn't see me going to pieces."

"Did you come here because of Lulu?" I asked gently.

She nodded and sniffed, but she didn't start to cry again. "When I heard the news on TV this morning, I didn't know where to go. I thought maybe if I came to the studio I'd find out there'd been a mistake, that Lulu was *here* and she was all right, that it was somebody else who . . ."

"I'm so sorry." I couldn't think of anything else to say.

Faye stopped walking, which forced Tuffy and me to stop, too. She looked directly at me, and I saw misery in her eyes. "It's my fault," she said. "I'm the reason she's dead."

"Oh, Faye, you're *wrong,*" I said. "Some terrible person —"

"No! It's God punishing me because of all the nights I used to lie in bed, wishing Daddy had married Lulu, and that she was really my mother."

"You've got to stop thinking like that," I said. "Your fantasy didn't cause Lulu's death. You weren't responsible, and I can't believe that Lulu would want you to suffer unreasonable guilt. Think about it: Would she?"

Faye squeezed her eyes shut. After a moment, she opened them. "No . . . I guess not."

We began to walk again, back toward the studio.

"Lulu's really gone, isn't she? I mean *really gone?*"

"I'm afraid she is," I said.

"I can't believe I'll never see her again." Faye took a deep breath. "She'd want me to grow up now, to be strong. Wouldn't she?"

"Yes, I'm sure she would," I said. "Actually, that's a way to honor her."

"I wish I'd had more time. There was so much I wanted to tell her." She looked exhausted, and her eyes glistened with tears she was holding back, but she was standing up straighter, and the first hint of healthy color was creeping back into her pale cheeks. As though having come to a decision, she said, "I'm going to go home."

"Can you call someone to stay with you?"

Faye glanced at her watch. "Not right now," she said. "But don't worry about me. I'll be okay. Really." She reached down to pet Tuffy and gave him a kiss on the top of his head. "Bye, boy."

We had nearly reached the studio doors when she indicated a lustrous green BMW parked near the entrance. "That's my car," she said. "Thank you for being so nice to me."

"Take care of yourself, Faye." I waved at her as she drove away.

Then I tossed Tuffy's baggie into the Dumpster and went into the studio to tape another show.

As soon as I neared my set I caught a delightful scent that made my mouth water. Stan Evans was holding a takeout bag from a good burger restaurant and grinning.

"I figured you hadn't had a chance to eat," he said, "so Mr. Hopkins let me go pick up something for you. I got you a double burger with everything on the side, 'cause I didn't know how you'd want it. And fries. That place makes the best fries. And I got your dog three double burgers without anything except the buns."

"That's very thoughtful of you, Stan. I really appreciate it." This was one of those times when a hamburger with the works was more appealing than filet mignon would have been. A filet would have taken too much energy to eat. "How much —"

He waved one hand in a dismissive gesture. "Mr. Hopkins paid. Oh, and I put fresh water in the bowl by your dog's bed."

"Thank you for all of that," I said sincerely.

Stan gave me a shy smile and hurried off toward the door to the front office.

I transferred Tuffy's hamburger patties onto a plate from the set and put it on the floor next to his water. I ate my hamburger and fries sitting on the kitchen stool behind the preparation counter. For take-out fast food, it was very good and restored my energy. As I washed Tuffy's plate and mine in the sink, I was not only ready, but eager to tape the next show.

It was three o'clock when I finally was able to leave the studio. I let Tuffy into the Mustang and clipped his auto safety harness to the rear seat belt. As soon as I climbed in myself, I took the cell phone out of my bag and called Shannon.

On hearing my voice, she said brightly, "Hi, Del. Look, I can't talk right now because I'm exercising to TV, but I'm dying to hear everything about what's going on with you! Can you come over tonight for dinner? Just us girls?"

"I'd like that," I said. In spite of my reluctance to call her, I meant it.

"Don't bring anything," she said. "I'll order Chinese. I remember what you like. Let's make it early. About six?"

"That's perfect. I've got to get up at dawn

to bake the finished main dishes I'm demonstrating on the two shows we're taping tomorrow."

"You've got to tell me everything tonight, but now I've got to get back to exercising. I've missed half of the step routine already!"

We said quick good-byes and I disconnected the phone. I was a bit concerned. Shannon sounded almost natural, but not quite. Just a little too *up.* I hoped that —

From the backseat, Tuffy's low growl interrupted my thoughts. I turned around to pet him and was startled half out of my wits by the sound of knuckles rapping on my driver's side window.

I swung back around in my seat and saw Nicholas D'Martino standing outside my car.

Lowering the window, I asked, "What are you doing here?"

"Investigating the Lulu Owens murder," he said. "But I saw you on the monitor when I was interviewing Gilmer York on the other side of the building."

"Did you learn anything?" I asked eagerly.

"You're good on TV. You almost made me think I could cook."

Amused, I replied, "I meant, did you learn anything useful to finding the killer?"

"As York would put it, 'bits and bobs.'

Nothing that seems like evidence. At least not yet."

"Good luck," I said, turning the key in the ignition.

"Hey, wait! Don't leave. You were about to drive over my foot. I was going to call you when I finished with York, to ask you something."

I kept the motor running, letting the car idle. "Ask me now."

NDM then uttered the last sentence in the world I would have expected to hear from him. "I'd like you to have dinner with me," he said.

I almost laughed. "Oh? Where did you plan to ask me to meet you?"

"I'll pick you up."

That was my second surprise in approximately five seconds. "Is the Nicholas D'Martino standing next to my car the real one, or am I looking at a perfect replica pod person?"

"*Invasion of the Body Snatchers,*" he said, getting my reference. "One of my favorite old movies. No, this is the real me." He craned his head down so that I could examine the back of his skull. "See? No telltale mark."

"Why are you asking me out?"

"Because I like you." He cocked his head

and squinted at me. "It hadn't occurred to me until this minute, but you look a little like the actress in that movie — Dana something. Dana Wynter. A brunette with big eyes."

"Don't you remember that her character became one of the monsters at the end?"

"What can I say? Women are trouble."

"I'll repeat my question: Why are you asking me out? I'm not at all your type."

"Frankly, I'm a little tired of the girls built for speed."

"So that makes me . . . what?"

"Built for endurance." He said that with a smile.

"Thanks," I said wryly, "but no thanks. I have zero intention of wasting my 'endurance' on you."

He looked as though I'd slapped him. "Why are you being so hostile? I just asked you out to dinner."

I realized that he had no idea why I reacted negatively to his invitation. I'd have to enlighten him. "If I don't seem thrilled, it's because you've insulted me by your arrogant condescension. You implied that you're willing to lower your standards, at least to your way of thinking, and try out the company of a woman who's been eligible to vote in five presidential elections.

Sorry, but I'm not going to be anyone's *experiment*."

"You're not only bad at reading people, you're no good at math," he said. "By my calculations, you've been able to vote in *six* presidential elections."

"Well, Mr. D'Martino, you can take your calculations and stick them — where your newspaper isn't delivered!"

25

John and Shannon O'Hara lived in a one-story Spanish hacienda in rustic Mandeville Canyon, several blocks north of Sunset Boulevard, and near Will Rogers State Park. They had bought the house a few months before Mack and I purchased ours in Santa Monica, when it was still possible to buy a home in a nice area on the salaries of working people.

As I approached the house, I saw that the only vehicle in the carport was Shannon's white Saturn. I hadn't expected John to be home because Eileen told me before she left for her study group that he was working this evening with Detective Hall. I was glad Shannon had asked for this to be an early evening. With any luck, I'd be back at my house before John got home to Mandeville Canyon. Before I went in, I sat in the car for a few minutes, remembering. . . .

Shannon was twenty-nine and Eileen was

two when John and Mack and I realized something was seriously wrong with Shannon. For several months her behavior had been erratic: She was often confused, couldn't make decisions; once an easygoing person, she began starting arguments for no apparent reason, and she seemed perpetually nervous. John took her to a doctor, who diagnosed postpartum depression and gave Shannon tranquilizers. All the pills did was make her sleepy, and we began to fear for little Eileen's safety with her mother falling asleep so often. John hired a live-in nanny, and Mack and I took Eileen on weekends and on my days off from teaching.

Then Shannon, who'd always been well groomed, began to neglect her personal hygiene and withdraw from her friends. Desperate to find out what was the matter, John took her to a different doctor. That one said Shannon was having "severe" postpartum depression, and gave her different tranquilizers.

The crisis came during Shannon's thirty-first birthday party. Her voice ringing with accusation, she demanded to know why I had invited Charles Manson to dinner when I knew that Manson was planning to kill her. For a moment I thought she was joking, but then she started screaming. She pointed to Mack and threw a wineglass at his head. She swore with absolute conviction that Mack wasn't Mack at all, but was really Charles Manson and that we had to kill him before he killed all of us.

Shannon refused to go to a hospital and fought John when he tried to take her to the car. He had to call for an ambulance. Shannon spent the next six weeks in a lockdown mental facility.

As horrible as those weeks were, for Shannon and for those of us who loved her, she was finally diagnosed as a paranoid schizophrenic. John wouldn't take the word of just one psychiatrist anymore, so he called in two others. Separately, they concurred: paranoid schizophrenia. We learned that this particular mental illness typically shows itself somewhere between the ages of eighteen and thirty-four. Shannon was twenty-nine when the symptoms began. The wrong diagnoses had wasted two years when she could have been helped.

In the hospital, the doctors experimented with several medications and dosages. Finally the right combination brought her symptoms under control, and she was judged well enough to come home. But John made sure she was never again alone with little Eileen.

John was patient and loving, but he couldn't be with Shannon twenty-four hours a day. Sometimes she'd forget to take her medication or only pretend to take it. Then, as was typical with a patient like Shannon, "the voices" that commanded her would return. She'd have an acute attack and need to be hospitalized again.

Over the years, as the effectiveness of one medication diminished, another was prescribed. Shannon had seemed much better over the past several months, and much more often she seemed like the Shannon I'd first known. She'd told me that her group therapy sessions were helping her understand the disease and were teaching her to function in a healthy way. When I'd visited her last week, she was talking about working again. Not going back to being a paralegal, as she was when she met John; that work was too stressful. What she had in mind was starting a home-based business by making novelty sweaters to sell in boutiques. She knitted beautifully.

My favorite sweater is the one she'd created for me as a Christmas present last year: sky blue, with a V neckline and a replica of Tuffy on the front. As a tribute to Shannon's new ambition, I was wearing it tonight with a plain denim wrap skirt.

Shannon greeted me at the door, fairly shimmering with energy. Her red curls sparkled from a fresh shampooing. An emerald green headband held the hair back from her pretty oval face. The color of the headband matched her eyes, and the flowing caftan she wore.

"That sweater looks gorgeous on you!" She seemed almost giddy with delight, admiring her creation. "But it's a little off-center." She made a minute adjustment to the way the sweater sat on my shoulders. "Perfect. Come in! Come in! You've got to see my workshop!"

Shannon closed the door behind us and guided me through the archway from the foyer into the long gallery-like living room. It was done in warm southwestern hues, with Native American rugs and wall hangings and artifacts. Shannon had grown up in New Mexico, and had collected furniture and pottery from that part of the country. The ambiance she'd created was relaxed and pleasing to the eyes.

But something new had been added. At the far end of the room a knitting machine had been set up. Beside it was a gateleg table covered with stacks of colorful yarn and little baskets full of buttons, sequins, and beads. She made a sweeping gesture.

"Ta da!"

"Very professional," I said. "You're serious about making novelty sweaters to sell."

"Absolutely! Eileen's working up a business plan for me: how much I'll need to spend on materials, what I should charge, what to do about taxes — all that stuff." She smiled happily. "I'm lucky to have a daughter who's a business major. By the way, she tells me she's doing the same thing for you."

"It's just an idea she's had. She wants me to go into the mail-order fudge business," I said.

Shannon laughed. "Maybe we can sell packages of your fudge with each of my sweaters. But if the customers eat your fudge, they probably won't look so good in my sweaters."

"I admit, you've got a point." I smiled at her, but I couldn't help wondering if she was a little too *up*, or just more enthusiastic than she had been in a long time. All at once I realized how painful it would be for Shannon, and how unfair to her, if she knew I was scrutinizing her for signs of the old problem. Resolutely, I decided to forget about her illness and simply enjoy her excitement about this new project.

Indicating her workshop, I said, "You're

already set up. I haven't had time to even think about making fudge commercially. Right now I'm too busy cooking for the TV shows."

"Speaking of — let's have dinner," Shannon said. "The order was delivered a few minutes ago, and I don't like cold Chinese food. Besides, after dinner, I have to get busy and sketch some new designs."

Shannon's kitchen continued the southwestern theme, with whitewashed walls, terra-cotta pots holding a variety of cactus plants, and an aged wooden sign that said "Shannon's Cantina."

We sat at her handsome pine trestle-base table inlaid with strips of cactus. Until Shannon bought that table years ago, I told her that I'd never thought of cactus as "wood." She'd explained that the natural death of cactus wood takes years, and during the period of decay, it's exposed to scorching desert sunlight and battering by the wind and sand. Nature's brutality gave the cactus wood its mellow golden tones.

Her description of how a dead cactus came to be turned into the beautiful surface of this table was the first time I'd thought of wood as something that died. Of course I knew that trees were cut down and new trees planted, but I never made the connection between lumber and death.

I forced myself to shake off the melancholy notion as Shannon spooned portions of rice, beef with snow peas, and sweet-and-sour chicken onto bright red crockery plates.

Before I'd swallowed the first mouthful, Shannon said, "Going into business is important because it will give me something interesting to talk to John about. For so long it's seemed as though the only subject we had in common was my health. He never shows it, but he's got to be bored out of his mind." She gave a mirthless little laugh. " 'Out of his mind.' That phrase must sound strange, coming from me. I mean, because I actually have been *out of my mind.* Believe me, the real thing is nothing like that cliché we throw around."

"You've overcome so much. John must be very proud of you."

Even though we were alone, she lowered her voice to a near whisper. "I'm afraid I'm losing him."

"Oh, Shannon, no. That's not true."

"No one knows my husband better than I do, Della," she said sharply. "He's *kind* to me, but his heart isn't here anymore. I think there's someone else. Do you have any idea who it could be?"

I reached for her hand to comfort her; her

skin was icy cold. "John *loves* you. He'll never leave you."

Shannon's eyes glistened with tears she was fighting to hold back. I heard the sadness in her voice as she said, "Loyalty and *love* are two separate things."

The visit with Shannon had shaken me. I felt so guilty about my feelings for John that I knew I had to do something radical to stamp them out, and I knew what that was. As my brother, Sean, the navy man, might say — or he might have said it if he was drunk and in the middle of World War II — "Full speed ahead and damn the torpedoes." Before I could change my mind, I found the card NDM had given me and phoned him.

He answered on the second ring. When I said hello, he recognized my voice.

"I want to see you," I told him. "But not in public. Where do you live?"

"You want to come over here?"

"Unless you're busy with one of your built-for-speed blondes."

"I don't bring them home." He gave me his address.

NDM lived in the bottom half of a townhouse in the Larchmont section of Los

Angeles, a residential area of sidewalks and slender trees that were surrounded by cement. It was more typical of New York City than of Southern California. I found a parking place several numbers down from NDM's building.

My heart was pounding, but determined to go through with my plan, I rang the bell.

He opened the door. I walked past him into his living room and said, "I'm calling your bluff."

"What bluff?"

During our marriage I'd initiated sex many times with Mack, but now I did something I'd never done when I was single: I kissed a man before he kissed me first.

It surprised him, but his reflexes were good; he caught up quickly. Just as I was about to break the kiss, his arms went around me, locking my body against his with a fierceness that made me gasp. Our mouths met again, but this time in a fully mutual joining of lips and tongues. I felt him swelling against me.

I had no concept of time or place. All I knew was that I was in the arms of a man who kissed me as hungrily as I kissed him. Hands roamed over bodies. Fingers fumbled with clothing, items fell to the floor. Then I was naked, lying on a couch, holding and caressing a naked man who was caressing me. My eyes were closed, but all of my other senses were heightened. The skin of this man's back was smooth; his scent was a pleasant amalgam of soap and sweat. . . . His body was strong and welcomed.

We finished — spent but not exhausted. Without speaking, he took my hand and led me into his bedroom. Under oath, I could not say what the room looked like — only that the sheets were fresh and clean. We melted into each other again. And again.

Afterward, lying beside NDM, my pulse began to return to normal. His eyes were closed and his breathing deep and even. Thinking that he was asleep, I carefully eased myself out of the circle of his arm and moved to the edge of the bed.

With his eyes still closed, he asked, "Where are you going?"

"Home." These were the first actual "words" we'd spoken since I'd kissed him.

He opened his eyes. Looking puzzled, he propped himself up on one elbow. "Why are you leaving?"

"I have to walk my dog, then get up early to bake two different kinds of meat loaf and a broccoli casserole."

He sat all the way up and stared at me. Ridiculous as it sounds, I felt embarrassed that I was standing in front of him without any clothes on. It was one thing to be kissing in this state, and another to be having a conversation in the nude. But I'd acted outrageously tonight; it was too late to be modest.

"Don't you leave your girls and go home when you've . . . after you've . . . ?"

"It's a little different," he said.

"Why?"

"Ask me when I've had a chance to figure it out."

"Good-bye," I said, backing toward the living room door. "I had a wonderful time."

He looked thoroughly nonplussed. "What happened here tonight?"

"You proved your theory that I'm built for endurance."

"Don't throw that stupid remark in my face."

In the living room, I scooped up my panties, sweater, skirt, and shoes from where they'd fallen and slipped into them at warp speed. Not wanting to delay an extra few seconds fumbling with the clasp, I stuffed my bra into my handbag and was out the front door.

26

The next morning Eileen was up and off to an early class when I called Liddy and asked her to come over as soon as Bill left for his office. Now Liddy was drinking coffee and watching me assemble ingredients for the TV taping while I told her about practically ravishing NDM last night.

"What in the name of Paula Deen were you *thinking?*" Liddy demanded.

"I wasn't thinking. It was pure lust."

Her eyes twinkled with humor. "He must have thought Santa came early and brought him a man's favorite thing."

"He couldn't have been more surprised if I'd come down his chimney. If he had a chimney. I didn't notice." I tried to visualize his living room and couldn't, but I had the vague impression that it was neat.

"What triggered that Vesuvian eruption of hormones?"

I described my visit to Shannon and how

terrible I felt when she talked about getting herself in shape and staying on her new medication so she could have a real married life again with John. "She said she was afraid she was losing him."

"Do you think she knows how John feels about you?"

"She suspects he's developed feelings for someone. She asked me if I had any idea who it might be."

"Of course you said no."

"I told her I believe absolutely that John loves her, and I do."

"A nonanswer answer." Liddy glanced meaningfully at the plant stand next to the refrigerator, where the pumpkin she'd carved for me sat with the profile of the elephant facing us.

"Shannon's smart," she said. "You're a widow now; the four of you were close for years. Propinquity. I think she invited you over to probe a little."

"I told her that I hardly ever saw John, but that I knew he was working with Detective Hall on what the papers are calling 'The Cable TV Murders.' She wanted me to tell her everything I knew, so she could talk to John about his work. I told her some, but not about being chased through Brentwood and calling John from Fred Priestly's carport."

"Be careful around Shannon," Liddy said. "We know what happens if she goes off her meds. Okay, let's get back to the reporter. How was he in bed?"

"Terrific. He did everything to make sure I enjoyed it as much as he did." I sat down opposite Liddy, refilled her cup, and poured coffee for myself. I wasn't comfortable talking about this, but I needed to. "Mack and I had a really good sex life. It transitioned naturally from that early couldn't-keep-our-hands-off-each-other heat to the luxury of making love whenever we felt like it. We had our fights and problems, like every couple, but we were happy, and well matched in bed. I had no idea how much I missed sex."

"Sex and credit cards — my two favorite parts of marriage," Liddy joked.

"When I felt those stirrings toward John, it was like I'd had amnesia and suddenly all the memories came flooding back."

"Bill and I are in that first stage again, now that the boys are out of the house. There were a lot of years there when the kids had to come first, and it seemed as though they *always* needed something. Even though they were twins, they never got sick at the same time."

I smiled. "Double jeopardy."

"No kidding. Bill and I used to fantasize about checking into one of those cheap motels on La Cienega under a phony name. Enough about me. I want more details about last night."

"I told you the sex was great."

"But what did you talk about?"

"We didn't talk," I said.

"Not at all? No little jokes in between the moans, no sweet murmurings of 'oh, you're so beautiful' and 'oh, you're so hard'?"

I shook my head. "From the moment I walked in and kissed him until I finally got out of bed, we didn't talk to each other."

"That's weird," Liddy said.

"I didn't know what to say, and apparently he didn't either. But he cooperated physically — *more* than cooperated. After all, that's why I was there."

"So it was an erotic exorcism. You exorcised John O'Hara by getting erotic with Nicholas D'Martino. Now what?"

"What do you mean?"

"When are you going to see him again?"

"I don't plan to. Last night was a kind of sexual *collision.* Out of bed, I don't even like him."

"The trouble is, you've released the beast," Liddy said. "Now it's going to want to be fed. Last night you just might have created a bigger problem than you think you solved."

27

By midmorning I'd finished making a broccoli casserole, my breadless meat loaf, a very different kind of meatloaf baked in a round of sourdough bread, and organized the ingredients for a heavenly pink ambrosia. The first three were the make-ahead dishes I'd be displaying at this afternoon's TV tapings. The ambrosia would be assembled on the set. I carefully packed all of those items and a package each of fresh spinach and spinach fettuccine into two grocery boxes. Finally, dressed in the simple dark green sweater and black slacks I'd wear for the first taping, I was ready to leave for the studio. A short garment bag contained the blouse and skirt I'd change into for the second show.

Tuffy was ready to go, too. He'd eaten his breakfast, and I'd taken him for a walk, brushed his shiny black coat, slipped his automobile safety harness over his head, and clipped his red leash to his red cloth collar. He'd always had soft collars because I would never put either a hard leather collar or a chain around his neck.

Leaving one of the two boxes, the garment bag, and Tuffy just inside the closed front door, I hefted the first box and started along the side path that led to my carport. I was thinking about Lulu, once again going over our conversation of Monday night, hoping that I'd discover something useful to catching her killer, a hint that I missed previously.

I hadn't succeeded in getting her to tell me whom she thought Mimi's mystery lover had been, but she'd come close to giving it up. She'd only stopped short of revealing the name because she said she wasn't completely sure, and didn't want to hurt someone. The name of the mystery man might have nothing to do with Lulu's murder, but I was willing to bet that Lulu and Mimi were killed by the same person. What better motive for murdering Lulu than fear of exposure? I was sure that the person who killed Lulu must believe she knew something that put him or her in jeopardy. Apparently, everyone at the channel knew Lulu liked to talk. I'd heard her say that to Detective Hall the night of Mimi's murder. Yesterday, Stan Evans told me that Car Guy referred to Lulu as the station's own *National Enquirer.*

Halfway to the Mustang, my musing was interrupted by the noise of a powerful engine roaring up my street. Recognizing that sound, I felt my pulse rate increase at least twenty thumps a minute from its usual steady fifty-eight.

The silver Maserati screeched to a stop and NDM vaulted out. He was the last person I wanted to see, but I had to admit that he was attractive in his pale gray shirt and navy blazer. I refused to let myself think about the skillful body under his clothes. No matter how much effort it took, I would adhere to my resolve not to let our one-time physical encounter go any further. My erotic exorcism, Liddy had called it. NDM pushed an unruly hunk of dark hair back from his forehead and marched purposefully across my lawn. I was tempted to ask him not to walk on the grass, but I didn't get the chance.

He smiled at me, but I didn't smile back. Positioning himself between me and the Mustang, he said softly, "We need to talk."

Hoping to discourage him, I tried to sound cool. "I'm sorry, I don't have time. I have to get to the studio."

NDM didn't discourage easily. "How about having dinner with me tonight? *Only* dinner. And conversation. I want to find out what you like to read." That was a subtle reference to our first fight, about those "very mature" young models he dated. Considering the harsh things I'd said then, I had to give him credit for being a good sport about it.

"No. I'm going to be busy. Do you mind stepping out of the way so I can get this box to the car? It's heavy."

Instead of moving, NDM took the box out of my arms and held it. "Okay, I know this is a little awkward, but I'd like to see you again."

I *wanted* to say, "Let's go to bed together as soon as I finish taping!" Liddy had been right; I'd released the "beast" of sexual desire. Now I had to control it, so what I *actually* said was, "It's not going to work."

NDM stared at me, an expression in his eyes that looked like hurt. But I couldn't believe I'd hurt him; he had all those gorgeous blonde actress-models.

"What was last night?" he asked quietly. "Did you just use me for sex?" He shook his head in amazement. "I can't believe I said that."

Gently, but not unkindly, I said, "How

does it feel to be used for sex? Why should it only be the privilege of *men?*"

"I never thought of it like that, but I get your point."

"Then you agree with me, that we should quit while we're ahead?"

"No, I don't. I'm saying that — under more traditional circumstances — I want to get to know you better."

I thought: *You know me pretty well in one respect right now.*

From inside the house, Tuffy began to woof; it was his special "the postman is coming" signal.

Simultaneously, I heard, "Hello, Mrs. Carmichael."

Recognizing the cheery voice of our neighborhood's pleasant Filipina mail carrier, I turned, waved at her, and called, "It's okay, Tuffy." He stopped barking.

The young woman's straight, shoulder-length black hair bounced as she hurried up from the sidewalk with a rubber-banded bundle of envelopes and magazines in her hand. Full of energy and good humor, she always seemed to enjoy her job. "Here's your mail," she said.

I took it from her. "Thanks, Vera."

Vera smiled at me and at NDM. "Happy Wednesday," she said, as she headed toward the next house on her route.

"I preferred Tuesday," NDM said pointedly. "Tuesday *night.*" Indicating my plain green sweater, he added, "You look good, but I'm kind of fond of what you wore last night — that silly blue sweater with the poodle on it."

Ignoring the remark, I pulled the letters from the bundle, tucked the magazines under one arm and riffled through the envelopes. A bill, a bill, an advertisement. When I came to one rectangle, I stopped flipping through them. It was from the Better Living Channel, and it looked like a check. I ripped it open and sighed in relief.

"Something good?" NDM asked.

"My paycheck." I knew what the gross would be, but not the net. Now I saw that even with all the deductions, the amount would get me through this month and next. If I kept my job, and if the school didn't lose more money, in a few months I could begin to save again, and I wouldn't have to admit to my accountant mother the financial trouble I was in. Folding the check to put into my pocket, I saw the envelope beneath it. The handwriting was unfamiliar, but the sight of the return address label startled me. I must have made some sound, because NDM moved quickly to stand beside me and look at the object in my hand.

"What is it?" he asked.

"This is from Lulu."

"Lulu *Owens?*" He put the box down on the path and leaned in for a closer look but didn't try to touch it.

The envelope was plain white and business size.

NDM said, "It's postmarked yesterday, the day after she was murdered."

With hands that were trembling, I opened the flap and carefully removed the single sheet of paper inside. So as not to destroy any possible prints, I held it at one corner, with just the tips of my thumb and index finger.

It was a page of ordinary white copy paper. At the top, Lulu had written in blue ink: "Glad to know you, Della. Enjoy!" Below that she had printed the recipe for her lasagna.

NDM said, "A recipe? I don't get it."

"I do. Lulu made us lasagna for dinner that night. I told her it was better than mine, and she said she'd give me her recipe. Lots of people say that when you compliment something they've made, but few actually take the trouble to do it. Lulu must have written it out after I left her house Monday night. . . ."

Visualizing her street, I remembered something. "There's a mail box at the corner, half a block from where she lived. She must have walked up to that box, mailed the letter, and — *Oh, no!*"

"What?"

"That's why she was killed outside her house," I said. "The murderer caught her before she could go in." I stooped down to the food box. With my free hand, I reached in and extracted one of the several zip-top plastic bags I'd tucked between the pan of breadless meatloaf and the package of spinach fettuccini. I used the bags as a cushiony buffer to keep the strands of dry fettuccini from breaking in case the meat loaf shifted in the box while I was driving.

NDM said, "The only snail mail I get anymore are bills. I'm surprised Lulu didn't e-mail you the recipe."

"She told me she didn't trust computers. She kept all of her recipes in big albums she showed me."

NDM watched me put Lulu's envelope and recipe into the baggie and zip the top closed.

"Not a bad emergency evidence bag," he said, "but I doubt there'll be any prints on the letter except Lulu's."

"Maybe you're right, but if there are other

prints, we'd know that someone else handled the paper. It could be a clue."

"It's a long shot, but you're right to be careful. We can't afford to assume the paper won't tell us anything. We'll give it to Hall for SID to go over."

I held on to the top of the plastic bag. "Would you put the box in my car for me? I've got to take that, another box, and Tuffy to the studio. I'll drop the letter off at the North Hollywood Station on my way."

"You can come with me, in my car," he said.

"No, thanks." I started walking ahead of him to unlock the Mustang's doors. "I'm taping two shows today and I don't know when I'll be through."

Just as I reached my car, I saw something so shocking that it sent me reeling backward. I collided with NDM. Both of us would have fallen if he hadn't grabbed my arm to steady me. At the same time, miraculously, he managed to keep the box of food upright.

"What happened?"

I pointed. Barely managing to croak out the word, I said, "Look."

Following my line of sight, he whispered, "Oh, Jeez."

We stared at the Mustang. The driver's

side window was smashed in and the contents of my glove compartment were scattered over the front seat. And someone had stuck a sheet of white paper under my windshield wiper. Scrawled in big black letters, it read:

U R Nxt

Without touching the paper, NDM read the message aloud. " 'You are next.' "

"I understand the text," I said. "It also means that the killer knows where I live."

28

I called Hall on his cell phone to tell him that my car had been broken into, and about the message on my windshield.

"Don't touch that car!" he shouted. "I'll be there in five minutes."

"Five minutes? From North Hollywood? How can you get here so fast?"

"I'm in Brentwood." He hung up before I could ask anything else.

Indicating the box, I said, "We should take the food into the house."

NDM, carrying the box, followed me into the house, picked up the second box, and put both of them onto the kitchen table for me.

I picked up Tuffy's leash and brought him outside with us while NDM and I sat together on the front stoop, waiting for Detective Hall.

"To be safe, I think you should move out of your house for a while," NDM said. "Is there someone you could stay with?"

"Of course." Liddy. In any disaster, she would take Tuffy, Emma, Eileen, and me in before I could ask for shelter. There was no way I was going to endanger Liddy and Bill by staying at their house with a killer threatening me, but perhaps Eileen could stay there for a while.

"After we see Hall, I'll take you wherever," NDM said.

"No. I'm not going to let anyone chase me from my home."

"The police won't be able to give you meaningful protection. At most, they'd have a patrol car circle the block every hour or so, but even that's doubtful, given all the crime in this city. I could stay here, if you like."

"Absolutely not!"

"I wasn't suggesting anything personal. I'd sleep on the couch in the living room. My being under your roof would be strictly business — the business of trying to catch a murderer."

"No. I don't need a bodyguard." Even as I said that, I felt my stomach muscles clench in fear at the thought of the killer having been here in the night, so close he was in my carport.

"Della, I have a friend at North Hollywood Station who told me that a guy chased you after you visited Faye Bond. Threatening you here at your home is an escalation. If you don't back off now and stop asking questions, he could proceed to the next step: killing you."

"I'm not going to be intimidated. I have a big advantage over Mimi and Lulu. Neither one of them had any reason to think they were in danger. I do. I can be careful not to let anyone surprise me. And I have Tuffy. He's strong and very protective. Just see what happens if you try to grab me."

"Don't tempt me," he said. He reached across my lap and scratched Tuffy behind an ear. "Nice dog. I'm not going to hurt your mistress." He straightened. "You'd be better off with a piece. Do you have your husband's service revolver?"

"No. I turned it in."

"He had a backup, didn't he? Something not on the official list?"

"I gave it to John," I said. "I don't like guns."

"Let's not debate gun ownership now. Tell me why the killer seems to think you're getting close to finding out who he is. What do you know that hasn't been made public? Hall is keeping a tight lid on the case. Even my friend at the station told me only about what happened to you in Brentwood. She wouldn't risk saying anything else."

She. *Why am I not surprised his informant is a* woman?

"I have no idea who the killer is," I said, "but I'm convinced that the person works at, or has some connection to, the channel."

"Why?"

I told him about discovering the car that pursued me was at the studio. "It's a Simba that Car Guy uses on his show. When he drove it onto his set, I recognized the rough sound it made. Then the damage to the front looked like it matched the damage to the back of my Mustang. I called Detective Hall, who had SID go over it. Car Guy told us the Simba was parked on the street outside the studio along with other employees' cars from Friday morning until Monday morning, because the parking lot was being paved on Friday. The street behind the studio is dark and pretty deserted. Car Guy had the key, but apparently anyone who knows how could have hot-wired it and driven without a key."

"So whoever took the car and drove to Mimi Bond's house didn't want his own vehicle to be recognized. The question is *why* did the driver go to the Bond house in a stolen car? He couldn't have known you'd be there, so what was he planning to do that he didn't want to use his own wheels for?"

I focused on that evening and remembered something that hadn't seemed significant at the time.

"Lulu was at the Bond house," I said. "I took flowers to Faye, as an excuse to question her. She was still too upset to say much, but Lulu and I talked. She was just about to tell me some things about people at the studio when we were interrupted. Faye was making noise upstairs and Lulu was concerned. That's when Lulu invited me to dinner at her house on Monday night, so we could keep talking." I was beginning to see part of the puzzle; the shape was starting to form. "What if the killer was really after Lulu but was distracted by seeing me there?"

"That was Friday. If the person planned to kill Lulu, why did he wait until Monday night to do it?"

I knew the answer to that. "Lulu told me she was staying at Faye's all weekend, to take care of her. The person wouldn't have had a chance to get Lulu alone until Monday night. There's something else that convinces me the person has a connection to the channel," I said. "Do you know how Lulu was killed?"

"She was stabbed to death."

"The murder weapon was a knife that was stolen from my kitchen at the studio. It had to have been taken after I left Monday afternoon because I used it during my rehearsal with Quinn Tanner."

He reached for my free hand and folded it into his. "That's got to be tough for you."

"I really liked Lulu. It's terrible that she's dead, and it makes me sick to know someone took a knife of mine — a tool I'd used to make good food — and . . . Yes, it is tough."

"Who did you see at the studio that day?"

"Quinn Tanner; George Hopkins; Car Guy; the day security guard, Stan; and the person at the desk who operates the gate buzzer. Gil York was taping his show at the other end of the building; I saw him on the monitor. And there was also whoever was working with him."

"Okay, those names are a start. We'll need to find out who else was there, or who might have come after you left."

At that moment, with the two of us sitting together on my front stoop and NDM holding my hand, Detective Hall drove up in the vehicle I'd nicknamed the Green Hornet.

And John O'Hara was with him.

29

Embarrassed to be seen with NDM holding my hand, I pulled away quickly and stood up. NDM stood up, too, and so did Tuffy. We made a line of three, facing the duo of investigators getting out of Hall's Rover. Detective Hall nodded at me and strode right for the Mustang.

John headed for us, threw a glare at NDM, and asked me, "What happened here?"

"Sometime during the night, that message was placed on my windshield."

John started toward the car. I followed, with Tuffy on his leash. Glancing back, I saw that NDM had remained by the stoop. Half turned away, he was speaking quietly into his cell phone.

Slipping on latex gloves, Hall removed the note. He and John studied the scrawled threat. John cursed softly and asked me, "Where's Eileen? Has she seen this?"

"She left early for school. I woke up in the middle of the night to be sure she was home and saw her car parked in the driveway behind mine. I'm sure she didn't see it, or she would have come back inside and told me."

Hall put the note in an evidence envelope and carefully examined the outside of the Mustang. "Is this car exactly the way you found it?"

"Yes. As soon as I saw the note I called you. I haven't touched anything."

On a case, John was usually the epitome of cool, but right now he couldn't hide the lines of worry etched in his face. "It isn't safe for you and Eileen to stay here."

"I've already had this argument once today and I'm not going to have it again."

John stiffened. "Does D'Martino want you to leave?"

"You two think alike. Look, I'm sure Eileen can stay with Liddy until you catch whoever did this, but I'm not leaving."

John turned to scowl at NDM. I saw the journalist disconnecting from his call.

"How long has *he* been here?" John asked.

Coming toward us, NDM heard the question. "I got here a couple of minutes before Della saw the break-in and the note. Not that it's any of your business, unless you

302

think I wrote that message."

John's voice was hard; he wasn't retreating an inch. "Do you have an alibi for last night?"

I almost choked, but I managed not to make a sound as I stood rigid with tension.

NDM was as smooth as cake batter. "Is that a serious question, asked in your professional capacity? If so, the answer is no, I don't have an alibi. I was alone all of last night."

I relaxed inside, but tried not to let my relief show. Then I thought, *What's the matter with me? I'm an adult and I can do anything I want to do, as long as it's legal.* But I knew my situation wasn't that simple.

John asked NDM, "What are you doing here this morning?'

"Visiting a friend," NDM said. "Lieutenant O'Hara, you're beginning to sound like a jealous husband, but you need to remember that you're not *Della's* husband."

John's face reddened, but Hall interrupted before the exchange could get more heated. "Cut it out, you two. We don't have time for a head-butting contest."

I held up the plastic baggie. "Detective Hall, John — this came in the mail just before I saw the car note. It's from Lulu Owens, the recipe for her lasagna. She must

303

have written it out after I left her house Monday night, and then mailed it at the post box on her street. That could explain why she was outside her door when she was killed."

Hall took the baggie out of my hand. He and John scrutinized the contents.

"Who touched this?" John asked.

"From the time the mail carrier brought it, about fifteen minutes ago, I'm the only one who handled the envelope and the page inside. As soon as I saw that it was from Lulu, I only touched the paper up at the corner." I pinched my thumb and index finger together to demonstrate.

Hall grunted. "There probably isn't anything we can get from the paper, but forensics will go over this letter, the windshield note, and the car." He extended a hand toward me. "Let's have the key to the Mustang."

I took it out of my pocket and gave it to him. "Be careful driving. It can be a little temperamental, but I'm used to its quirks."

"A flatbed tow truck is on the way to haul it to the station house. You're coming with us."

"All right," I said, "but I have to tape two shows today. Will somebody take me to the studio from there?"

NDM said, "I will. I'll put your boxes of TV food and the garment bag in my car. We can follow Detective Hall and Lieutenant O'Hara."

"No," Hall said, in a tone that discouraged argument. "Mrs. Carmichael comes with us. If you want to, you can follow with her stuff."

John didn't look happy about that plan, but he clenched his jaws.

I turned to Hall. "It will save time if you question me while we drive. I need to be able to let the station know when I'll be there for the taping. We're on a tight schedule, and they have everything set up."

Hall looked at his watch. "Tell them you'll be there in a couple of hours."

A flatbed tow truck with the LAPD logo rumbled up my quiet street. Hall hurried down to the sidewalk and signaled to it, directing the driver to back it up my driveway.

Once the truck was correctly positioned, the driver conferred with Hall and got out of the cab to secure the Mustang with a chain.

Hall supervised the winching of the Mustang up onto the flatbed as NDM loaded the food boxes and my change of clothing into the trunk of the Maserati.

John drew me a few yards away from the activity and spoke in low tones. Indicating NDM, he said, "Be careful of that guy, Del. He's bad news."

"What do you mean?"

"He's a reporter with a reputation for having no scruples when he's out to get a story. And he chases anything in a skirt."

"I wear mostly slacks," I said.

John glowered. "This isn't a joke. If he's after you, he could have sneaked over here and planted the note to scare you. He admits he doesn't have an alibi for last night. Did he offer to let you stay at his place?"

"No, he didn't." I thought it best not to tell John that NDM offered to stay with me in *my* house. "You can't really think he would leave that message."

"No, I don't," John admitted, "although I believe he's capable of pulling any stunt to get a headline. I think the person who killed the two women broke into your car and wrote that threat, but I'm not ruling D'Martino out. With your life in danger, I can't afford to rule anyone out."

"I appreciate that," I said softly. "Really. I don't know what I'd do without your friendship. You and Shannon and Eileen are as much my family as my own blood, but I know how to take care of myself. I haven't made any terrible mistakes in the last two years on my own, have I?"

"No, you haven't. You've been amazing." He attempted a smile, but there was sadness in his eyes. John's smile was a painful echo of Shannon's.

I wanted to put my arms around him, to comfort him, to assure him that everything would be fine, just as I had when we discovered how ill Shannon was. But giving physical comfort to John O'Hara was something I could never do again.

To break what had become an awkward silence, I said, "I saw Shannon last evening."

"I know. She told me. It was good of you to have dinner with her."

"Not at all, she's my friend. She's excited about making sweaters to sell. You know how talented she is. I think she'll be a success at it."

John nodded. "I'm glad to see her happy."

"Do you want me to call Liddy about Eileen staying with her for a while, or would you rather she come home to you and her mother?"

John's reaction was immediate, and firm. "Call Liddy. I'd love to have her at home, but it's better if she just comes over to visit once or twice a week. Shannon doesn't need the extra stress right now."

I felt a twinge of concern, and was about to ask John what he meant, but Hall waved at us, calling, "Hey, let's go!"

With the flatbed tow truck leading the way, our three-vehicle convoy took off for North Hollywood.

Detective Hall was at the controls of the Green Hornet, John was in the passenger seat next to him, and Tuffy and I occupied the backseat. I'd clipped Tuffy's auto safety harness to the seat belt on his side. He was sitting up, staring out his window.

I turned around to check on NDM through the rear window. He had his steering wheel in a death grip, and looked impatient. I guessed that being forced to keep to the speed limit was probably making him a little nuts.

As we covered the miles, I explained to Detective Hall and to John my theory that the person who stole the car from the studio and chased me had come to Brentwood because he was really stalking Lulu, and my belief that he hadn't been able to kill Lulu until Monday night because she spent the weekend with Faye.

"Whoever it is must either work at the studio or have access to it," I said. "First, in order to doctor the mousse with the peanuts that killed Mimi. Second, to steal the Simba — which makes me think that the person knows enough about cars to hot-wire it. Third, to steal the knife from my kitchen set."

John said, "We've already come to the same conclusion."

"Okay, that's good. I presume you've made a list of the people who were at the studio on Monday, those who were still there when I left, or those who came in later?" I named the people I'd seen on Monday.

"Mickey Jordan was there late in the day," Hall said. "He'd called a staff meeting."

"The publicity man was there," John said. "Phil Logan."

Phil Logan? I made a mental note to ask NDM what he knew about the man who'd had my photos retouched and who arranged the interview with NDM, which had led to this new complication in my life.

Even though the Green Hornet and NDM's Maserati were trailing the flatbed, we were still making pretty good time on the freeway. I checked the clock on the dashboard and saw that we should be reaching our off-ramp into North Hollywood in another five more minutes or so.

Hall's usual driving position was to bend

over the steering wheel, practically embracing it, but suddenly he snapped upright in his seat.

"What the hell?" He slammed on the brakes, jerking me harshly against my seat belt. Tuffy's safety harness kept him from slamming into the back of Hall's seat.

Through the windshield, I saw the tow truck bouncing over a spilled load of telephone poles — and on the flatbed my Mustang was bucking like a rodeo rider.

The poles had come loose from the big truck just ahead of the tow truck and were rolling over the freeway. Cars on both sides of us were swerving to get out of the way. More drivers were honking loudly as their vehicles careened into other lanes and collided with machines already there.

Then, with indescribable horror, I saw my precious Mustang *explode* into a million jagged pieces!

30

The force of the blast sent chunks of metal shooting up into the air to rain down on everything below. I heard a clang and a thud on the roof of the Rover, but nothing pierced the steel skin. I looked back at NDM and saw a twisted part of something hit the hood of the Maserati. It bounced off and left a nasty dent, but NDM wasn't hurt. He didn't even seem upset; he was busy talking on his cell phone.

On our side of the freeway, traffic had come to a jumbled halt amid the reverberating crunches and bangs of collisions.

John told me, "Stay here!" and sprang from the Rover. Through the window, I watched him run toward the cab of the tow truck. Everything on our side of the freeway had come to a stop.

Working his phone, Hall called for emergency medical vehicles, the highway patrol, and the fire department. I saw John pull the tow truck driver out of the cab. The man's head was bleeding, but with John's help he was able to walk away from the flatbed.

Tuffy was sitting up straight, calmly watching the activity going on around us. "Good boy," I said, patting him.

Hall unsnapped his seat belt. "Stay put!" While he continued to shout instructions into his phone, he got out onto the freeway and raced into the middle of the tangle of cars.

"To hell with 'stay put.' This isn't Victorian England where women were shut indoors as soon as there was trouble in the street."

I was squeezing through the space between the driver's and passenger's sides to get into the front of the Rover when NDM opened the driver's door. "Della — are you okay?" he called.

"Yes, but my car exploded!"

Pocketing his cell phone, he said, "Stay where you are," and sprinted off to help John give aid to drivers and passengers.

If one more man tells me to stay where I am, I'm going to scream.

I saw Hall directing those cars that were able to operate away from the tow truck, but the jam was so severe most couldn't move more than a few feet. For some it was only inches.

I gave silent thanks that it was a very cool and overcast day. No sun, and no need for air conditioning. I turned on the Rover's ignition so I could let the windows down enough for Tuffy to have plenty of fresh air. He'd be comfortable and safe in the Green Hornet. There was no need to worry about anyone trying to steal it because we were landlocked.

Hall's ignition key was on a ring with two other keys and a Swiss army knife. I took the ring, got out of the vehicle, and locked it behind me.

The smell that filled the air was an acrid combination of smoke, hot metal, and spilled oil and gasoline. Not pleasant, but it was bearable. It would have been worse on a warm day.

Stuffing Hall's fat key ring in my pants pocket, I plunged into a veritable sea of fender benders, looking for whoever could use my help.

Most of the cars around me were wedged together. Some had suffered only minimal damage and looked able to operate, but they were blocked in by those that had smashed front ends and weren't drivable. Tow trucks would have to remove the disabled vehicles to open up an escape lane for the cars that could make it out of here on their own.

Some of the stuck drivers had gotten out and were sitting or standing on the tops of their cars, trying to see what was happening up ahead, or were looking back at the massive tie-up behind us. Several drivers had abandoned their own cars and had formed pairs or trios atop the biggest SUVs.

I'd lost sight of John and Hall and NDM. My last glimpse of John had been when he was pressing one of his handkerchiefs against the cut on the head of the police tow truck driver, to stop the bleeding. Now both he and the wounded driver had disappeared.

As I clambered around battered cars, looking for some way to be useful, I heard raucous music pouring from a couple of radios and strident voices from all-talk or all-news stations coming from others. The result was babble, underscored with rock and rap.

The din lessened for a few seconds, and I heard a woman's piercing cries of pain, followed by a man's shouted plea for help. His voice was hoarse, the timbre of an elderly person. I couldn't see the source of the cries and the shout, but they had to be only three or four cars behind Hall's Rover.

Following the woman's cries, I squeezed between cars and scrambled over fenders and bumpers.

The cries were louder now. There was enough space for me to squeeze past the final car — and then I was facing a sight that stunned me into momentary immobility. An elderly Asian man was in the driver's seat of a newish Buick. His airbag had deployed and deflated. He didn't seem to be injured, but he was frantic.

"Please help my daughter," he cried.

The reason for his panic was lying across the backseat: a young Asian woman, drenched in sweat, and twisting her body to try to ease her agony. Her knees were up, and she was holding them a shoulder's width apart, but she'd pulled her floral, ankle-length skirt down for modesty. In spite of the pain she was in, and the perspiration that plastered her jet-black hair to her scalp, I could see that she had a lovely face — and a very pregnant belly. A big, wet stain covered the upholstery beneath her.

The moment she saw me, she cried out in relief and tried to raise herself onto her elbows. "Help me, please! My baby is coming!" Relief was followed immediately by another scream of pain.

Oh, no!

The famous line from *Gone with the Wind*

pounded in my head — "Lordy, Miss Scarlett, I don't know nothin' about birthing babies!" — as I looked around frantically, hoping to spot anyone who could help her.

I stood up, surveyed the sea of stalled vehicles, and yelled, "Help! We need a doctor or a nurse! There's a woman here in labor!"

No response.

I leaned over to speak to the young woman. "It's going to be all right." My voice rang with conviction, but I was faking it. I'd never had a child; I hadn't even seen a birth for twenty years, not since Liddy had her twins. Her husband had been too nervous to be in the delivery room, so I'd been her Lamaze partner. Fighting panic, I tried to remember anything I'd seen or heard way back then.

Talk. "Conversation calms a woman in labor," or so I remember someone in Lamaze class saying. *I hope it hadn't been a man.*

I forced a cheerful smile and asked, "What's your name?"

Her answer was a gasp. "Mia."

"I'm Della. Don't worry, Mia. We'll get through this." *Somehow.*

Even with her features contorted in pain, I saw she was dubious. I couldn't blame her;

she was in labor, trapped in a car, facing a stranger.

About two feet separated the Buick from the empty car beside it. The Buick's rear door had sprung partially open, but only a couple of inches. Not even the skinniest supermodel would have been able to squeeze inside. I pulled at the door, trying to open it wider, but the miserable thing wouldn't budge.

Bracing my right foot against the outside frame, I planted my left on the ground and put every ounce of strength I had into the job — and *yanked.* Metal screeched, but the door gave enough for me to be able to wiggle most of my body inside.

"Mia, scoot back," I said. "Press your shoulders up against the far door."

She did as I asked. "Thank . . . you for . . . your help," she said, gasping.

I struggled my way through the narrow space until I was mostly inside the car, kneeling on the seat with my derriere sticking out in the pungent breeze.

The presence of another woman seemed to comfort her. Little did she know! There were probably a hundred women in this traffic jam who could help her more than I could, but it looked as though I was all she had.

Mia let out another cry of pain, and then puff, puff, puffed.

"Oh, good, Mia — you've had Lamaze."

She nodded and puffed.

On the floor of the car, I saw a crumpled pair of maternity underpants.

"Has your water broken?" The moment those words were out of my mouth I knew that was a stupid question. What else could the dark stain around her lower body be?

"Yes. . . . When the cars . . ." Mia cried out, then puff, puff, puffed.

I remembered another question from twenty years ago: "How close together are your pains?"

"Each . . . minute." She cried out again, this time a long wail. No puffing.

"Keep breathing!" I leaned forward and reached for the hem of her skirt.

She screamed, "It's coming!"

Probably more terrified of what was about to happen than Mia was, I lifted her skirt, turned it back onto her knees — and saw the top of a dark little head.

Thank God it's the head and not the feet! I knew enough to realize that seeing feet would mean a breach birth, requiring an expert. But the head coming first is "basic."

Out of the corner of one eye I saw a folded blanket on the shelf in front of the rear window. I grabbed it and spread it below the head and up across my own knees.

"Push!" I said, praying that was the right instruction. "Push, Mia!"

She pushed, and pushed, and I saw the head inch forward, then I saw the baby twist slightly — and I saw a little shoulder — and with Mia pushing and me praying, the baby came out. It was in my hands, all slimy and covered with goop. It was the most beautiful thing I'd ever seen in my life.

The mother was weeping, but with joy. The baby started to cry — it was breathing. I gave an enormous sigh of relief. And then I saw the cord. The umbilical cord. All I knew about an umbilical cord was that it had to be cut. But how?

I asked the elderly man in the front seat, "Do you have scissors or a knife?"

"No, no." Now he was sobbing.

It was as though the Patron Saint of the Inexperienced was watching over me, because at that moment I knew what to do. Cradling the baby against my chest with one arm, I worked my free hand into my pocket and pulled out Detective Hall's ring of keys and his Swiss army knife. Among the assorted gadgets, I pulled out the small knife blade. I didn't have anything to sterilize it with, but I had no choice except to use it. I put the baby down carefully between my knees and pulled the blade open. Clenching my jaws to keep from gagging, I cut the cord.

Looking up, I saw NDM staring at me through the window on the other side of the car. He put his cell phone back in a pocket and came around to my side of the car. At that moment, I heard the *whup-whup-whup* of a helicopter above and the shriek of sirens racing toward us from the other side of the freeway.

I wrapped the baby in the blanket and put him — yes, it was a boy — into Mia's arms.

NDM pushed the airbag away from the woman's father and asked him if he was all right. The man replied that his arm hurt. As I worked my way backward out of the car, I heard NDM urge the elderly man to stay where he was until help arrived.

Standing, my legs were a little wobbly. I leaned against the Buick, took a couple of deep gulps of air, and felt steady again.

Just then, John found me. When he looked into the car and saw Mia and her baby, he hurried off to get one of the emergency medical technicians who'd arrived.

"I cut the cord, but the knife wasn't sterile," I told the young blond EMT who appeared with John a few minutes later.

"And I didn't know how to clean out his eyes."

"Don't worry," the medical tech said, waving me away. "We'll take care of everything."

Mia's father wanted to get out of the car. I helped him up, careful not to touch the arm that was giving him pain, and guided him over to another EMT.

NDM stayed behind. I saw him bend forward into the Buick. Then Detective Hall pulled me out of the way of a tow truck, and I lost sight of NDM.

John got some sterile wipes from the medical supplies and gave them to me so I could clean up a little. At least my face and hands.

In a few minutes, NDM joined us. "Mother, baby, and grandfather are going to be taken to the hospital for a complete examination, but it looks as though they're all going to be fine," he said.

Tow trucks had cleared a narrow path out of the snarl and some cars were finally able to leave the scene.

Miraculously, no one had been killed in our monster traffic tie-up. Only a few people were hurt, and while they were taken to area hospitals, one of the EMTs told us he thought most of their injuries were minor.

Detective Hall approached. "O'Hara and

I have to stay here. D'Martino, you can take Ms. Carmichael and go."

Down at my side, and out of his view, I used the last of my wipes to clean the blade on Detective Hall's Swiss army knife. "I'll get Tuffy and my handbag out of your car, and bring you back your keys," I said.

Hall nodded and began directing the clearing of an exit path in front of NDM's Maserati.

Moments later, I let Tuffy into the back-seat of the most expensive car he'd ever been in, clipped his harness to the seat belt, and I got into the passenger seat.

NDM said, "I checked on your show food. It's okay."

"Thank you."

"Go tape your shows," Hall told me.

As NDM climbed in behind the wheel, John leaned in the passenger window of the Maserati, and reached behind me to give Tuffy a quick ear scratch. "I'll let you know what happened as soon as we find out," he told me. Because he'd made no secret of his dislike of NDM, it must have been difficult for John, but he looked at NDM and said, "Thanks for the help out there."

"No problem."

As we finally left the freeway and the turmoil behind, I asked NDM, "Do you have any idea why my car exploded? Was there a gas leak? Did that bouncing over the telephone poles crack something open?"

He was silent for a moment. "I think there was a bomb."

"A *bomb?*" Even as my voice expressed surprise, I realized that "bomb" had been the deep, visceral fear that I hadn't allowed myself to consider consciously.

"I worked my way through college doing construction work, and I have some demolition experience," NDM said. "I've done stories on bombings. From the way the car went up, I'm willing to bet explosives were rigged to the undercarriage."

I believed that, but it didn't make sense. "Why would someone put a warning note on the windshield if they were going to kill me with a bomb?"

"My guess is that the killer thought you'd take the note and the car to the cops. While you were driving . . . boom."

This was too much. I began to shake uncontrollably.

NDM immediately turned the car into a quiet residential street and cut the engine. Without saying a word he took me in his arms and held me tight against him until my trembling subsided.

When I was breathing more normally, I

said, "I don't know what's the matter with me —"

And then his lips were on mine. Softly, he kissed my mouth, my eyes. Without thinking, beyond thinking, my arms went around his neck, and I returned his kisses until they were hard and probing and took my breath away.

When we finally pulled slightly apart, I tried to reclaim my composure. "Thank you for heading off my meltdown."

With a tender touch, he smoothed a strand of hair back from my face and smiled. "You were in shock. I didn't want to slap you, and I didn't have a bucket of cold water to toss in your face, so . . ."

We kissed again. One more kiss. Deep, but gentle. If I had to describe it, I'd say it was a survivors' kiss. Not sexual, or rather not *just* sexual.

Slowly, we released each other. I looked around and saw that we were parked on a street with lots of soft green grass between the sidewalk and the curb.

"Tuffy needs a walk," I said. *And I need to clear my head.*

Opening my purse, I removed a disposal bag that was on a wire frame and had a cardboard handle. It was designed to scoop and snap shut, then be dropped into the nearest garbage can. I turned in the seat, unhooked Tuffy's safety harness, and grabbed the end of Tuffy's leash.

"Want me to come with you?" NDM asked.

"No. I'll just be a few minutes, and then we can go on to the studio."

As I opened the rear door and let Tuffy out of the Maserati, I saw NDM reaching for his cell phone.

31

Quinn Tanner greeted me with, "You look bloody awful!"

"I got here, Quinn, against major odds. As soon as I wash up, I'll be ready to work." The truth was that after what I'd gone through on the freeway, I *needed* to work. If I didn't tape the shows, I was afraid I'd go to pieces. Even though it hadn't always been true, I like to think of myself as the "she doesn't go to pieces" type.

NDM had parked near the double doors into the studio and carried both boxes of food inside behind me, while I held Tuffy's leash and carried the garment bag.

"There's a shower room behind Car Guy's set," Quinn said. "But your clothes are filthy. What in the world is all over the front of you?"

"Afterbirth," I said.

"There is no need to be *sarcastic,*" she snapped. "I only inquired because you can't go on camera like that."

Sometimes the way to make people think you're joking is to tell the truth.

"I have a change in the garment bag," I said, "but it's for the second show and to wear home. I can cover my slacks by tucking a dish towel into my belt, but do you have a sweater or shirt I could borrow to wear on top?"

Scanning me with a critical frown, she said, "Nothing of mine would fit. I'm a size two. You are . . . *not.*"

NDM put the boxes of food on the prep counter. Indicating the auto shop set, he told Quinn, "I see a couple of Car's jumpsuits in dry cleaners' plastic hanging up over there. Della could wear one of those. I think she'd look kind of cute."

"Do you really?" Quinn's tone was frosty. "But I suppose that would be better than how she looks now."

She'd been so hostile to him and to me that I didn't trust Quinn to be alone with Tuffy. I asked NDM, "Would you look after him while I shower and change? I won't be long."

"Sure," he said, taking the leash.

Quinn began unpacking the food and putting the items where she wanted them to be while I grabbed one of Car Guy's clean uniform jumpsuits and headed off to find the shower.

The door was in the set's rear wall, partially concealed behind a tower of tires. I expected it to look something like a gas station bathroom, but Car Guy's cleanup facility turned out to be an almost luxurious room done in green and white tiles, with a new toilet, ceramic pedestal sink, and glass-enclosed stall. All were on the higher rather than lower end of the quality scale. There was even a shelf piled with fresh towels. In the mirrored cabinet over the sink, I found several unopened bars of soap and several plastic laundry bags. All the comforts of a decent hotel. Remembering what Lulu had said about the large amount of advertising revenue Car Guy pulled in, I guessed that he had extracted this facility from Mickey about the same time he insisted Mimi be fired.

After a quick but thorough soaping and rinsing, I dried myself. Folding my soiled sweater and slacks, I put them into one of the laundry bags. Along with what I was going to wear of Car Guy's, they would go to the dry cleaners in the morning. I'd probably have to explain what those stains on my clothes were so they'd know what to use on them.

Wearing only underwear, I stepped into Car Guy's dark blue uniform. It was a couple of sizes too big, and an inch or so too long, but by cinching the waist with my belt, I solved both problems.

When I returned to my own set and modeled my new look, NDM laughed, but said, "That's not bad."

Quinn called across the prep counter. "Everything is laid out properly. We're behind schedule, so let's get started, shall we?"

NDM handed Tuffy's leash to me. "I'm going to North Hollywood Station to see what I can find out. How long will you be here? A couple of hours?"

"Don't worry about coming back for me," I said. "I'm going to call Liddy or Eileen and ask one of them to take me home."

"I'll take you home," Mickey Jordan said, startling me. I hadn't seen him come into the studio. "Now let's get to work. Time is money."

It took another few minutes for the lights to be set and the camera adjusted. I used the opportunity to phone Liddy, tell her what happened, and ask if Eileen could stay at her house for a few days. As I knew she would, she agreed immediately, but she wanted me to stay at Casa Marshall, too.

"I'll be fine at the house. I have Tuffy and an old baseball bat from when Mack played. My mind is made up, but I appreciate the offer."

"All right, but I'm still going to worry," she said with a sigh. "Do you want me to tell Eileen?"

Quinn gestured to me impatiently and headed up to the director's booth.

"Yes, please call Eileen. That would be a big help," I said. "Have to go now. Talk to you later."

Positioning myself behind the prep counter, I did a quick scan of the surfaces and saw that Quinn had arranged everything perfectly. The necessary ingredients in front of me, and pre-prepared dishes on the rear counter, ready to be brought forward to display at the end of the show. She'd even preheated the ovens. Quinn might not be a joy to know, but she was very good at her job.

In my earpiece, I heard Quinn's ten-second countdown. I gave a friendly wave to Jada Powell, who was taping the show today. She responded with a pleasant nod and Camera One's red light went on.

I looked into the lens and smiled at the unseen audience. "Hello, everybody. I'm

Della Carmichael. Welcome to *In the Kitchen with Della*." I fingered the uniform's shirt pocket that said "Car Guy" in bright red thread. "You may be wondering why I'm dressed like this. Well, the show is coming to you from Southern California, the home of freeway chases and traffic tie-ups. As I was on my way here today, we had a mess on the freeway. My own clothes got dirty, so I'm wearing one of Car Guy's outfits. He's my next-door neighbor here at the Better Living Channel. I'll have to bake him something tonight to thank him for the use of his clothes. When you do this kind of 'real' show, there isn't a costume department. They have those in studios where they film movies and TV series. We just wear things we have in our own closets. I'm grateful that my TV kitchen isn't next door to *Sesame Street.* It would be pretty hard to do what I do in a Big Bird suit." I smiled, hoping that if the *Sesame Street* people — who had a reputation for being very protective of their characters — saw this, they would know I was joking.

"Speaking of TV and the movies, today I'm making recipes that came from a show business husband and wife. First up is an Italian meatloaf baked in a big round of sourdough bread, the recipe courtesy of ac-

331

tor and director Tom Troupe. With it, for dessert, is the best ambrosia I've ever had. That recipe is from his wife, actress Carole Cook, who got it from her sister, Regina Cocanougher, in Decatur, Texas. My thanks to you all for sharing. Now, let's get cooking!"

Both half-hour shows went smoothly. I talked and chopped, talked and stirred, sautéed, mixed, and tasted. Nothing happened that required stopping the tape to do it over again. Even Tuffy behaved like a performing pro. He was the perfect foil, gazing at me when appropriate, and cocking his head for comic punctuation.

When the shows were finally over, the adrenaline rush on which I'd been operating began to dissipate. I hardly remembered a word of what I'd said, but Mickey, who'd been watching on a monitor in the control room, told me he was pleased by what he saw.

Nodding in Tuffy's direction, he added, "The mutt's a good touch. Gals will love it."

Inwardly, I flinched at the words "mutt" and "gals," but that was just Mickey, whose slang was stuck in a 1950s time warp.

I left the pre-prepared dishes and the on-set prepared food from the two shows for the studio staff to enjoy, and gathered the laundry bag with my dirty clothes, the empty garment bag, Car Guy's uniform, and Tuffy, and put them in the back of Mickey's yellow SUV.

When we drove out through the security gate, Mickey gestured at the new billboard. Grinning with pride, he asked, "How do you like that?"

"It was a wonderful surprise. I was absolutely stunned."

"Yeah, well, I spent the money for *you.* Cost an' arm an' a leg to get it so quick. But forget I said anything about the money. You're attracting a lot of new subscribers to the cable package we're in. My market research people found that out."

Although I hated the thought, what went through my mind was: *Don't you mean that* two murders *have stirred up all this interest?* What I said was, "If I'm helping the channel, I'm glad. I love teaching, and you've given me the biggest classroom I've ever had."

"Iva got it right when she talked me into giving you a shot."

"Maybe you should put Iva on your billboard," I joked.

He took me seriously. "Nah. I got her a diamond bracelet."

We were on Ventura Boulevard, heading for Beverly Glen Canyon. Mickey, a New Yorker who hadn't learned to drive until he was forty years old, didn't like the freeways. "They're death traps on asphalt," he'd said.

"Mickey, if you have a few minutes to talk, can we stop for coffee? There are some things I need to tell you."

"Sure, Iva's having a spa day, whatever that is. She won't be home until late. Where's a nice restaurant out here?"

"There's a fast-food drive-through on the next block. Let's get our coffee there. I don't want to go inside and leave Tuffy out in the car."

"Great. I don't feel fancy right now myself."

A few minutes later we were parked, with two large coffees for ourselves and a bowl of water for Tuffy.

I told Mickey about the note on my windshield and my car destroyed in a suspicious explosion while it was being transported to the North Hollywood Station.

Mickey let out a stream of curses and banged his fist on the dashboard. He hit it so hard, he cracked the surface veneer and hurt himself. Shaking out his bruised hand, he growled, "What the f— is going on? Somebody's trying to off you, too? Who's

334

next — Car and Gil? I'll have a network with nobody on it! Twenty-four hours a day of f—ing cheapo infomercials!"

"I don't think there's any danger to Car Guy or Gilmer York, but I'm absolutely convinced that whoever murdered Mimi Bond and Lulu Owens, and whoever destroyed my car, is connected to your channel."

Staring out the window, scowling, he listened as I recounted the events that led to my conclusion: "The killer has to be someone with access to your studio."

After a few seconds of silence, Mickey turned in his seat to face me. "I must say, you got guts. We're out here in a parking lot, pretty much alone. You're taking a big chance, telling me how you're figuring this. What makes you think it's not *me?*"

32

A chill swept over me, but it only lasted for a moment. "No," I told Mickey Jordan firmly, "I don't believe you're a killer."

To my surprise, he looked a little disappointed. I added, "Not that I don't think you're capable of it, if you had a strong enough motive, but I'm sure you didn't murder Mimi and Lulu, or blow up my car. You're off the hook with me. Not with Detective Hall, though. He found out you really were in New York when Mimi died, but he's not ruling out the possibility that you hired someone to kill her for you. I don't believe you did that."

"You're right. I'm not the killer, and I didn't pay for it. But I'm curious why you don't think so."

"If it makes you feel any better, I did suspect you for about a minute, but I crossed you off my mental list. When you approached me about doing a show on your channel, I made it a point to find out as much as I could about you."

He snorted. "The f—ing Internet! I don't make a great impression on some of those sites."

"I didn't learn about you just on the Internet. Someone checked you out." I wouldn't tell him that John O'Hara, using his law enforcement connections, had done a thorough background search on Mickey. At first I was annoyed that John was interfering in my life, but I had to admit his report made for colorful reading.

First, there were the rumors about the murky origin of Mickey's fortune, in particular, speculation about where he got the initial investment money, but nothing illegal had been proven. Then there had been gaudy mutual charges in his several divorce cases, but they'd eventually been settled without bloodshed. What facts could be proved showed Mickey Jordan to be an astute businessman who bought dead or dying companies, brought them back to life, and sold them at a handsome profit. He was a hard negotiator. Some men whose businesses he'd bought low and sold high were unhappy with the deals they made and had strong words to say about Mickey, but he'd never lost a lawsuit or been charged with a crime.

I said, "The thing that seems to be most consistent about you is that you carefully plan everything you do. Last Friday I surprised you when I said I wanted to visit Faye Bond. Did you tell anyone where I was going when I left your house?"

He shook his head. "Nobody. I had more important things on my mind."

"Then you were the only one who knew where I would be, but you didn't have time to get to North Hollywood, hot-wire the car — even if you had known it would be there — and come back to chase me through Brentwood. I don't think you'd hire a killer, because I can't see you putting yourself in the power of somebody who could betray you."

"You got that right." I heard bitterness in his voice. He took a swallow of his coffee, as though to wash the taste away.

"Whoever tried to frighten me in Brentwood went to the Bond house without expecting to find me there," I said. "I think that person was after *Lulu* because Lulu knew something that could expose Mimi Bond's killer."

"You're smart," he said. "How about coming into business with me?"

"No, thank you. I just want to keep cooking."

Mickey frowned, squeezed his eyes shut, and drummed his fingertips on the steering wheel. I sipped coffee in our companionable silence.

Opening his eyes again, he said, "Let's keep this simple. Your take on the case is that Mimi was the target, an' Lulu was collateral damage, an' you were almost collateral?"

"Yes. I think the killer only intended to commit one murder: Mimi's. But Lulu became a dangerous loose end because of something she knew. I was asking questions, and I spent time with Lulu, so that made me a possible danger to him. Or *her*."

"Forget the 'her' part. I never met a gal who could hot-wire a car."

"You're sitting next to one," I said. "My husband showed me how to do it."

"Your old man was a car thief?"

"A police detective who had a habit of losing his keys."

He aimed a half-smile at me. "Next time I lose my keys, maybe I'll call you instead of Triple A."

With the usually taciturn Mickey in a talkative mood, I decided to ask him about my show's bad-tempered director. "Were

Quinn Tanner and Mimi Bond close friends?"

Mickey let out a derisive snort. " 'Friends'? They liked each other about as much as Churchill and Hitler liked each other. Why'd you figure they were pals?"

"After Mimi collapsed, Quinn accused me of having caused her death. She was so unpleasant, I thought she might be upset because they were close."

"Those two porcupines? No way. Quinn was Mimi's director. Each one of them came to me, trying to get me to fire the other one."

"I'm not complaining about Quinn, because I can work with her, but do you have any idea why she's so hostile to me?"

"That's a no-brainer. Quinn wanted to replace Mimi. She even made me a demo tape of herself, but she's cold as a meat locker on camera. Iva calls her 'charisma challenged.' " Mickey's mouth curved up and his eyes warmed, as they always did when he spoke of Iva. "My gal looks like the cover of a fashion magazine, but when we're alone she makes me laugh. Maybe you know I was married more often than was good for me. What the hell, I was young an' stupid, an' then I was middle-aged an' stupid. But when I met Iva, I knew she was the prize in my box of Cracker Jacks. The possibility of getting caught an' losing Iva . . . She's the *real* reason I wouldn't have murdered Mimi." He took the last swallow of his coffee and added, "Or at least I wouldn't kill anybody I've met so far."

It was close to four thirty when Mickey eased his yellow behemoth to a stop in front of my house.

"You gonna be all right tonight?" he asked.

I wondered which "all right" he had in mind: all right after the possibility of somebody having put a bomb in my car, or all right alone in my house while a killer is loose. I decided to give him the thinking-positive answer.

"I'll be fine," I said.

"You have a security system?"

"No."

"I'll treat you to one an' deduct the cost as a business expense."

"No, please, but thanks for the offer. With a dog and a cat and a college student houseguest, it would probably keep going off at all hours."

"You want some unregistered fire power? I can get it for you. But here's a tip: If you shoot somebody trying to break in, be sure you drag him all the way inside the house before you call the cops."

"No, Mickey. If I had a gun, I might accidentally shoot myself in the foot."

"Okay, but you can't say I didn't try. Call me if you change your mind." He put the big yellow SUV in gear and drove away in a cloud of exhaust fumes.

I started up the path, but paused to look at my little English cottage. The pink camellia bush was in bloom on one side of the front door, and my hand-planted night-blooming jasmine was growing tall and shiny on the other. For the first time in the years I'd lived there, I wasn't eager to rush inside. Except for Emma and Tuffy, I was going to be alone tonight. As much as I hated to admit it, I was nervous. No, the truth was that I was more than a little afraid.

Tuffy tugged on his leash and looked up at me, communicating his need for a walk.

Reaching down to pet him, I said, "Okay, boy, you got it."

I put the garment bag full of dirty clothes on my doorstep and took a scoop bag out of my purse, and we headed back down the path to tour the neighborhood.

No one followed us.

As soon as I unlocked the front door, I heard Emma's soft little pads loping across the living room to meet us. She greeted Tuffy first, stretching her neck up to touch her soft gray nose to his wet black nose. He wagged his tail. I unhooked Tuffy's leash and started toward the kitchen. Eight paws trotted behind me.

Once I'd taken care of the pets and given Emma some affectionate strokes, I went to the bedroom, reached for the phone, and dialed Ed Gardner's number at Western Alliance Insurance. It was after five thirty; I wasn't sure if he'd still be in his office, but he answered the phone.

"Hi, Ed. It's Della Carmichael."

"How's the TV star? If you're calling about the policy changes, we had computer troubles here, so I'll get the new bill out to you on Friday."

"No, I wasn't calling about that. I have to make a claim."

"A claim." He was silent for a moment; I pictured him frowning unhappily at the prospect of having to pay money *out.* "What kind of a claim?"

"Auto. My car has been totaled."

"If somebody hit you, I hope the driver was in a Rolls." He sounded cheerful at that thought.

"Nobody hit me. My Mustang exploded."

"Exploded? Was it a mechanical malfunction? Something Ford did wrong?"

I had to be careful how I answered because I didn't have any proof yet. "There's some suspicion it was a bomb, but thankfully nobody was in the car when it went off."

"Glad to hear that, but a *bomb?* This is a first for me."

"If it turns out to be true, am I covered for that?"

"Oh, yes. You've got both collision and comprehensive. Comprehensive covers everything, even the extraordinarily unusual."

I began to relax. "That's a relief. How soon will I be able to buy another car?"

"Are you asking when will you get a check?"

"Yes. If you need to see the wreckage, it's at the North Hollywood police station, or wherever they took it."

"I'll have an adjuster go out and get pictures for the files, and I'll process the claim as quickly as possible."

"Thank you."

"But if you're waiting for the check before you buy a new car, I've got some bad news for you."

A cold ball of dread formed in my stomach. "What is it?" *What now?*

"Your Mustang is eighteen years old, so —"

"But I've kept it in perfect condition. I have all of the service records, going back to when Mack bought it new."

"I believe you, but no matter how well it's been cared for, an eighteen-year-old car isn't a collector's item, Della. According to the evaluation tables, it's just an *old car*. Frankly, you won't be getting more than a small fraction of what a new Mustang, or any comparably priced car, will cost you. And, of course, when you buy a new car, you'll have the registration fees and all that. As soon as you pick something out, call me from the dealer's office so I can cover your new vehicle before you leave the lot."

"Yes, I will, Ed. I'll call you." We said good-bye.

More debt. How in the world am I going to . . .

Then I took a breath and made myself stop the internal whining; I hate people who whine. I reminded myself that I'm alive and healthy, and that there's a solution to my problem: I have to keep my TV job. If Mickey sells the channel, as he's sold other businesses when they start to make money, the new owner might not want me if I'm still under suspicion of murder. Which

345

meant that I had to find out who killed Mimi Bond and clear my name.

33

I turned on the inside and outside lights and found Mack's old baseball bat in the storage closet. Followed by Tuffy and Emma, I took it to the kitchen and began to figure out what I could have for dinner. I needed a hot meal to be able to think clearly. No standing up over the sink while I ate a peanut butter sandwich tonight.

Too tired to cook, I turned to the stash of emergency meals that I kept in the freezer. What appealed to me most, because it was delicious and would take the least amount of energy to consume, was Barbara Rush's special chili.

The actress was a friend of one of my Happy Table students. When I learned that this movie and TV star was well known in the entertainment community for her cooking skills, I invited her to be a guest speaker at class. She was a big hit, and her chili was so good I keep several Tupperware portions in the freezer.

After giving Tuffy and Emma each a treat, and while the chili was defrosting, I sat down at the kitchen table. Using my grocery pad and a pen, I began to make a list of murder suspects, people who knew Mimi and also had access to the studio facilities:

George Hopkins
  (where was he before my show went on the air?)
Quinn Tanner
  (wanted Mimi's job, but I got it, so why would she kill Mimi?)
Car Guy
  (Mimi tried to humiliate him by saying he couldn't perform sexually.)
Gilmer York
  (Mimi pursued him, and when rebuffed, lied that he was a drug addict.)
Stan Evans
  (once drove for Mimi, and she got him the daytime security job.)
Al Franklin
  (night security man; no known personal link to Mimi.)
Ernie Ramirez and Jada Powell
  (worked with Mimi, but no known animosity.)

Faye Bond
(had no access to backstage.)

I didn't bother to consider Mickey or Iva
Jordan as suspects in Mimi's murder.
Mickey was off my list for the reasons I
explained to him. Not only did Iva have no
apparent motive — she certainly could not
have been worried about Mimi as a rival for
her husband! — the more important reason
I didn't suspect her was that she had arrived at the studio with Lulu to see my first
show, and she was continuously in Lulu's
company until Lulu took her home after
Detective Hall let them leave. I knew this
from my chat with Lulu at Faye Bond's
house. Lulu also told me that while Mimi
was a pain in the solar plexus to her camera
operators, Ernie and Jada, they had no connection with Mimi outside the studio. Lulu,
who had been around them all for years,
hadn't been able to imagine why either
Ernie or Jada would kill Mimi.

As for Faye, Lulu told me that Faye was
an unhappy child who adored her late father
and had a tense relationship with her
mother. Even if Faye had a powerful motive
for killing Mimi, she had no opportunity to
doctor the mousse. According to Lulu, from
the time Faye arrived at the studio that

night, just after Lulu — and while Mimi was throwing a fit at me in the dressing room — Faye was outside with the other people who would be in the audience, waiting to go into the studio. Then she never got out of her seat in the front row. Lulu could swear to it. Faye had looked so unhappy and fragile that night, Lulu had kept an eye on her.

That brought me to Stan Evans. Lulu said he'd worked for Mimi as a chauffeur. They must have parted on amicable terms, because when she let him go, she got him a job with the studio so he wouldn't be out of work. That was a nice gesture from a woman who wasn't known to be as kind to human beings as she was to animals.

While I was thinking and making notes, Liddy called twice to see how I was. In between Liddy's calls, Eileen phoned. She insisted that she wasn't afraid to stay at the house with me, but I managed to convince her that I would feel better if she was at Liddy's for the time being. It took a few minutes, but she agreed.

Immediately following Liddy's second call, John phoned.

"Did you lock all the doors?" he asked.

I wanted to scream at his treating me like a child, but I controlled myself. "Please,

I'm not ten years old. Of course I did. Now tell me what you've found out."

"A bomb was attached to the Mustang's undercarriage."

So NDM's guess was right.

"Della? Are you there?"

"Yes. I was just . . . Was there anything left that could lead to finding out who made it?"

"Not a professional," John said. "It was a crude device. Anyone with a computer could have learned how to make it on the Internet."

On John's end of the call, I heard a woman's voice, but I couldn't understand the words. John must have covered the mouthpiece, because all I could make out was a few seconds of murmuring. Back on the line, he said, "Shannon wants to say hello."

My still-guilty heart skipped a couple of beats. "Oh, good." I tried to sound sincere.

I heard Shannon laugh as she took the phone. "Men! I don't want to say 'hello' — I want to find out how you *are!* John told me what happened today. Are you all right?"

"Yes, I'm fine." *Maybe I should make a recording of the answer and just push a button when people ask me if I'm all right.* "Eileen's with Liddy, so you mustn't worry."

"I know. I've been on the phone with her," Shannon said. "Why don't you come and stay with us until that monster is caught?"

"It's sweet of you, really, but I'm not going to be chased out of my home."

"Well, for protection, how about I send John over to stay with you tonight?"

"Absolutely not!" My response was too quick and too loud. I dialed the volume down. "That's a kind offer, Shan, but no." To cut off this line of discussion I decided to lie. "Actually, Mickey Jordan — the man who owns the channel — hired a security company to watch the house."

"Oh, what a nice employer." Shannon laughed again, a merry trill. Her tone was teasing as she asked, "Is there something delightful going on between you two?"

The thought was so ridiculous I couldn't suppress a chuckle. "No. He's happily married, and even if he weren't, I have no desire to become the *fifth* Mrs. Jordan."

"Goodness! What is he, the bluebeard of cable TV?"

"He's nicer than it sounds. I think the incumbent Mrs. Jordan is finally 'the one.' "

John said something in the background, and I heard Shannon tell him that Mickey Jordan hired security for me. "So you don't have to worry about her, sweetheart."

Shannon came back to me. "We're so glad to know you're safe, but if you need anything, just call us. Doesn't matter how late."

I thanked her warmly and we said good night.

With all of my heart, I wanted Shannon to be well and for her and John to be as happy together as they once were. And I wanted to stop having guilt pangs about something I had only *felt,* but not done.

The phone rang again. When I picked it up and heard the voice on the other end, I knew that Fate was hitting me tonight with a guilt trifecta.

NDM said, "I'm not going to ask if you're all right."

I expelled a great sigh of relief. "Thank you for that. I've heard that question too many times tonight."

"I'm not asking because I know you are."

"How do you know?"

"Because I'm outside your house. With dinner and some information."

Dinner was the best pizza I'd ever tasted, and the information was about George Hopkins.

"His problem is that he's a sick gambler," NDM told me as I poured us each a second glass of the merlot he'd brought along with the three-cheese and pepperoni pizza with the thin crust, still hot when he came through the door.

NDM went on, "Hopkins is so much in debt, he's on the verge of bankruptcy. His wife, who left him night before last, told me that a week before Mimi Bond was murdered, Hopkins tried to borrow money from her. Mimi refused."

"I can see how George might have killed her in a rage, but a week later? Have you talked to George?"

"He's disappeared," NDM said.

"George *could* have killed Mimi, I suppose," I said. "He knew about her allergy; he could have ground up peanuts and put them in the mousse without being seen. But it bothers me that there was a week between her refusal to lend him money and her death. It would be easier to believe that George is the killer if it had happened when she said no, but what good would her dying a week later do him?"

"Nobody knows where Hopkins is. Vanishing makes him look guilty."

"Couldn't he be hiding from the gamblers?"

"He could," NDM said. "We should know pretty soon, because the story's going to be in tomorrow's papers. If he's innocent, he'd be smart to come forward."

"And get killed?"

"Nobody forced him to lose everything. I'm not sympathetic to reckless gamblers."

I was surprised by the bitterness in his voice, and wondered if at some time NDM had had an experience with a sick gambler. "But I admit that the time lag bothers me, too," he said. "There's another possibility I'm investigating."

"Tell me."

"I'm giving a hard look at Mickey Jordan's business dealings. He's done some pretty ruthless things to get where he is. It's possible that an enemy is out to ruin him by destroying the Better Living Channel. There's been a big uptick in subscriber numbers, but our business guy tells me that if there are rumors of financial or management problems, stockholders could start running. I've got an article tomorrow, speculating about that."

"Isn't it early to put that theory in the paper?"

"It's covering several bases," NDM said. "If the killer isn't George Hopkins, and it isn't someone out to torpedo Jordan's cable network, then the real murderer is likely to feel safe because he'll see us looking in these other directions." NDM paused and rotated his shoulders to ease tight muscles. I saw the tension in his body begin to lessen. "If he believes our focus is elsewhere, he won't need to target you. Tomorrow, after the paper comes out, I think you'll be safer than you are tonight."

Tonight . . .

"I'd like to stay here to protect you tonight." He raised his right hand in a three-finger pledge. "Scout's honor — I won't make a move on you. Your couch doesn't look very comfortable, but we're adults. We can share a bed, and just *sleep.*"

"Do you mean it? We'll spend the night together as friends? Like buddies? Nothing else?"

"Not unless you start something," NDM said.

We played three hands of gin rummy — I won two of them — and together gave Tuffy his final walk of the night.

In the bedroom, NDM stripped down to his shorts, laid his clothes neatly across the chaise next to the window, and got under the covers.

I undressed in the bathroom, put on sweatpants and a T-shirt, and joined him in bed. We were on opposite sides, with at least eighteen inches of space between us.

Tuffy settled down on the carpet next to my side and Emma curled up on top of the television cabinet. NDM and I said good night, turned away from each other, and fell asleep.

Sometime during the night, and while not fully conscious, one of us touched the other and "started something."

I awoke to find my hand caressing NDM's bare chest and his hand slipping up under my T-shirt. The sensation of his fingertips stroking my breasts was electric. The touch of my hand was having a similar effect on him. Slowly, with gentle exploration, our kisses deepened, our clothing was peeled away, and we were naked in each other's arms.

This time, we talked a little.

34

Movement on the opposite side of the bed awakened me. In moonlight filtering through the sheer curtains, I saw NDM in silhouette, reaching for his clothes. I turned my head and peered at the glowing green numerals on my bedside clock.

"It's only four thirty," I said.

"It's seven thirty in New York. My business sleuth is already in his office, where he's digging for more information about Mickey Jordan's enemies. Go back to sleep."

Instead, I turned on the night table lamp. "Be careful not to step on Tuffy or Emma."

Indicating Tuffy with a nod, NDM smiled. "I'm grateful he didn't go for my throat in the middle of the night." He fastened his belt and leaned over to give me a light kiss on the forehead. "I'll let myself out."

"Bye."

At the doorway he turned. "What time is your *Chronicle* delivered?"

"About six a.m."

"Good," he said, and was gone.

I turned off the light, lay down, and snuggled my head into the pillow, luxuriating in the warm sheets, and the faint, pleasant scent of NDM. It had been a long time since two human beings had shared this bed.

Within a few minutes, I knew I wasn't going to be able to go back to sleep. There was too much to do this morning. Even though I had taped a pair of half hour shows on Tuesday and two more yesterday, today was Thursday, and this evening would be my second live TV hour.

Has it only been one week since my debut? I feel as though I've lived a year in these seven days. Two women have been murdered, my car was blown up, and I've been to bed — twice — with a man I hardly know.

Wryly, I remembered many years ago, in elementary school, receiving this comment on my report card: "Della makes good use of time." I was proud of that.

By five fifteen I had showered, shampooed, dried my hair, dressed in comfortable jeans and a sweatshirt, plugged in the coffeemaker, and given the pets their breakfasts and fresh bowls of water. I fastened Tuffy's leash to his collar and headed out the front door to take him for his morning walk.

Tuffy and I were halfway down the path to the sidewalk when I recognized the man sitting in a not-very-new black car with red and yellow flames painted along the side parked outside my house. He was wearing a wrinkled Los Angeles Lakers jacket zipped up to his chin, and he needed a shave.

"What are you doing here?" I asked the channel's red-haired daytime security guard, Stan Evans.

"Hi, Ms. Carmichael. You're up early."

"Yes, but why are you here, Stan?"

"Mr. Jordan told me to come watch your house last night. He's paying me extra."

I couldn't help laughing.

Stan cocked his head and squinted at me with an expression of concern. "You okay, Ms. Carmichael?"

"I was just surprised to see you." I couldn't tell him what was funny to me: that the lie I'd told Shannon and John O'Hara to keep them away last night — about Mickey Jordan having hired security to guard me — had turned out to be the truth.

"What about your job at the studio?" I asked.

"Don't you worry about me. Mr. Jordan said I could leave here at six. I'll catch a few hours sleep and get to the studio at ten. Al

Franklin — the night man — he's going to fill in for me from eight to ten this morning."

"Look, I'm about to take Tuffy for a walk. We'll be back in a little while and then you come inside with me. I'll make you a hot breakfast."

"Gee, thanks, Ms. Carmichael!"

Last night, before NDM came over with the pizza, I'd defrosted the Barbara Rush chili, so I heated it this morning to go with the omelets I made for Stan Evans and myself. While I poured us each a second mug of coffee, I asked, "I wonder how Faye Bond is doing. Have you seen her again, since the other day at the studio?"

"No, ma'am. Not since I left her with you in the parking lot. I don't really know her. I just happened to be around when she came in crying."

"This must be a hard time for her. In the space of a few days, she lost both of her mother figures."

At that moment, the doorbell rang. It startled Stan so much he spilled coffee on the table.

"Oh, Jeez, I'm sorry!"

"That's all right. Don't worry about it." I grabbed the roll of paper towels from next to the sink.

The doorbell rang again, more insistently.

"Let me clean it up," Stan said.

I handed him the roll and hurried toward the front door. It still wasn't quite six a.m. yet. *Who in the world . . . ?*

A glance through the living room window revealed the channel's publicity man, Phil Logan, fidgeting impatiently at the front door.

I opened it just as he aimed an index finger at the bell again. Under his other arm, I saw several folded newspapers, and in his free hand was my copy of the *Los Angeles Chronicle* in its red plastic wrapper.

He smiled broadly. "Oh, boy, have I got a surprise for *you!*"

"Good morning, Phil. You're here early." I moved aside to let him in. He fast-stepped past me, sniffed the air and said, "Is that coffee I smell?"

"We're having breakfast. Come join us."

The light in his eyes brightened; he looked as eager as Tuffy waiting for a treat. " 'Us'? Is Eileen here?"

Before I could answer the question, we were at the kitchen door. Phil stopped so abruptly on seeing Stan that I expected to find skid marks on the floor when I looked down.

I didn't want Phil to misunderstand the young man's presence in my house at this hour. "Mickey hired Stan to sit in his car and guard the house last night."

"Oh . . . good. Hi, Stan." Phil acknowledged Stan with a nod.

"Hi, Mr. Logan." Stan stood up. "I gotta go. Thanks for breakfast."

"You're welcome, Stan." Before I could thank him for doing guard duty, he was out of there.

With Stan gone, Phil was all business. "Wait 'til you see what I've got."

I took a coffee mug from the cabinet, but before I could pour some for Phil, he'd spread out the front page of a copy of the *Los Angeles Chronicle*.

"You're above the fold! Look!"

I did — and gasped. The upper part of the front page featured a picture of me holding Mia's newborn. NDM must have taken it with his cell phone camera. I was so focused on what was happening with Mia that I hadn't seen anything else.

Beaming, Phil read aloud, " 'In the middle of yesterday's massive tie-up on Los Angeles's one-oh-one freeway, the Better Living Channel's new cooking star, Della Carmichael, forty-seven, was the heroine of the day when she climbed over stalled vehicles and forced open a car door to deliver the baby of Mrs. Mia Nugent, twenty-three, wife of Sergeant Andrew J. Nugent, currently deployed in the Middle East. Without help, supplies, or equipment, Carmichael brought infant William Chang Nugent safely into the world. Emergency Medical Technician James Gibbons, twenty-seven, who arrived on the scene following the birth, said of Carmichael: "That woman did a good job." Carmichael, who hosts cable TV's *In the Kitchen with Della,* is no stranger to dramatic events. During the airing of her first show, Mimi Bond, the network's previous West Coast cooking personality, died on camera when . . .' " Phil looked up. "Yada, yada, yada. It goes on from there, talking about the murders."

My immediate reaction was monumental embarrassment. "I'm not a heroine, Phil! Nature mostly delivered the baby. I didn't do much more than *be* there. Did you persuade him to write that?"

Phil guffawed. "You don't know that guy very well. I couldn't persuade D'Martino to take a drink if he was thirsty. He wrote that story the way he saw it." Frowning, he added, "I wish he hadn't said you're forty-seven." He shrugged. "But the forties aren't as old as they used to be. Lots of gorgeous actresses are admitting to it, even to being older." Phil pointed to another part of the page. "Look, he wrote a sidebar from the interview you gave him, about how you come from a family of accountants and doctors, but you became a school teacher, married a cop, and run a cooking school. We struck publicity *gold* today. No, platinum, or whatever's better than platinum. Aren't you glad I gave D'Martino a week's exclusive with you?"

Hearing that, I felt a sudden chill. "An exclusive? What do you mean?"

"To get you — formerly a total unknown — some ink in the *Chronicle,* I gave him a week when I wouldn't schedule any other interviews for you. Believe me, this was a good deal; the *Chronicle's* one of the most important papers in California. Online it goes all over the country. The wire services are already picking up the baby delivery story. And what perfect timing this thing is, because you go on the air again tonight. I bet your numbers will get a big bump."

Phil gulped down half a mug of coffee. "Here are three copies of the *Chronicle,* and the one I picked up from your lawn. I thought you might like a few, to send clips to your family."

After hurriedly swallowing the rest of his

coffee, Phil said good-bye and left, jaunty and smiling.

I sat down with the paper and read the story to the right of the piece about Mia's baby. Below a wide helicopter shot of the wreckage on the flatbed tow truck and the backed-up traffic behind, the accompanying article had few details. I was relieved to see that it said that the mess on the freeway had been caused by the explosion of a car being transported "to a repair shop." Detective Hall had managed to keep the word "bomb" out of the paper, and there was no mention of who owned the car. I was thankful for that.

I made myself read the baby article. It was just as embarrassing as it was when Phil had read it, but now I saw at the bottom of the story, in small print, the words "related article in C 1."

Quickly shuffling through the paper, I found Section C: Business. There on the first page was another D'Martino byline, this time speculating about what affect the murders of Mimi Bond and Lulu Owens would have on the stock price of the Better Living Channel. The piece stated that two theories of the crimes were currently being pursued by the police. One was the possibility that the killings were linked to business enemies of Mickey Jordan. The second centered on TV producer George Hopkins.

It had been learned that Hopkins had sought a substantial loan from Mimi Bond and been refused, and that Hopkins, who was known to be a serious gambler, had disappeared. Hopkins was urged to contact the North Hollywood Division to arrange to come in for questioning. The information was attributed to "knowledgeable sources close to the case." When asked, Detective Emil Hall, in charge of the investigation, "replied with a terse 'No comment.' " The article was accompanied by headshots of Mimi Bond, Lulu Owens, George Hopkins, and Mickey Jordan. The photo they used of Mickey was a candid, scowling shot that made him look sinister.

I put the paper down and thought about the fact that Phil had given NDM a week's "exclusive" with me. Now the week was over.

Would I see NDM again?

Did I *want* to see him again? I didn't know the answer to that.

There was no time to think about it now, with several hours of baking and decorating to do to prepare the finished exhibits for tonight's "Halloween Cakes and Cookies" show.

With the investigation focusing on Mickey Jordan's enemies and on George Hopkins's personal problems, I had the sense that things were coming to a head.

35

Before I managed to get the first batch of cookies into the oven, Liddy called. She'd seen the front page of the *Chronicle* and wanted to hear all about how I managed to deliver a baby. Eileen was on an extension, so I was able to tell both of them at the same time that the story was greatly exaggerated. I said that what little I knew came from being in the delivery room with Liddy twenty years ago. They laughed when I added that *finally* I was grateful that Bill Marshall was a dentist who got queasy at the thought of birth, otherwise he would have been with Liddy and I wouldn't have known anything at all about the process.

"What are you going to do about a ride?" Liddy asked next. "I can take you to the show tonight."

"That would be great," I said. "I plan to start looking for a car tomorrow."

"Don't get another Mustang," Liddy said.

"That car was *Mack;* it wasn't you. Besides, you need something bigger for all that you've got to haul around."

"More space would be useful," I said.

"A Jeep," Liddy said. "What about getting a Jeep?"

"I hadn't thought about it. I like the look of Jeeps, and it would be the right size."

"One of Bill's patients has a Jeep dealership. Believe me, the guy will give you a bargain." Liddy chuckled. "We'll make sure he gets the message that if he doesn't treat you like a member of his own family, he won't enjoy his next visit to Bill's office."

On Liddy's extension, Eileen giggled. "That's *scary.*"

Because I hadn't yet fallen behind in any bills, my credit rating must be good enough to get financing, but it had been years since I bought a car. Liddy, who changed vehicles every two years for both herself and for Bill, was an experienced negotiator.

"That would be a huge help," I said.

"We'll go tomorrow morning. Now, when shall I pick you up for tonight? Same time as last week?"

"Perfect. By the way, because it's a Halloween show, the audience will be made up mostly of people I invited by e-mail from the Mommy and Me classes. And Detective

Hall and some of his people will be there."

"Then there probably won't be another murder tonight," Liddy said cheerfully.

"Don't even joke about that."

Liddy, Eileen, and I said good-bye, and I went back to work.

When the phone rang a few minutes later, it was a four-way conference call set up by my sister Keely for herself, our sister Jean, my mother, and me.

"I found the story on the Internet this morning when I logged on to check my e-mail," Keely said. " 'Cook Show Host Delivers Baby!' Why didn't you call and tell us?"

I repeated that the paper's version of events was a major exaggeration, and that I didn't deserve the credit I was given. Reassuring them that all was well with me, I changed the subject to tonight's TV show. "It's a Halloween theme."

Jean asked, "What kind of a costume are you going to wear?"

"I have a witch's hat and cape from when I used to take Eileen trick or treating."

My mother protested, "Oh, no. Wear an outfit that makes you look pretty. But not too sexy, because children will be watching."

"Try to appeal to the fathers without

alienating the mothers," Keely said.

"I'll think of something middle-of-the-road," I promised.

My mother and sisters said they'd be watching tonight, they wished me luck, and we did a round of good-byes.

I turned off the phone to let voice mail take messages in order to concentrate on the baking.

And then the doorbell rang.

Wiping my flour-dusted hands on a dish towel, I hurried through the living room and looked out the front window. On the stoop, and pressing the bell again, was a dark-haired woman in her late thirties, with a sharp, pointed nose and thin lips. Expensively dressed in a navy blue wool suit with a large gold broach in the shape of an owl on one lapel, she would have been almost attractive, if not for the scowl on her face. I'd never seen her before.

I opened the door. "Yes?"

"Are you Della Carmichael?"

"Yes, I am. What can I do for you?"

"I'm Lily Robbins." Her tone implied that I should know who she was, but I didn't have even a glimmer of an idea.

I don't like to play guess-who-I-am games. "This is a very busy morning for me. I don't mean to be rude, but would you tell me why you're here?"

"I'm Lily Robbins — Lily *Owens* Robbins. Lulu Owens's daughter." Her manner was cold, her tone arrogant, but I decided to make allowances because she'd just lost her mother.

"Come in." I opened the door wider and stepped aside. She marched past me into the middle of the living room.

I said, "I'm so sorry about what happened to your mother. Won't you sit down?"

"No."

My expression of sympathy hadn't made her any more charming. "Then what can I do for you?"

"I heard you were the last one to see my mother alive."

Matching her tone, I said, "That's not precisely true. I was with your mother early on the evening she was killed, but I left before that happened. Incidentally, how is it that you know where I live?"

"In Mother's desk, there was a list of all the personnel at the channel, with addresses and phone numbers. That's not important. What I want to know is, was she wearing her diamond rings when you were with her?"

"Diamond rings?" Mentally, I kicked myself for sounding like an echo. I took a moment to visualize Lulu that night at her house. "She wasn't wearing rings."

"They're missing," Lily Robbins announced. "They're supposed to come to me, but they're gone."

So this icy character was grieving for *jewelry*. I felt like throwing her out of the house, but I restrained myself and remained civil. "Perhaps she kept them in a safety deposit —"

"No. Mother used to wear them all the time, even after she and my father divorced. She said she would give them to me one day, along with her diamond earrings, but they're gone! I've been all through that ridiculous house of hers. The jewelry wasn't insured, but she photographed the pieces anyway and kept them with her homeowner's policy."

My pulse quickened with excitement. "Tracing the missing jewelry could be the way to find your mother's killer. You've got to give those pictures to the police." I reached for the telephone.

"Who are you calling?"

"Detective Hall and Lieutenant O'Hara. They're running the investigation."

I reached Detective Hall at the North Hollywood Station, told him about Lulu Owens's missing jewelry, and put Lily Robbins on the phone.

Hall must have asked her where she was staying because I heard her say, "The Beverly Hills Hotel." She then told him essentially what she had told me. Afterward, she listened briefly and replied, "All right. I'll go back and wait for him — but tell him to hurry up. And when you find the killer, remember that jewelry is supposed to come to me."

Without saying good-bye to Hall, or asking me if I wanted to speak to him again, she hung up the phone. "A Lieutenant O'Hara is going to pick me up at the hotel." With that, she stalked toward the front door.

"You're welcome," I said to her back.

She didn't reply. When the door closed behind Lily Owens Robbins, I thought, *Poor Lulu. With a harpy like that for a daughter, no wonder she was so fond of Faye.*

I went back to my baking but decided to start answering the phone again. Two hours later, John called.

"I deserve hazard pay for spending time with that woman, but the missing jewelry could be the break we need," he said. "We're making copies of the photos to get them to high-end pawn shops and fences."

"Keep me posted?"

"You bet," he said.

■ ■ ■ ■

Before Liddy and I packed her SUV for the show, I took Tuffy for a walk. Tonight's broadcast was going to be live, with an audience; too many people would be there for me to take Tuffy. If Mickey Jordan wanted me to do more taped half-hours, Tuff could resume his TV career then.

Peering into a box of cookies, Liddy said, "I want to be your taster tonight."

"As my friend, you'd be considered a 'plant.' I'm going to let a couple of mothers and kids taste. But I'll save you the goodie of your choice."

"I want one of those little ghosts made out of meringue."

We climbed into her SUV. I put the tote bag with my Halloween costume in it on the floor next to my feet and strapped on my seat belt.

Liddy turned the key in the ignition. "I called Derek Sloan for you," she said.

"Who?"

"Bill's patient, the Jeep dealer. We have an appointment for ten o'clock tomorrow morning."

I said, "Great." But silently, I was hoping

I'd be able to afford Liddy's idea of a bargain.

We were backing down the driveway when a loud series of honks caused Liddy to jam her foot on the brake. I turned around to see a green BMW pulling up to the curb in front of my house.

"It's Faye Bond." I unhooked my seat belt. "Stay here. I'll go see what she wants."

"Tell her not to blast her horn like that. She nearly gave me a heart attack."

Faye got out of her car and hurried to meet me at the bottom of the driveway.

I was surprised, and pleased, to note that she looked much better than she had the times I had seen her before. Her hair used to hang to her shoulders without a style, but recently had been shaped by an expert. Nor was it any longer lifeless beige, but glowed with subtle highlights. Instead of the clothes I'd seen her wear before — too big, and suitable for a much older woman — this afternoon she was in a trendy short skirt and cropped jacket. It was a becoming outfit. She had once seemed skinny, but in these clothes that fit, she was slender, with attractive, if minimal, curves.

"I'm glad I caught you," Faye said.

"It's nice to see you. Is there something you wanted?"

"To go to the TV show with you tonight, if you don't mind. After last week — I mean, I *need* to go again, when it's just *normal*." She clasped her hands and pressed them up under her chin. "I'm having nightmares. . . . Is this . . . ? Am I making any sense?"

"Oh, Faye, I'm so sorry." I reached out to touch her in sympathy and she grabbed my hand in both of hers. Her fingers were cold. "If it will help, of course you can come."

Liddy leaned out the driver's window and waved at Faye. "Hello."

I said to Faye, "You met my friend, Liddy Marshall. Ride with us."

"No, thanks, I'll follow you in my own car, in case it gets to be too hard and I have to leave."

"Of course. I understand."

"I know I'll be early," Faye said. "Do you think they'll let me stay in Lulu's set for a while?"

"It should be all right. Mine is the only show working tonight."

"Thank you," she said, giving me a quick hug. "See you there." She hurried back to her car and I returned to Liddy's.

As I climbed back into the passenger seat, Liddy said, "Faye certainly looks better. What did she want?"

"To be at the show tonight."

Liddy's eyes widened. "Oh, Jeez, I hope that's not a bad omen!"

36

At the Better Living Channel's gate, I identified myself to Angie, the female security woman whose voice I recognized on the intercom.

"Hi, Della," she said. "Congratulations. We got a *lot* more requests for tickets than we have seats."

Liddy grinned and pumped the air with her fist. "Way to go!"

"That's encouraging," I said. "Angie, you remember Faye Bond, Mimi's daughter? She's in the BMW right behind us. She's my guest tonight."

"Oh, that poor little thing. I'll keep the gate open 'til she's in, and I'll get somebody to set up an extra seat."

"Thanks, Angie. See you later."

The big iron gate swung open and we drove though. I told Liddy, "Park beside the double doors into the studio so we can unload."

She stopped where I indicated. Faye drove around us and on into the lot behind the studio. By the time Liddy and I got out and opened the back of the SUV, Faye had joined us.

Seeing three big cardboard boxes, she asked. "Can I help carry?"

"Yes, thanks." I hooked my tote bag over one arm and handed her the lightest box of the three, the one filled with cookies and meringues. Liddy and I each took one of the others.

As we entered the studio, I was surprised to see Stan Evans in his guard uniform. He stretched out his arms toward the boxes. "Let me take those."

"Gladly, but what are you doing here, Stan? Don't you get off at five?"

"Al Franklin's wife had to go to the hospital," he said, "so I'm subbing for him tonight."

He hefted my load and Liddy's, and I relieved Faye of hers. Stan acknowledged Liddy and Faye with a smile and a "Hi."

"I'm sorry about Al's wife," I said. "I hope it isn't serious."

He lifted his shoulders in a "don't know" gesture. "It's surgery of some kind," he said. "She's at St. Joe's in Burbank."

I made a mental note to send her flowers

381

tomorrow morning.

Because the studio was being prepared for the broadcast, the lights were on. There was no danger of tripping as we followed Stan past Car Guy's repair shop set to my kitchen area. We put the three boxes on my preparation counter.

"Oh, look," Liddy said, gesturing at the kitchen. "Somebody's decorated it for Halloween."

Somebody had, and very cleverly. "I like it," I said with enthusiasm. The refrigerator and the front of the oven were bedecked with fake spiderwebs. Black cardboard bats in different sizes hung down from almost invisible wires attached to the bank of lights above. The white sheet and black eyeholes of a ghost fluttered over the sink. A Vampire mask with a pair of bloodred glowing eyes was fixed to the wall of the rear display counter. Another ghost and a witch's broomstick "flew" from more wires above the spectators' seats.

Liddy leaned close to me and whispered, "I wonder if that nasty director of yours brought the spiderwebs and the witch's broom from her place."

I put a finger to my lips to quiet Liddy.

Examining the embellishments, Faye said, "Cool."

She'd been so quiet, I'd almost forgotten she was there and what she wanted to do. I asked Stan, "Is the sound wall locked?"

"Nope. You're the only one shooting tonight." He indicated the red phone on the studio wall. I knew it reached the other sets, the director's control booth, and the security office. The list of extension numbers was posted next to it. "I'll be in the office 'til the audience starts coming. If there's anything you need, just press the 'Two' button and I'll come running."

"Thanks again."

Stan ambled off to the left, toward the door to the front office.

"Do you know where Lulu's set is?" I asked Faye.

"Yes. She used to let me sit behind the camera and watch her while they taped."

"Would you like me to come with you?"

She shook her head. "I'll be all right. I just want to be around her things for a while."

I watched Faye's small figure as she headed to the right, toward the door in the sound wall that led to the two sets at the front of the building. As I joined Liddy behind the counter to begin unpacking the boxes, I glanced up to see that Stan — who'd paused at the doorway to the security office — was gazing at Faye. When he saw me observing him, he quickly retreated into the office and closed the door.

"That boy is interested in Faye," Liddy said. "Even though he didn't say anything to her when we all came in, I could feel it. It's not surprising. Now that she's fixed herself up, she's a cute girl, although I certainly wouldn't have described her as 'cute' a week ago."

"She coming out of her shell," I said.

We went back to arranging the finished Halloween candies and cookies and cupcakes onto the presentation platters and put them on the rear counter. There were a lot of them; I'd made enough for everyone in the audience, plus the studio staff and whatever members of law enforcement Detective Hall might bring with him this evening.

Half an hour before the audience was due to be let into the studio, Liddy and I were in the little dressing room behind the set. I had slipped into my makeshift cat costume. It consisted of a black long-sleeve leotard and black tights, and a short black fake fur skirt. The skirt had once been part of an old costume of Eileen's. She's two sizes smaller than I am, but I'd opened the back seam and stitched in a strip of black fabric a couple of inches wide to make it fit. Another part of her costume was on my head: a pair of black cat ears standing up from a wire frame that was concealed in my hair.

The outfit got an admiring "Me*ooow*," from Liddy. "Now for the finishing touches. Sit."

I sat, and Liddy used her eyebrow pencil to make little dots on either side of my nose and draw cat whiskers on my cheeks. Stepping back to view her handiwork, she said, "Purrrr-fect."

We were interrupted by a staccato series of taps on the door. A man called, "You decent in there?"

I recognized the voice. "Come in, Mickey."

Mickey Jordan opened the door and immediately started to say something, but he saw Liddy and stopped. I introduced them. Liddy gave him a warm hello.

Mickey told her, "Nice to meet you," and in the same breath asked her if she minded leaving so he could talk to me.

Liddy wasn't offended by his brusque manner; I'd told her about Mickey so she knew what to expect. "I have to go and move my car into the parking lot," she said.

Mickey closed the door behind her. Ignoring my costume and my face full of whiskers, he got right to the point.

"F—ing reporters have been all over me since the police got the idea my business enemies are behind what's happened."

"I'm sorry about that, Mickey —"

He waved a hand dismissively. "Don't be sorry. Fact is, the trash talk is good for me."

"How could that be good?"

"Makes people think I'm a dangerous character. Gives me an edge if I want to make a deal with somebody for something they don't want to sell."

"I hadn't thought of being suspected of murder as a business strategy," I said.

"Yeah, well, that's why I'm practically a billionaire and you cook for a living. But, hey, everybody should do what they're good at, right? Anyway, since he's taken a powder, it looks like Hopkins is the son-of-a-bee who killed Mimi and Lulu. I just hope the cops don't find him right away. I want to stay under suspicion for a while longer."

"You are amazing, Mickey." My tone was a combination of awe and irony.

"Thank you," he said. Apparently, he heard the awe but not the irony.

I asked, "What did you want to talk to me about?"

"Faye Bond. Why's that kid here? Angie

said she came with you."

"She was very close to Lulu and wanted to spend a little time in Lulu's set. It's all right that I brought her, isn't it?"

Mickey grimaced. "Personally, I don't give a flying Fig Newton where she goes. She's one rich little chick now that her mother's dead, but I tell you, I'd hate to see a nice guy like Gil get involved with her."

"Gil York? I didn't realize they knew each other."

"They do now. Gil rode out to the studio with me tonight, to see your show. We went to his set so he could try to talk me into buying him an expensive new piece of equipment. She was next door, at Lulu's. I didn't recognize her at first, until I saw her eyes. She's got bad news eyes, Della."

"What do you mean by 'bad news eyes'?"

"I can't explain it in words, but half the money I made was from knowing how to read people's eyes." He smiled ruefully and shrugged. "Ah, what the hell. I'm not getting involved. People are gonna do what they're gonna do. You can't stop 'em, especially if they want to do something stupid." He turned to leave.

"Mickey, wait. I forgot to thank you for having Stan guard my house last night."

"That's okay, but you don't need protection anymore, what with me being innocent — only don't repeat that — and George Hopkins a fugitive. His jig is up, and with the cops looking for him, there's no incentive for Hopkins to try to off you again."

"What if he isn't the killer?"

Mickey caught the doubt in my voice. "You don't think Hopkins is the guy?"

"I don't know, but something doesn't feel right about it. George *might* have killed Mimi. No one seems to know where he was before the show began, so he had opportunity to sabotage the mousse, and his motive might have been revenge. I heard he wasn't at the studio Monday night, so he *might* have killed Lulu and stolen her jewelry because he's apparently in desperate need of money. But what would he gain by killing me? There's at least one big missing piece here, Mickey."

"When he's caught, we'll find out." As Mickey opened the door, he added, "Now go do a great show. You've got nothing to worry about."

I wasn't so sure.

37

My show's theme music was full of eerie notes tonight. A long, sinister "boo" and soft, maniacal laughter accompanied the slightly discordant melody. Quinn Tanner's new recording was a good touch for our Halloween show.

As the tune was beginning to fade down, I entered the set in my cat costume and waved at the expanded audience. Every one of the original thirty seats was filled, and a dozen more had been set up. These formed a new front row just for the children. Most of them were from my Mommy and Me classes, so I knew that the adults sitting immediately behind them were their parents, ready to grab a child if one suddenly decided to get up and wander around.

Ernie Ramirez was at Camera One and Jada Powell operated Camera Two. A pair of large monitors, one on either side of the set, faced the audience to enable everyone to see a close-up of what I'd be concocting.

"Hi," I said, "I'm Della Carmichael. Welcome to this special Halloween edition of *In the Kitchen with Della.* Tonight our subject is *scar-rrr-y* treats. Let's get cooking."

In the far corner of the third row, I saw Faye Bond and Gilmer York sitting together. He whispered something to her; she smiled at him. Mickey would probably think that little exchange was "scary."

"First up," I said, "we're going to bake devilish red velvet cupcakes that we'll decorate with ghosts and bats and creepy crawlies: treats that give you the shivers. For the red velvet cupcakes, we prepare the batter for a red velvet cake, but pour it into cupcake pans instead of regular round cake molds. Cakes made from scratch usually taste better than mix cakes, and they're just about as easy. Think: 'easy scratch' and that will take the fear away. Here's a tip: The two eggs, the two sticks of butter, and the cup of buttermilk" — I indicated the ingredients on the prep counter as I mentioned them — "should all be at room temperature before you begin."

As I beat the sugar and the butter together with the hand mixer, then added the eggs, cocoa, and red food coloring, I explained what I was doing. At the same time, I was keeping an eye on the audience.

Detective Hall stood between Camera One and the monitor. In that spot, he had an unobstructed view of the set and, by turning his head, of the spectators, too.

Scattered through the seats, I saw Officer Cutler, the woman who was the first uniform to responded to George Hopkins's 911 call, and also three men in their twenties who were wearing casual clothes but who looked like police officers. Others might not pick them out as such, but I'd been married to a member of the LAPD for twenty years and recognized the similar short haircuts and the intense concentration of young gladiators on duty.

I didn't catch sight of John anywhere.

Smiling, chatting, and recounting the story of how I learned to make red velvet cake from my grandmother — and once made the mistake of using the dregs of an old bottle of wine vinegar instead of the correct white distilled vinegar in the batter, with *awful* results — I continued the process of combining and mixing until the batter was glossy and ready to pour.

I saw that Liddy was in the same place where she'd been standing last week, behind Camera Two. Once again, my loyal friend was smiling at me with encouragement.

Although I had no reason to expect it, I'd thought that NDM might come to the studio tonight, but he wasn't here. He hadn't said anything about it, but then we hadn't talked since he left my house at four thirty this morning.

Was it only this morning? The day had been so busy, it seemed as though it already had been forty-eight hours long.

Pushing personal thoughts away, I distributed the red velvet cupcake batter into a prepared twelve-cup baking pan, slid it into the oven, and brought up the already baked cupcakes from where they'd been resting on the back counter.

"Here are some that I baked earlier, to show you how they look when they're finished and cool."

I turned them out onto a platter and demonstrated how to assemble creepy creatures to put on the cupcakes.

"First, we cover the tops with frosting: chocolate, vanilla, and *bloodred* to drip down the sides. We get the 'blood' by stirring a few drops of this red food coloring — the same kind that I used in our devilish red cake batter — into some of the vanilla frosting."

Next, I showed them how to shape marshmallows into ghosts and skulls, using mini chocolate chips for the eyeholes.

In my earpiece, I heard Quinn start the countdown for the first commercial break.

"Okay, kids," I said, "we're all going to have some of these tasty creations later. But when we come back in a couple of minutes — and your parents are going to hate me for this — I'm going to show you how to *gross out* your friends."

That elicited wild "yeahs" from the children and groans from the parents.

While we were off the air, I reached down to the shelf below the prep counter and brought out two large plastic containers and removed the tops. No one in the seats out front could see that one was full of peeled grapes and the other of thick spaghetti.

Waiting for the red light to come back on, I spoke to the kids, asking what they would be wearing for Halloween. This was a trick I used in teaching the cooking classes that included children: You keep their attention by getting them to talk about themselves.

Commercials over. Camera One's red light came on.

I smiled into the lens and said, "Welcome back. I'm Della Carmichael, and this is our special Halloween *In the Kitchen with Della*. Now, you kids in the front row. I want a couple of volunteers. Who is daring enough to come up here and, with your eyes closed, stick your hands into my bowls of horror?"

Lots of giggling and nudging. One hand went up. Then another. A girl and a boy.

"Okay," I said, pointing to those two. "Let's see how brave you are."

Camera Two swung around to catch the young volunteers as they left their seats and approached me. In our classes, these children always had been comfortable with me, so I wasn't concerned about the game I was going to play with them. I wouldn't have done this with a child I didn't know.

I asked the girl, "Would you like to go first?" She nodded slowly, a little nervous but full of the spirit of adventure. Even though I knew it, I asked, "What's your name?"

"Olivia," she said softly.

"Olivia, that's a pretty name." Turning to the boy, I asked, "And what's your name, young man?"

"Brian."

"When I was little, I had a boyfriend named Brian. Are you married?"

"No!" He shook his head with such vehemence that the audience laughed.

"Okay, Olivia and Brian, close your eyes. That's right. Good. Olivia, give me your hand." She did, but tentatively. I guided it to the bowl of peeled grapes. "Now put your hand right in here."

She did, with a shivery squeal of "Ee-ewww."

"Eeewww is right," I said. "You're holding a handful of *eyeballs!*"

Little Olivia screamed and jerked her hand out, but when she opened her eyes and she saw the real contents of the bowl, she giggled.

Brian still had his eyelids squeezed tight. "Do me! Do me!" He was practically jumping up and down with excitement.

"Brian, you certainly are brave." I took his hand and guided it toward the bowl of spaghetti. "Now reach in — reach deep."

He did.

"Squish your hand around," I told him. "Do you have any idea what you're holding?"

Brian shook his head. "No."

"It's a bowl full of big, long, juicy . . . *worms!*"

Brian said, "Yuck," but he kept squishing, and he was grinning.

"I guess Brian must really like fat, juicy worms," I said.

The audience was chuckling. As we went to the next commercial break, I cleaned the children's hands with paper towels, escorted them back to their chairs, and showed the audience the real food.

I returned to my prep counter and organized the candies and cookies for the next segment.

When Camera Two's red light came on, I said, "Now we're going to turn red gumdrops into devils, make spiders out of black licorice, and decorate sugar cookies with spiderwebs made out of melted chocolate."

I moved down the counter and picked up several strings of the licorice. Before I could make the first twist, there was a bright flash in the rigging above me as one of the powerful bulbs burst. The heavy light casing crashed down onto the counter. With a sickening lurch, I realized it was the very spot where I'd been standing scant seconds before.

Too surprised — or too shocked — to be afraid, I grinned at Camera Two and said, "Welcome to the thrills of live television. We just lost one of our lights, folks. That's all."

In my earpiece, I heard Quinn yell at the engineer, "Punch up fourteen!" On the small monitor in front of my counter, I saw a commercial for auto insurance go out over the air.

Hall started toward me, and in the audience, the North Hollywood police contingent stood up, but he waved them back down. A few of the parents had gasped when the light fell, but otherwise they were staying calm so that the children didn't panic. Luckily, other than the flying ghost and the witch's broom, there was nothing above their heads that might fall.

Over the loud speaker from the director's booth, we all heard Quinn Tanner say, "Keep your places. No one was hurt. Once in a great while a little mishap will occur."

Hall ignored her command and was around to my side of the counter in seconds.

Right behind him, having raced down from the director's control booth, was Mickey Jordan, eyes blazing with fury.

"What the —" Realizing that children were in the room, he swallowed the expletive on the tip of his tongue and instead growled, "What happened?"

Detective Hall slipped on a pair of latex gloves; I thought he must keep them in every pocket. He picked up the light and the wire attached to it and peered at them.

He said quietly to Mickey and me, "This just looks like an old wire. I'll take it to the lab, but I don't see any evidence of tampering."

"So it was only an accident?" I asked.

397

"Looks that way right now, but I want my people to go over all the rigging up there."

Mickey balled his hands into fists. "The bastard I bought this channel from never replaced anything. Maintenance? It's like he never heard the word."

Outside of camera range, a studio electrician had opened up a ladder, climbed it, and was aiming a handheld spotlight so that it filled in the illumination we'd lost when the light casing fell. I saw him speak softly into his mobile phone.

Quinn's voice came over the loud speaker again. "We're ready to broadcast. Della, get back into your place. Mickey, Mister Hall, please clear the set so we can do our final segment."

Using one sheet of paper towel to brush tiny shards of fallen glass from the burst bulb off of my prep counter, I caught the sharp little bits in a second sheet I held below the edge. Then I balled them up and dropped them into the trash container. At the moment, there was nothing I could do about the pieces that crunched under my feet, but I'd make sure that the cleaning crew swept them up.

Hall took the fallen light with him as he and Mickey stepped back behind Camera One. The red light went on.

I'd made the decision not to refer to the incident again, so I said brightly, "In the time we have left, we're going to make our monsters and decorate our cookies. Then everyone in the audience will have little bags of goodies to take home. Even the grown-ups."

The show finished without any further problems. As the end credits rolled on the screen, I began passing around the platters of decorated cookies and cupcakes, and handing out the take-home bags. The children chose what they wanted while the adults applauded.

Except for the near miss, the Halloween show had gone as planned.

As I smiled at the spectators and waved good night, I noticed that at some point Gilmer York and Faye had left the studio.

When the members of the audience, excepting Hall, his people, and Liddy, had filed out, Stan Evans closed the studio door and stood in front of it. His mouth was turned down and his lower lip stuck out in a pout. Or perhaps he was simply exhausted from having had to stay awake all night, guarding my house.

Quinn Tanner came down from the control booth, conferred with Mickey, and addressed the two electricians on the scene. She pointed to the racks of lights above the set. "No one goes home," she told them, "until every single thing up there is checked for stability. Not only on this set, but also on Car Guy's. Tomorrow morning, before anyone steps onto either of the sets in front, I want everything there checked, too."

Liddy and I were in the dressing room where I packed the tote bag with the clothes I'd worn to the studio.

"I'm too tired to change again," I said. "Since I'm wearing a cat costume three days before Halloween, please try not to get stopped for speeding."

In a teasing tone, she said, "I wonder if there's a law against being disguised as an animal when it's not Halloween."

The door was open, but Detective Hall knocked anyway.

"Come in," I said.

"No. I wanted to say that you two can go home. We'll examine the wire attachment, but I don't think there was any crime in that falling light. Except neglect. I've told Jordan he has two weeks to make sure everything in the studio is the way it should be, because then I'm sending a city inspector to check it out."

Liddy said, "So it was an accident — no

one *tried* to hurt Della tonight?"

"Things fall." Detective Hall looked at me, and with just a hint of a smile on his lips, he added, "As the man said, 'sometimes a cigar is just a cigar.' "

That night I dreamed of cigars: cigars that exploded into the air, and fell to earth in pieces of what had once been a Mustang.

38

Liddy picked me up Friday morning for our trip to the Jeep dealership.

"Now when you see something you love, don't tell Derek you love it," Liddy cautioned. "We can get an even better deal if he thinks he's talking you into something."

I smiled, remembering that about eighteen years ago I'd had this same conversation with Mack, but in reverse. We were on our way to look for the Mustang he'd always wanted. As excited as a teenager, he'd told me, "When we get to the lot, I'm going to play it as though I'm not really interested in a Mustang, but I'm just there because I'm looking at lots of different makes. As soon as I spot the one I want, that's when I'll start criticizing it. Play along with me, okay? Back me up in whatever I say?"

I promised. Then we got to the lot and strolled down a line of preowned Mustangs. As soon as Mack spotted the one he wanted he said to the salesman, "That's it! How much?" The result was that while Mack negotiated a little, I knew that he wanted that particular car more than he wanted the best possible deal on it. In the end, the salesman was happy, which secretly I felt wasn't good news for us. But Mack was happy, and that's what mattered. He treasured and babied that car until the day he died.

Sloan's Jeeps was on Vineland Avenue, in the San Fernando Valley, not far from the Better Living Channel. The dealership covered most of a city block along Vineland. Festooned with bright red, green, and blue triangular flags flapping in the breeze all along its length, Sloan's Jeeps was impossible to miss.

Liddy turned into the driveway and stopped next to the bungalow-style office.

"There's Derek Sloan," she said, pointing to an exceptionally good-looking man in his early forties who stood in the office doorway, making a note on a clipboard. His skin was the color of Godiva chocolate. He wore a custom-tailored sports jacket the color of Cream of Wheat, and brown twill slacks. If I'd seen him anywhere else, I would have guessed he was an actor.

Sloan looked up, saw Liddy, and grinned.

Radiating good cheer, he headed toward us as we got out of her SUV.

"Hi, Derek," Liddy said. "This is my friend, Della Carmichael. She wants to see your best Jeeps."

I extended my hand to Derek Sloan; he took it in a warm grasp. "I want to see your most *practical* Jeeps," I said, hoping that he would correctly interpret my choice of the word "practical" to mean "economical."

He patted my hand that was still in his, and said, "Got it." He let go. "Now, what kind of vehicle are you looking for? I mean, what are your daily needs?"

Liddy jumped in and explained that I ran a cooking school and so had to cart boxes to my classes.

"I don't want anything too big," I said. "I'm used to small cars."

"Were you planning to keep your present car or trade it in?"

"Neither," I said. I didn't feel like telling him that my Mustang had been reduced to hunks of barely identifiable metal. Although I hadn't thought to ask her to, Liddy remained discreetly silent.

"Okay," Sloan said. "Let's take a walk around the lot and you tell me what speaks to you."

"I like the way you put that," I said, and

began to feel more comfortable in this venture.

Derek Sloan's property was a festival of bright, gleaming vehicles in vivid colors.

As the three of us worked our way up one aisle and down another, I said, "I had no idea there were so many different types."

Some Jeeps were much larger than I'd expected, with different features and configurations than I'd noticed in the course of driving around town. Each time I paused to inspect a particular model, I looked at the sticker price. I was unfamiliar with the cost of Jeeps, and most of them were more expensive than I'd hoped they'd be.

"I do like that one," I said, pointing to a silver gray Jeep that was a bit smaller than the other designs. It had sleek lines that appealed to me. "What is it?"

"That's the new Compass," Sloan said. "It's an excellent choice if you need storage space and four doors but don't want one of the big guys." He opened the driver's door. "Get in and see how it feels."

I climbed in and settled myself behind the wheel.

"It has generous head room, shoulder room, and leg room. And your passengers have good leg room, too."

While I touched the various knobs and dials and checked the position of the hand brake, he talked about cargo capacity, rack and pinion steering, independent front suspension, and front and rear disc brakes. I liked what I heard, but even though the Compass was less expensive than the other Jeeps I'd seen, the price was still higher than I'd hoped to pay.

"This one is *you*," Liddy said.

"It's very nice," I told Sloan, "but . . ."

"I know, price is a factor, but if you don't have your heart set on any particular color I can make you a marvelous deal," he said.

"I hadn't even thought about color. What do you mean?"

He politely offered his hand to help me out of the Compass. "I want you ladies to see something I have behind the office."

Sloan set a rapid pace, but Liddy and I kept up easily. As we rounded the corner of the office-bungalow, I saw another Compass, this one in a beautiful shade of blue. I felt the fluttering of excitement in my chest. This vehicle "spoke" to me.

"I'm forced to make you a great deal on this one," Sloan said.

Liddy asked, "Why? What's wrong with it?"

"I can't sell it as new because it has 196 miles on it. It left the lot two days ago but came back yesterday. A case of buyer's remorse. Actually, it was the buyer's *wife's* remorse; she wanted a Lexus."

This sounded a little too good to be true. "The man drove it for almost 200 miles. Are you sure there's nothing wrong with it mechanically?" I asked.

"Absolutely," Sloan said. "I was suspicious, too, but my mechanics went over it carefully before I refunded his money. It's in new-car condition and comes with a complete warranty, but according to the rules, it's now a used car."

I took it for a test drive, with Sloan in front and Liddy in back. Before I'd circled the second block, I knew that I wanted this vehicle. "How much?" I asked.

Sloan named the price that was almost as low as I'd hoped, and much better than I had feared.

It took about an hour of paperwork, arranging financing, filling out forms, and calling Ed Gardner at Western Alliance Insurance to cover the car, but a little before noon, the vehicle was mine.

I hugged Liddy and thanked her for bringing me to Derek Sloan, thanked Sloan, said good-bye to the two of them, and climbed into the driver's seat of my new marine blue Jeep Compass with the medium slate gray interior.

Driving home, it was easy to get used to the controls. I liked its smooth ride and the way the steering wheel fit my hand. I thought that this vehicle and I were going to have a long, pleasant relationship, and I was thankful for its first owner's buyer's remorse.

Eileen was backing down the driveway in her red VW Rabbit just as I approached my house. Seeing me wave at her, she stopped, got out of her car, and came running over to me.

"Wow," she said. "Nice wheels. When did you get this?"

"About thirty-five minutes ago."

"It's just right for you, Aunt Del. Conservative, but sort of hot."

"Thank you, I think. But why are you here? I'd rather you stay at Liddy's for a few more days, until we're sure it's safe for you to be here again."

"I came by to pick up clothes because I'm going up to Lake Arrowhead with some friends. We don't have any classes Monday, so we'll come back Monday night."

"Have fun," I said. Because I wasn't her mother, and because she was twenty years old, I resisted the urge to ask her if any of those friends were male. *Lord, with Eileen, I've turned into my own mother.*

Eileen's eyes were bright with excitement. "I left a note for you on the kitchen table, but you don't have to read it now because I'll tell you. It's great news! Not only did I finish your business plan, and ran it by my professor who said it was good work, but . . ." She drew out that one syllable word to the length of a short sentence.

"But . . . What?"

"You're going to be thrilled! I found us an *investor!*"

I couldn't believe that I understood her. "You can't mean — someone wants to invest in fudge?"

"In the fudge *business,*" she said. "The start-up money isn't much, but we had to have a backer. Of course, we'll need a lawyer to draw up the contract."

"Who is the backer?"

"I don't want to tell you right now," she said.

My Suspicion Alarm was going *ding, ding, ding.* Afraid of the answer, I said, "You didn't ask Liddy for the money, did you? Or your father?"

She raised her right hand as though on the witness stand. "Absolutely not."

"That's a relief."

"I wouldn't go to family or friends. Our backer is strictly a businessperson. Okay? Trust me?"

"Of course I trust you."

"All you have to do is make enough fudge for thirty boxes, two dozen pieces per box, and have them ready by Monday night. I'll bring simple white boxes, and we'll fill them up. The backer has a distribution plan that he — I mean that this *person* — needs to test, and wants to start on Tuesday."

I did a quick mental calculation of twenty-four pieces of fudge times thirty. "That's seven hundred and twenty pieces of fudge."

"You can do it, Aunt Del," she said confidently. "Gotta go meet my friends. See you Monday night!"

With a happy wave, Eileen raced back to her car and drove away.

Seven hundred and twenty pieces of fudge by Monday. That was going to take time and a lot of sugar and butter and chocolate and the rest.

I started to drive up into the carport when I heard a familiar engine roar behind me. Turning, I saw NDM screech to a stop behind my Jeep. I winced to see the dent in the middle of the Maserati's hood from a piece of my exploding Mustang.

NDM got out of his muscle car. Before he

came up to my driver's side window, he took a good look at the Compass.

"Your new car?" he asked.

I nodded in the affirmative. "As of an hour or so ago."

"It suits you."

"What do you mean by that?"

"It's built for endurance." He smiled at me in a way that made my insides blush. "I'd like to take a ride with you," he said, "but I've got to go out of town."

"Where?"

"My source in North Hollywood tells me Hall has proof that George Hopkins sold Lulu Owens's jewelry."

"That's pretty damning evidence, isn't it?"

"It's the best he's got so far. Hall doesn't know it yet, but on my own, I've tracked Hopkins to Las Vegas, and I think I know where to find him there."

"If you're right, what will you do?"

"Get a story. Then I'll notify Hall where he is and let the Las Vegas PD hang on to him until he can be extradited back here. You don't need anyone to guard your house now."

"How did you know about that?"

"I saw the studio kid — Stan — outside when I left yesterday morning." NDM shook his head in annoyance. "He wasn't

411

doing you any good; he was sound sleep in his car. Forget him. New subject. When I get back from Vegas, I'd like to take you to dinner."

"You still want to find out what I like to read?"

"Among other things," he said.

39

The next day, there was no time to think about anything except my work. Saturday's cooking school classes were on advanced cake baking: a frosted, layered angel food cake topped with fresh fruit, my own red velvet cake variation with cherry filling and a warm sauce, a moist Bundt that a friend calls her "Orange Funeral Cake," and finally two types of cheesecake. One was a chocolate that I'd developed through many experiments, and the other was a vanilla with a chocolate brownie crust.

Since I'd gone on TV, my classes were filled, with a waiting list. I almost missed the early, easier days when I had only a few students. *Almost.* This cooking school had to be my security, because there were no guarantees in television.

As much as I enjoyed the Saturday classes, after a long day of tasting batters and frostings, all I'd wanted for dinner was a bowl of soup. I was relieved that there were no classes scheduled for Sunday this week. It would be Halloween, and a majority of my regular students had said they'd be getting ready to give or to attend costume parties.

First thing Sunday morning, I organized the wicker picnic basket full of different kinds of miniature candy bars and individual boxes of raisins and bags of dried fruits that I would pass out to the horde of costumed children I expected to come trick or treating after dark. I put the basket on the table by the front door so it would be handy when the time came.

By midmorning, I was up to my eyebrows in fudge. I'd already made five batches of the thirty that Eileen needed by Monday evening. My right arm was beginning to ache from the necessary stirring. Glancing at the clock, I saw that I could enjoy a guilt-free respite by taking Tuffy for a brisk walk.

About twenty minutes before, he'd scratched on the door to go out into the backyard. On unusually warm days, as this one had turned out to be, he liked to sun himself on the patio or nap in the soft grass.

I quickly washed and dried my hands, and took his leash down from the hook on the wall beside the refrigerator. After first making sure that Emma was not near enough to dash outside, I opened the door. Tuffy was dozing on the grass, near the back gate.

"Here, Tuffy. Let's go for a walk."

I saw him moving where he lay on the ground, but he didn't get up and come trotting toward me as he always did when he heard the magic word, "walk." Even before I could form the thought, an icy jab of fear pierced me. Instinctively, I dropped the leash and ran to him.

What I saw made me gasp in alarm: Tuffy's muscles were twitching. He was having a seizure!

"Oh, dear God, no!" I was about to fly back into the house to call his veterinarian when I spotted something near his head: a ball of ground meat. I snatched it up and saw little pellets inside. I recognized what they were: snail bait. I'd seen Liddy use it. Snail bait was poison. Tuffy could die!

Clutching the ball of meat, I raced inside, grabbed the wall phone and dialed the number for Dr. Jeffrey Marks's Rancho Park Veterinary Clinic. Even though it was Sunday, some staff was always on duty before their two p.m. opening time.

A young woman receptionist answered, and I identified myself as Tuffy's owner.

"He's eaten some snail bait. Is Dr. Marks there?"

"No, he isn't, but Dr. Fernandez is. I'll tell her you're on your way."

"Thank you." My hands were shaking so much I almost dropped the receiver.

I had to get Tuffy to the car, but how? He weighed seventy-four pounds. Too big for me to carry, but — I grabbed a fresh bath towel from the top of the washing machine and ran back outside.

Tuffy was still having seizures. By lifting first his shoulders and then his hips, I maneuvered him onto the towel. Using it as a litter, I dragged it to the back door and gave silent thanks that the door was set flush with the patio. No steps.

Faster than I would have thought possible, I managed to drag the towel with Tuffy on it through the house. From a crystal dish on the front table, I snatched my house and car keys. No time to go to the bedroom for my wallet. If I was stopped for speeding without having my license with me, I didn't care.

Outside the front door were two concrete steps before I could get to the path leading to the carport. By holding the top half of his body and the towel, I managed to ease him down the steps without hurting him, but I knew that I wouldn't be able to get him up into the Jeep without help.

Desperate, I looked out at the street. Cars moving meant people driving.

I ran toward the street, waving my arms, yelling, "Help, please! Help me!"

An older man saw me, slammed on his brakes, and called out, "What's the matter?"

"I need help to lift my dog into the Jeep so I can get him to the hospital."

Quick as lightning, this silver-haired stranger got out of his car and hurried beside me across the front lawn.

I opened the rear door of the Jeep. With each of us taking one end of the makeshift litter, we managed to get Tuffy up onto the rear seat, where he lay, his body convulsing.

Tears streamed down my cheeks as I thanked the man and climbed into the driver's seat.

I heard him call, "Good luck," as I drove away as fast as I dared, praying that I wouldn't have to stop suddenly and throw Tuffy off the seat and onto the floor.

Dr. Jeffrey Marks's Rancho Park Veterinary Clinic was a one-story building in West Los Angeles, on Pico Boulevard, east of Overland. With every second precious, it was a tremendous break that the Sunday traffic was relatively light. I made it to the back door of the hospital in eleven minutes.

One of Jeffrey Marks's associate veterinarians, Dr. Rina Fernandez, was waiting for us at the door. She was petite, with long curly brown hair and warm green eyes, and seeing her gave me a surge of hope. A young male assistant was with her; his face was familiar, but I was in such a state I couldn't recall his name. He opened the rear door and lifted Tuffy into his arms.

With Dr. Fernandez leading the way, and me following the assistant carrying Tuffy, we hurried into a treatment room. The young man — now I remembered, Juan — lowered Tuffy carefully onto the exam table.

"I reached Dr. Marks," Dr. Fernandez said. "He's on his —"

Before she could finish the sentence, I saw the familiar figure of Tuffy's longtime veterinarian coming into the room.

He wasted not a second. "What happened?"

I told him about finding Tuffy, and pulled the smashed ball of meat and snail bait pellets out of my pocket. Using a paper towel, Dr. Fernandez took it from me and went into the laboratory.

I hadn't seen her come in behind him, but

I was suddenly aware of Dr. Marks's pretty blonde wife, Mari. She took my hand and said softly, "Let's go sit down."

I wanted to stay with Tuffy, as I had through all of his inoculations and blood tests over the years, but I knew she was right. She led me to the waiting room as Dr. Marks and Dr. Fernandez, who'd returned from the lab, went to work trying to save Tuffy's life.

Because the hospital hadn't yet opened for its Sunday hours, Mari and I were alone in the waiting area, which was divided by a whimsical stained glass panel into the "canine" section and the "feline" section. When the office was busy, separating dogs and cats kept things relatively tranquil.

After a few minutes, when her quiet voice and pleasant chat had calmed me, I realized part of the job description of a veterinarian's wife was that she be an amateur psychologist. When I was breathing normally and was no longer in tears, I became aware that she'd settled one of the hospital's pet Siamese cats in my lap. I was stroking its soft fur as she told me about the female German shepherd they'd adopted and about what their college-age children were doing.

Dr. Marks finally emerged from the treatment room.

I felt my heart pound with fear. "How is he?"

"He's going to make it," Dr. Marks said. "You got him here just in time."

Tears started streaming down my face again, but this time I was weeping with relief.

Mari handed me a box of Kleenex.

Dr. Marks said, "We put in an IV catheter to decrease the seizures and muscle tremors. He'll have to stay here overnight. Maybe for a couple of nights. I'll know tomorrow, but the good news is that he's going to be all right."

"Someone tried to poison him," I said.

"I know. I saw the snail bait in the hamburger ball."

He ran a hand over his thick brown hair and his handsome features tightened with anger. I sensed that we were united in rage against anyone who would do such a thing.

40

Driving home from the veterinary hospital, my heart was full of gratitude for the skills of Doctors Marks and Fernandez, and to Mrs. Marks, for her kindness to me. Tuffy would survive. In spite of my happiness about that, I ached with sadness. This would be the first time Tuffy had been away from home overnight since he was a puppy.

My pain at almost losing him turned to fury at whoever had tried to kill him with poisoned meat. I tried to imagine who could have done such a terrible thing, to try to kill an innocent animal that had never hurt a soul.

A troublesome teenage boy lived around the corner. I saw him throw a rock at Tuffy last year, but after I spoke to his mother, he hadn't bothered us again. Since that one incident, I hadn't had a problem with anyone in the area. It was a pleasant neighborhood of people who kept their lawns neat, cleaned up after their dogs, and didn't leave the garbage cans out after pickup.

Pulling into the carport, I told myself that there was no point in trying to figure it out now. There was too much to do before tonight. As I walked up the path, I stopped to straighten two of the Halloween cutouts on the lawn. The black cat with its back arched was leaning to one side, and the cardboard ghost beside it had fallen onto the grass, where I'd knocked it over in my rush to get Tuffy into the Jeep.

I straightened the cat, and with the heel of my hand, I pushed the stake that held the ghost back into the ground. The rest of the Halloween figures were standing up as they were supposed to, and the grinning orange crepe paper jack-o'-lantern I'd hung above the bell was still in place.

Emma met me when I opened the door. She hadn't come running at the sound of my key in the lock. She was sitting there, looking worried. I believe absolutely that animals can worry, as well as feel other emotions. Emma's secure world was turned upside down when I rushed out of the house with Tuffy. Now I had come back alone. She stared up at me, and I read in her eyes the words she couldn't speak.

I picked her up and nestled her against

my chest, taking some comfort in the warmth of her fur and the feel of her little heartbeat. Stroking her, I said softly, "Tuffy's going to be all right. He'll come home tomorrow."

I carried her with me into the kitchen and gently set her down on the floor next to the sink. I refilled Tuffy's water bowl, because she liked to drink out of it, and put it down beside her. She took a few laps, then curled up to watch me work.

It was four o'clock. In two hours or so, the children would start coming around in their costumes, with parents, most of which would be costumed, too. As soon as I showered and put on my Halloween cat outfit — but only the black leotard top with black slacks and the cat ears on my head — I'd have to continue making the batches of fudge that Eileen was going to give to our mystery backer on Tuesday morning.

I was glad I'd already made the eight little individual white ramekins of crème brûlée I'd promised Liddy for her dinner party. She was entertaining three of Bill's fraternity brothers and their wives tonight.

When Liddy arrived just after five, my right arm and shoulder were stiff again from stirring multiple batches of fudge. I had decided not to tell her about Tuffy being in the hospital because I knew it would upset her. I'd tell her when he was home again.

"The custard is ready," I said as I led her into the kitchen. "All I have to do is make the hard sugar crust on top."

"You look so cute in those cat ears," she said. "But you forgot your face." She took her eyebrow pencil from her purse and quickly replicated the dots and whiskers she'd drawn on me Thursday evening.

Finished, she stepped back, viewed her handiwork, and uttered a self-satisfied, "Excellent."

"Thanks again."

Liddy looked at the counter where the pumpkin she'd carved with the elephant sat. "You keeping that other elephant out of the room?" she asked.

"I'm managing." But I wasn't going to tell her *how.* Not just yet.

"Good girl."

I got my cook's torch from the counter and removed the eight individual dishes of crème brûlée out of the refrigerator. Liddy sprinkled a coating of sugar on top of the custards as I switched on the torch and flamed the sugar until each of the custards had a hard crust. Together, we packed them in the box in which she'd carry them home.

"Enjoy your party," I said. "Tell me all

about it tomorrow."

"I will. One of those wives was a girl Bill liked in college. I hope she's gained a ton of weight."

Chuckling, I hurried ahead to open the front door for her — and Liddy almost collided with Faye Bond. The young girl's eyes were so red, it was clear she'd been crying.

"Oh!" Faye said to me. "I'm sorry. You're busy. I'll go."

"No, it's all right. Come in."

Liddy said "Hello, Faye. Happy Halloween." With a cheerful grin, she hurried to her car with the pots of crème brûlée.

Closing the door behind Liddy, I asked, "Are you all right, Faye? Has something happened?"

"Halloween." Her voice was little more than a whisper; I had to lean forward to hear her. "This is the first Halloween in eight years I haven't spent with Lulu."

"Come into the kitchen with me. I'm making fudge."

"Can I help?"

"You certainly can. I could use an extra arm for stirring."

I offered Faye a piece of the fudge that I'd made earlier. She bit into it, and her reaction was a gratifying, "Wow, yummy." While she ate a second piece, she perched on the kitchen stool and watched me take out a new pot and put together the ingredients for another batch of fudge.

"Tell me about your Halloweens with Lulu," I said.

"When I was little, she used to take me trick or treating. Mother said Halloween was low class, but she let us go. I guess she thought we were low class. Anyway, when I got too old to go around in a costume, Lulu let me help her give out the stuff to the little kids who came to her house. She called me her Halloween elf. . . . I really loved Lulu."

Faye took to stirring fudge with enthusiasm. I rewarded her by putting the crown from an old Halloween princess costume of Eileen's on her head.

Both of our fudge-stirring arms were getting tired by the time I realized it was after six. I poured the last of our new batches into the pans in which they would harden.

Faye followed me into the living room. We looked out the front window and saw the first wave coming down the street: little ghosts and witches and pirates and superheroes, accompanied by men and women dressed as a nurse, vampires, and a baseball player. There was also an Incredible Hulk among the chaperones, and a ninja garbed all in black.

Faye began to whimper. "I can't do this."

I showed her to Eileen's bedroom. "Lie down," I said. "I'll check on you later."

Trick or treating lasted for two hours. By then, Faye was in a deep sleep. I covered her with a light blanket and turned off the bedside lamp. I thought it might be a good thing for her if she slept there all night.

It was quiet inside my house, and quiet outside. The adorable children in their costumes and their accompanying parents were gone. I pictured moms and dads in their homes, washing painted little faces or dividing the contents of treat bags into portions for the kids to enjoy over the coming days.

By nine o'clock I was exhausted, from the trauma of nearly losing Tuffy and from making all those batches of fudge. I was looking forward to falling into bed . . . but then a faint uneasiness began to creep into my senses.

I held my breath and listened intently. The house was quiet. Too quiet . . . I told myself that I was imagining things because Tuffy wasn't here. Even when he was asleep, I had still felt his presence in the house. No, this silence was different somehow.

Had I locked the back door when I left

the house in such a frenzy to get Tuffy to the doctor?

Yes, I'd locked it.

I'm sure I locked it.

Just to reassure myself, I went through the laundry room to the back door.

Yes, it was locked. I shook my head, silently chiding myself for letting my imagination conjure a goblin that didn't exist.

A line from one of Shakespeare's plays popped into my head. I'd used it when I taught English, the bit from *A Midsummer Night's Dream:* "Or in the night, imagining some fear, how easy is a bush supposed a *bear.*"

Shakespeare's characters didn't have telephones to use to call their best friends, but I did. I'd ask Liddy if Bill's college girlfriend had, indeed, put on weight.

I reached for the wall receiver and put it too my ear.

No dial tone. The phone was dead.

Suddenly Emma let out a bloodcurdling *yowl* behind me.

I whirled around — just in time to see a masked figure swing a hatchet at my head!

41

Lunging to the side, I twisted away just in time for the blow to miss my head, but I stumbled against the kitchen stool and went down. Before I could get up, he was on me.

We rolled across the floor, with me kicking and scratching at any part of him I could touch. He grunted and cursed at me, but his voice was muffled by the mask that covered his face; I couldn't recognize his voice.

Whoever he was, he was in what I realized was a ninja costume, and he was a lot stronger than I and crazed enough to kill me. On the floor, I was so vulnerable that he *would* kill me.

He had a hatchet, and superior strength.

I needed a weapon.

Desperation, and a powerful will to live, pumped me full of adrenaline. It gave me the strength to yank out of his grasp, grab the edge of the counter, and pull myself up.

Knowing this might be my only chance, I lunged for the object at the back of the counter. My ribs smashed painfully against the edge as I stretched to reach my baker's torch.

I managed to grab it just as he jumped me from behind, wrenched me away from the counter, and shoved me hard against the kitchen table. The hand that held the little torch was at my side as I hung on to the plastic pistol grip.

My attacker's arm went around my throat; he was squeezing so tight I could barely breathe.

I gave him a powerful shot in the side with my left elbow. It sent shock waves of pain streaking up my arm and into my shoulder. Probably it hurt me more than it hurt him, but it forced him to loosen his grip just enough for me to coil around.

I clicked the switch on the torch, brought my right hand up, and gave him a blast of fire on the side of his face. It burned through the ninja mask, into the flesh of his cheek.

Screaming, he dropped his grip on me, slapped at his face, and yanked the smoldering fabric over his head, revealing the seared flesh on his cheek — and his face.

Stan Evans!

Without taking a precious second to process the thought, I gave him another blast of fire on his chest. He screamed again and flailed out at me. His wild blows missed.

I dropped the torch, grabbed the kitchen stool, and swung it at him, catching him smack on his collarbone. I heard a *crack* as he reeled backward. He lost his balance. As he fell, the back of his head caught the corner of the table, and he collapsed on the floor, unconscious.

Stan Evans lay there, not moving. But I didn't know how long he'd be out.

I yanked open a kitchen drawer and grabbed one of my chef's knives and the roll of duct tape I'd used to repair an old electric cord until I was able to replace it.

Stan was lying on his face, blood from the blow to his head seeping through his tangle of red hair. Quickly, I pulled both of his arms behind him and, using the tape, bound his wrists together tightly. Then I rolled him over onto his back. The burn on his face was red and ugly. The spot on his chest where I'd given him the second blast of fire was red, too. When he regained consciousness, those burns would be painful. After what I'd had to do to save myself, I knew that I'd never be able to use that torch again for cooking.

I cut more tape off the roll and bound his ankles together. It was time to call John.

My telephone was dead; Stan must have cut the line outside.

Cell phone. It was on the counter next to the stove, where I'd put it this afternoon when I came home from Dr. Marks's hospital.

Bless whoever developed the cell phone.

I heard footsteps in the hall and looked up to see Faye Bond standing in the kitchen doorway.

She was holding Mack's baseball bat in both hands, and she looked ready to swing it — at me.

42

I said, "You can put the bat down, Faye. There's nothing to worry about now. Everything's under control."

Faye didn't put the bat down. She was staring at me, but there was such a strange look in her eyes that I wasn't sure she was actually *seeing* me.

On the floor, Stan groaned. His eyes blinked open. "Oh, God, I hurt."

The sound of his voice seemed to bring Faye back to the present. Her eyes focused on Stan. Still holding the bat, she demanded of him, "What happened?"

"I need a doctor." He began to whimper.

"He tried to kill me." I brought the cell phone up and pressed one key.

"Put that down," Faye snapped.

"I'm calling —"

She moved a few feet closer to me, near enough to knock my head off if she swung the bat. "Put that phone down. Now."

I did, placing it on the counter beside me. "Hands where I can see them," she said.

I brought my hands around to the front and let them hang at my sides.

Stan was groaning louder. "Please, it hurts so much!"

"Do something for him," Faye said.

"I have burn ointment in the bathroom —"

"Stay where you are." Inclining her head toward the refrigerator, she said, "Ice. That's good for burns. Put some ice on his face."

Carefully stepping around Stan, I took several paper towels from the roll next to the sink. Crossing to the refrigerator, I pressed the lever on the icemaker function and used the towels to catch the handful of cubes that came tumbling out.

Like the ice cubes falling into my hand, suddenly the disconnected pieces of the murder puzzle that I'd seen out of context were falling into place. I began to make out a coherent picture.

I knelt beside Stan and pressed the wrapped ice cubes against his cheek. The cold gave him a little bit of relief.

"You threw poisoned meat over the fence to kill my dog, didn't you? You wanted to get him out of the way so you could get into the house tonight."

He didn't reply, but I knew I was right.

"Let me call the police, Faye. Stan murdered your mother."

She wasn't surprised. Almost casually, Faye said, "We were in love. Mother wouldn't have let us be together. She'd have said Stan wasn't 'suitable,' so we had to get rid of her. She deserved to die anyway because I know she killed my father."

Stan's eyes snapped wide open. "Faye, shut up!"

"Why?" Referring to me, Faye said, "She can't tell anybody. She's going to die, too." Faye's calm tone was even more chilling than her words.

I had to keep her talking. That one digit I'd pressed on the keypad was a number on speed dial. If the call got through, and if what was being said in this kitchen could be heard . . .

A big "if." I couldn't count on it. My mind was swirling with questions and glimpses of answers.

Mimi, Lulu, me . . . Why me, then not me, but now me again? What were they trying to hide? No, wait — maybe it was Stan who was trying to hide something. Maybe the two of them weren't entirely equal partners.

"Cut him free." Faye waved the bat at me. "Now. If you don't . . ."

"All right," I said, "but I need my knife."

"Do you think I'm stupid? I'm not going to let you get your hands on a knife. Unwrap the tape."

That would buy me a little time. I needed it because I was about to make a guess. Pretending to tug at the tape holding Stan's feet, I was watching Stan's face as I told Faye, "I'm surprised you'd want to be with this man, after he'd been your mother's lover."

Faye gasped in shock because the expression on Stan's face was as good as a signed confession. I should have guessed about that relationship sooner. Lulu had almost told me when she said she would have named Mimi's mystery lover, except that it would hurt someone. I couldn't imagine whose feelings she would care about more than Faye's.

Faye was staring at Stan, her eyes full of horror and disgust. "No . . . no, you couldn't have. . . ." Her voice was little more than a strangled whisper.

Pressing my luck, I said to Faye, "So you didn't know about Stan and your mother? Lulu knew, but she wanted to protect you so she kept quiet. Stan killed her because he was afraid she'd slip and tell you."

I watched Faye's eyes darken with fury.

All her attention was on Stan.

"*You* killed Lulu? You told me Della did it! You said that's why we had to come here tonight and kill her!"

"I didn't kill Lulu," I told Faye. "Now you know who did."

"No, no, she's lying!" But Stan's face betrayed him.

Keeping up the pressure to divide these two, I said, "With your mother dead, you're rich, Faye. Your potential as an heiress — *that's* why Stan went after you when you came home from college. He'd been your mother's lover, but that couldn't have been much fun." I stood up as I spoke and slowly backed toward the counter. "You were young, and with Mimi dead, you'd have all that money. Stan couldn't let you find out about his past with the mother you hated, so he killed Lulu. Then he thought Lulu might have told me, that night when we were at your house. He chased me all over Brentwood in a stolen studio car — he had access to all of them — but I got away. After he murdered Lulu, he convinced you that I had to be killed because I'd done it. But that's not true, Faye, and in your heart you know it."

I kept my eyes on Faye as I asked Stan, "Why did you pick *tonight* to kill me? Was it because you saw Faye with Gilmer York? Did you blame me for putting them together? You had to know she came with me because you were in the security office when Angie let us in. Gil York is very good-looking. He's on television. You were afraid that a young girl like Faye might fall for him, and then where would you be? You would have murdered Mimi and Lulu so you could marry Faye for her money, but with another man finding Faye attractive, she might realize she had more choices than just you. You probably saw the possibility that the big-money prize you killed for could slip away."

"It was Faye's idea to kill Mimi," Stan cried. "She figured out how to do it — she ground up peanuts and put 'em in a little bag, and she used some pudding to show me how to mix them in so Mimi wouldn't suspect anything. All I did was what she told me to do!"

"You used your keys to sneak into the studio; you cut the cord on the refrigerator," Faye snapped.

I saw the look of insane hatred in Faye's eyes. Stan saw it, too.

Faye's mind seemed to be focused on a single thought. "You killed Lulu — even though you knew how much I loved her."

He whined. "That old woman was going to keep us from being together. But we can still have everything we planned, baby. It's not too late!"

"Yes, it is," Faye said softly.

Desperate, cowering against the wall, Stan looked at me and cried, "Hit her, baby! We'll get out of here and go someplace and be together like we planned."

Faye was standing over Stan now, concentrating on him, as though there was no one else in the room except that whimpering, begging man on the floor.

Slowly, I reached my right hand out along the counter, until I touched . . .

Faye raised the bat high over her head. With a blood-chilling wail she was about to crash the weapon down onto his skull, but —

My fingers closed around the top of Liddy's carved pumpkin. I heaved it at Faye.

The big orange vegetable — Liddy's elephant in the room — smashed against the side of Faye's head and splattered, but the force of the blow sent her reeling over onto her side, against the stove. The bat flew out of her hand.

I jumped at Faye, grabbed her by one wrist and twisted it up behind her back until she screamed in agony. I was bigger and stronger than Faye and managed to pull her by the twisted arm until I'd dragged her close enough to the cell phone —

John O'Hara and four uniformed officers in Kevlar vests crashed through my back door.

My cell phone call *had* gone through, and John had heard enough of what was going on to send him racing here, with his posse. It wasn't exactly a race to the rescue, because I'd managed to save myself, but I was glad that I'd kept his number on my speed dial.

I warned John and his men, "Don't slip on the pumpkin pieces." My kitchen floor was going to need a good mopping. Strange, the silly things you think about when you've just escaped death.

Two of the police officers hoisted Stan off the floor, and another handcuffed Faye. I heard somebody reading our modern Bonnie and Clyde their rights.

"What's going to happen to those two," I asked John.

"Jail, right now. When they're arraigned, it's a pretty sure thing the DA's going to ask for remand."

"You mean that they be held without bail until their trial. Do you think the judge will agree?"

John nodded. "With two murders and one attempted to their credit, I can't see a sane judge giving them a chance to flee. But I wouldn't be surprised if some expensive lawyer tries to get Faye off on an insanity plea."

"I'm remembering something Mickey Jordan told me. He knew Faye when she was a troubled child. He said that with a mother like Mimi she never really had a chance."

"A lot of people have bad childhoods and they don't commit murder. I'm sympathetic to their victims," John said grimly. After a moment, he added, "Hall is at North Hollywood Station waiting for us. Are you up to coming?"

I thought of kindly Lulu, stabbed to death, and Tuffy, having convulsions and almost dead from poison.

"You couldn't keep me away," I said. "But first I have to find Emma. I think Stan stepped on her. Her cry saved my life."

I found Emma under my bed. She came out when I coaxed her. By gently exploring her body, I discovered that her right front paw was tender. That must have been where Stan Evans stepped on her.

Carefully, I examined the paw. She was sore, but no permanent damage had been done.

NDM arrived at North Hollywood Station a few minutes after we got there with Stan Evans and Faye Bond. He hadn't known about the drama at my house; he was bringing George Hopkins back from Las Vegas to give Detective Hall a statement.

George had come with NDM willingly, to clear himself.

He told us that it was true; he *had* sold Lulu's jewelry. But he produced a piece of paper in Lulu's handwriting that gave him the right to sell the jewelry. The money from the sale was to be a loan to George, for three years, at 10 percent interest per annum; the paper had been notarized.

George had taken the money he'd received for the diamonds and gone to Las Vegas to try to win enough money to pay off his gambling debts. Instead, he'd lost it all.

43

NDM and I finally had our dinner date. It was two nights later, after Tuffy had recovered and come home, and after NDM's front-page story in the *Chronicle* about the murders had been picked up by the wire services and reprinted all over the country.

He called for me at my home, in his Maserati, which still had the dent in its hood, and we drove down the coast to a lovely restaurant that looked out over the ocean.

Along the way, I told him about Eileen's plan to turn me into the Famous Amos of fudge, and that the mysterious investor she'd approached was Mickey Jordan. Her pitch to him was that because I appeared on his network, commercial fudge with my name on it was a natural fit in his business empire. He agreed to give her concept a try and was about to test-market it with the thirty boxes of fudge I'd made.

"If this thing fails," he'd told Eileen, "I'll

just give everybody in my companies fudge for Thanksgiving."

During a very good meal of fresh grilled fish and warm spinach salad, NDM and I talked about books and entertainment and politics. In fiction, we both liked to read the classics and mystery novels, and in nonfiction, our favorites were biographies and history. We both like a wide range of entertainment, except anything involving cruelty to animals. In sports, he liked football and I liked basketball, but we both liked baseball.

Things were going well until we came to politics. His opinions, so opposite to mine, made me furious.

I said, "I don't understand how you can possibly believe that!"

He said, "For a smart woman, I don't know how you can take that position!"

Just as on the subject of guns, we agreed to disagree, but it didn't look as though either of us was going to change our views.

After dinner, as we drove along the ocean, NDM said, "Let's forget the fight. I'd like to hold you in my arms tonight."

"That's the first one of your ideas that appeals to me," I said.

"Your place or mine?"

"Mine is closer. And I have pets to care for."

As soon as we returned from walking Tuffy, NDM kissed me. We wanted each other so badly that we barely made it into the bedroom.

Afterward, relaxing in each other's arms, NDM asked, "I've noticed that you never call me by my name. Why not?"

I lifted my head and looked at him. "Because Nicholas D'Martino is a mouthful."

He smiled at me in such a *knowing* way that it made me blush.

"What do you want me to call you?" I asked.

"Nicholas. Not Nick, unless you're mad at me."

I closed my eyes and rested my cheek against his bare chest. As angry as he made me when we discussed politics, I doubted that it would be very long before I called him "Nick."

RECIPES

DELLA'S
KILLER MOUSSE

7 ounces semisweet chocolate, plus 1 ounce
   grated
1 ounce unsweetened chocolate
4 tablespoons sugar
4 tablespoons milk
4 eggs, separated
1 pint whipping cream
1 teaspoon vanilla

Melt the 7 ounces semisweet and 1 ounce
unsweetened chocolate in the top of a
double boiler. Add sugar and milk to egg
yolks and mix. Add egg mixture to melted
chocolate. (Put a little warm chocolate into
egg mixture first, to warm the egg mixture,
then add remaining melted chocolate.) Pour
into large bowl to cool.

Beat egg whites until stiff. Fold into chocolate. Beat cream until stiff. Fold into chocolate. Add vanilla and half of the grated chocolate. Refrigerate for at least two hours. (If it's more convenient, you can make it in the morning.)

Top with the rest of the grated chocolate and serve. (You can also top with a dollop of whipped cream, but I think that's over*kill!)

NOTE: I wanted to make the most delicious chocolate mousse I'd ever tasted. It took five or six experiments with ingredients, but I finally came up with this version. It's not quite as good as sex, but if you aren't in love, this dish could make you forget about it for a while.

HILDA ASHLEY'S
EASY CRANBERRY CHICKEN

1 can of whole-berry cranberry sauce (16 ounces)
1 envelope of onion soup mix
3/4 cup Russian dressing
6 chicken pieces (breasts and thighs)

Preheat oven to 350 degrees.

Mix cranberry sauce, onion soup mix, and Russian dressing together. Dip chicken pieces into mixture. Place chicken pieces on a foil-lined cookie sheet. If any mix is left, pour over chicken pieces.

Bake chicken for 1–1 1/2 hours. During last half hour, cover loosely with foil to avoid over-browning.

NOTE: If you prefer to use skinless and boneless chicken breasts, reduce baking time to 55–60 minutes, depending on your oven. Chicken with skin and bones will take longer to bake until done.

Della's
"Gangster Chicken" Cacciatore

4 tablespoons extra virgin olive oil
3 garlic cloves, chopped
1 large onion, peeled and chopped
2 large green bell peppers, seeded and cut
　　into silver dollar–size hunks
1 jar of marinara sauce (4 pounds)
1 can whole tomatoes (28 ounces)
1 teaspoon dried basil
1 teaspoon dried oregano
2 teaspoons granulated sugar
1 package sliced mushrooms (1 1/2–2 cups)
Salt and pepper
1 can stewed tomatoes (14.5–15 ounces)
12 chicken breasts and thighs, raw (with or

without skins)

Put 2 tablespoons extra virgin olive oil into a big Dutch oven. Heat gently — don't let the oil get "smoking hot." Add garlic and onion. Cook for a few minutes, until onion is transparent. (Be careful not to burn the garlic.) Add bell peppers and cook, while stirring, for a few more minutes. Add marinara sauce, whole tomatoes, basil, oregano, sugar, and mushrooms. Stir to incorporate. Salt and pepper to taste. Simmer over medium heat while you prepare the chicken pieces. If the sauce seems a little too thick, add stewed tomatoes or the equivalent amount of marinara sauce.

Heat 2 tablespoons of extra virgin olive oil in a heavy skillet and cook the chicken pieces until they are *just slightly browned* on both sides. Do not overcook. Drain chicken for 1 or 2 minutes on paper towels to get rid of any extra oil. I like to use only skinless and boneless half breasts that I cut into halves again. (If you use chicken pieces with the skin on, remove the skins after baking but just before serving the cacciatore.)

Put the chicken pieces into the cacciatore sauce and turn off the heat. Cover and let stand on the stove while you preheat the oven to 350 degrees. When the oven has reached 350 degrees, uncover the cacciatore and bake it for 45 minutes. Remove from heat. Here's the secret for the most tender, juiciest chicken pieces: *Let the cacciatore rest (covered) for a couple of hours; then bake it again for another 40–45 minutes.* Serve after this second baking.

This batch of cacciatore serves 8 (or 2 people can eat well for 4 days).

NOTE: When all the chicken has been consumed, if there's any sauce left, save it to serve over scrambled eggs. If you're not going to use the sauce the next day, freeze it until needed.

LULU'S
LASAGNA

3 hot Italian sausages (approximately 1 pound)
3 sweet Italian sausages (approximately 1 pound)
1 pound fresh mushrooms
1 tablespoon butter
6–7 tablespoons extra virgin olive oil
4 garlic cloves, minced
1 pound lean ground beef
Dried rosemary

3/4 cup dry white wine (good enough quality to drink)

1 can peeled whole tomatoes (28 ounces), chopped

1 can peeled and chopped tomatoes (15 ounces) **or** 1 can diced tomatoes (15 ounces)

1 can tomato paste (6 ounces)

1 jar pasta sauce (28 ounces)

1/2 teaspoon dried oregano

1/2 teaspoon dried basil

1 tablespoon granulated sugar

Salt and fresh-ground pepper

1 pound lasagna noodles

1 1/2 pounds ricotta cheese (regular or part-skim)

1 pound mozzarella cheese, thinly sliced

3/4 cup Parmesan cheese, freshly grated or shaved

Parboil sausages, then remove casing and crumble. Set aside. Sauté mushrooms in butter and 2 tablespoons extra virgin olive oil for approximately 10 minutes over medium flame. Set aside for later.

In a heavy-bottom pot or Dutch oven, sauté garlic in 4–5 tablespoons extra virgin olive oil until garlic is lightly tan. (Be careful not to burn the garlic.) Add sausage meat, ground beef, and a generous pinch of rosemary. When browned, add wine and simmer for about 10 minutes. Add tomatoes, tomato paste, pasta sauce, oregano, basil, and sugar. Sprinkle salt and fresh-ground pepper to taste. Bring to boil. Stir occasionally for about 5 minutes, then lower flame and simmer (stirring occasionally) for 1 hour. Turn off flame and let stand in covered pot while you prepare the pasta.

Cook pasta noodles according to package directions. Add a drop of oil to the pasta water to keep pasta from sticking together. Cook until al dente. Don't overcook and let it get too soft.

Preheat oven to 400 degrees. Get ready to use ricotta, mozzarella, and Parmesan cheese. Prepare a rectangular baking dish by ladling a little of the sauce (a couple of big spoonfuls) into the bottom of the dish to keep the bottom layer of pasta from sticking. Over the sauce, spread a layer of pasta, another layer of sauce with the sausage and ground beef, some mushrooms, a layer of ricotta, and a layer of mozzarella slices. Sprinkle Parmesan over this and repeat the layering process until you've used *almost* all the ingredients; save a little of the sauce and ricotta. To finish, top lasagna with spoonfuls of sauce and dot with ricotta. Bake for

25–30 minutes.

NOTE: Whatever is left over keeps well under plastic wrap and in a glass or ceramic baking dish. It can be reheated in the microwave until you're tired of it.

BARBARA RUSH'S
CHILI

When I heard from one of the students at my cooking school that movie and TV star Barbara Rush was a very good cook, I invited her to be a guest speaker. She's as generous with her recipes as she is beautiful. Here's her special chili.

4 pounds ground beef (good grade)
4 onions
Several cloves garlic, minced **or** 1 teaspoon garlic powder
1 can whole tomatoes (15 ounces), sliced
1 can tomato paste (12 ounces)
1 can tomato sauce (15 ounces each), an additional can is optional
1 small can tomato sauce with tomato bits
3–4 tablespoons 4-Alarm Chili Powder *without* red peppers **or** regular chili powder
1 package Texas chili preparation spice with masa flour, optional
1 teaspoon thyme

1 teaspoon oregano
1 teaspoon tarragon
1 teaspoon sweet basil
1 teaspoon rosemary
5 teaspoons Worcestershire sauce
4 cans kidney beans (27 ounces each)
1 small can Hunt's chili beans
Vegetable oil

Brown the beef with the onions and garlic. Add tomatoes, tomato paste, tomato sauce, and tomato sauce with tomato bits. Add additional pasta sauce until mixture reaches your desired consistency.

In a bowl, mix 3 or 4 tablespoons of 4-Alarm Chili Powder with a little water to make a paste before adding to chili. (If you can't get 4-Alarm, use regular chili powder.) Start with 3 tablespoons, and taste as you go along. Add another tablespoon if you want it a bit stronger.

NOTE: You can optionally use a Texas chili preparation spice, which comes with masa flour. If you decide to use it, also mix 1/4 cup masa flour with a little water. Add this paste to the chili. Taste as you go along.

To chili, add thyme, oregano, tarragon, basil, rosemary, Worcestershire sauce, kidney beans, and Hunt's chili beans.

NOTE: *If you prefer to use garlic powder instead of minced cloves, then sprinkle the powder into chili after you've put in all the beans. Taste as you do this to get the right amount. You may want a little more. Or not.*

Cook the chili over a medium-low to medium flame for approximately 1 hour. (Barbara says, "You can cook it for *days* if you just keep adding liquid so it doesn't get too thick.")

Have available for your guests: bowls of finely chopped onions, shredded cheddar cheese, and sour cream, so they can add spoonfuls of these to their chili if they wish. Also, have a bottle of Tabasco sauce on the table in case anyone wants the chili hotter.

This recipe serves 8–10 guests, but it can be doubled for a crowd. If you have fewer than 8–10 guests, freeze what's left over; it's just as good when it's thawed out.

RAMONA HENNESSY'S
BROCCOLI CASSEROLE

This delicious side dish is courtesy of Ramona Hennessy, sister of actress Barbara

Rush. Ramona and Barbara cook big Thanksgiving and Christmas dinners for their "family" of friends, and this dish is always part of the huge buffet. One year Ramona said she might make something different, and there was a *huge* outcry of protest. Ramona told me, "This casserole is so easy, it's embarrassing."

1 package frozen broccoli (10 ounces)
1 cup half-and-half
1 heaping tablespoon all-purpose flour
1 cup prepared stuffing
1/4 cup water
1/4 cup melted butter
Salt and pepper

Cook broccoli until tender, but don't overcook. Drain off water.

Make white sauce by mixing half-and-half and flour, and cook over a medium heat until thick. (Use a wooden spoon and stir continuously.) This thickens quickly, in 2 or 3 minutes. You'll know the white sauce is ready when it makes a thick coat on the back of the wooden spoon.

Combine stuffing mix with water and butter. Preheat oven to 350 degrees.

Mix together cooked broccoli and white

sauce. Add salt and pepper to taste. Put broccoli mixture into a lightly greased baking dish. Scatter stuffing mixture on top. Bake for 35 minutes.

This recipe serves 4, but it can be doubled easily. Warning: No matter how much you make for your dinner guests, don't expect to have any left over for yourself the next day.

DELLA'S
LATKES

4 russet potatoes, peeled and grated
1 medium onion, 1/3 grated, 2/3 chopped
2 eggs
3 tablespoons matzo meal **or** 2 tablespoons matzo meal and 1 tablespoon all-purpose flour
Salt and pepper
Vegetable oil

Drain the grated potatoes by forcing them through a sieve until as much liquid as possible is squeezed out. In a large bowl, combine potatoes, onion, eggs, and matzo meal (or the matzo meal and flour mixture). Add a generous pinch of salt and a few grinds of fresh black pepper and mix well. (It will be gooey and look like a mess.)

Put a depth of about 1/2 inch of vegetable oil into a *heavy* skillet and heat until tiny bubbles begin to form on the bottom.

Shape the potato mixture into thick patties about the circumference of a silver dollar and drop into the hot oil. Cook the latkes about 3 or 4 minutes on each side. They will be golden brown. Remove with slotted spoon and drain onto 3 or 4 layers of paper towels. Serve hot or warm with dollops of applesauce and/or sour cream.

This recipe makes 10–12 latkes, depending on thickness desired.

DELLA'S
CHUNKY CINNAMON APPLESAUCE

12 large apples (Pippin, Granny Smith, or a tart red — don't use Red Delicious because they're too soft)
Sugar
Cinnamon

Peel and core the apples, put them into a heavy pot with *a little water,* and cover the pot. Cook the fruit over medium heat until soft, or approximately 20 minutes. Remove from heat and mash apples, but leave the applesauce a bit chunky. Add sugar and cinnamon to taste. Put into a glass container (not plastic) and chill in the refrigerator until ready to serve.

NOTE: When money was tight, I'd make up jars of this applesauce to give as holiday presents. You can create cute personal labels on the computer, or buy premade labels in most office supply or stationery stores. You don't have to spend extra money for the jars if you save glass jars during the year. (Be sure to sterilize the jars so the taste of the previous occupant doesn't taint your applesauce.)

CAROLE MOORE ADAMS'S
QUICK AND EASY NUT-BUTTER FUDGE

1/2 cup honey (butter inside of measuring cup to make honey slide out easily)
1/4 cup butter (half a 1/4-pound stick)
1 cup dark or semisweet chocolate chips
1 cup nut butter (smooth or crunchy, any kind such as almond, cashew, peanut; butter inside of measuring cup so nut butter will slide out smoothly after measuring)
1 teaspoon vanilla extract

Line an 8×8×2 inch pan with parchment or wax paper. Put honey, butter, and chocolate chips into the top of a double boiler — over hot, not boiling water — and stir constantly until ingredients are melted and thoroughly mixed together. Remove top part of double boiler and stir in nut butter and vanilla. Pour fudge mixture into prepared pan. Chill in refrigerator until set, about 1 hour. Cut fudge into 1-inch squares. Insert a toothpick into each square for easy pick-up.

NOTE: Carole told me that the first time she made this fudge, her sister Chris came over to trim her hair, tasted the fudge, and took a third of it home for her family's evening dessert. It's the best fudge I've ever had.

REGINA COCANOUGHER'S FUNERAL SALAD

1 can cherry pie filling (21 ounces)
1 can of pineapple tidbits (20 ounces) **or** crushed chunks, drain juice
1 can of sweetened condensed milk, Regina likes Eagle Brand (14 ounces)
1 cup of miniature marshmallows
1 cup chopped pecans
1 tub of Cool Whip (16 ounces)

Whip it all together and refrigerate until ready to serve.

NOTE: Regina lives in Decatur, Texas. Her sister, Broadway, movie, and TV actress

Carole Cook, taught me how to make this delicious creation, which can either be a buffet side dish or a dessert. I call it "Ambrosia," but Carole says Regina calls it "Funeral Salad" because she always keeps the ingredients on hand in her pantry. When someone she knows passes away, Regina whips up a big bowl of this and takes it over to the family.

ABOUT THE AUTHOR

Melinda Wells was born in Georgia and grew up wanting to be a writer. She wasn't interested in cooking until she was living in New York City and engaged to marry a talent agent. "Most of the time we went out to dinner with his clients, but one night we were home and I made dinner for him: Beef Stroganoff. He raved about how good it was, and how impressed he was. I was embarrassed to tell him that it was the only dish I knew how to make, so the next day I enrolled in a cooking school." Melinda's black standard poodle (the original "Tuffy") passed away after sixteen happy and healthy years. Now, she's making plans to adopt another standard from a poodle rescue organization. Currently, Melinda Wells lives in Los Angeles with rescued pets and enjoys cooking for friends. Please visit her website at dellacooks.com.

The employees of Thorndike Press hope you have enjoyed this Large Print book. All our Thorndike and Wheeler Large Print titles are designed for easy reading, and all our books are made to last. Other Thorndike Press Large Print books are available at your library, through selected bookstores, or directly from us.

For information about titles, please call:
    (800) 223-1244

or visit our Web site at:
    http://gale.cengage.com/thorndike

To share your comments, please write:
    Publisher
    Thorndike Press
    295 Kennedy Memorial Drive
    Waterville, ME 04901